Canine
Confessions

BERNADETTE GRIFFIN

 LASKIN PUBLISHING

~~~~~

First Edition – May 2013

978-0-9879300-6-4 (Paperback)
978-0-9879300-7-1 (eBook)

~~~~~

Front Cover design: Alain Reno
www.alainreno.com

Print Jacket & Interior Layout & Design: Mallory Rock
www.novelpublicity.com

LASKIN PUBLISHING
www.laskinpublishing.ca

Distributed to the trade by The Ingram Book Company

Library and Archives Canada Cataloguing in Publication
Griffin, Bernadette, 1938-
Canine confessions / Bernadette Griffin.
ISBN 978-0-9879300-6-4 (print)
ISBN 978-0-9879300-7-1 (ebook)
I. Title.
PS8613.R534C36 2013   C813'.6   C2013-902042-X
I. Title.
PS8613.R534C36 2013   C813'.6   C2013-902043-8

Acknowledgements

I am indebted to the many poets whose words have found their way into this book, in particular to Walt Whitman and to Rainer Marie Rilke whose *Letters on Life* and *The Poet's Guide to Life* were a source of inspiration to this novel's narrator.

I am also grateful to Ian McGillis for his expert guidance and support throughout the course of writing this book, to Mary Metcalfe and Jacques Chenail for their painstaking and thoughtful editing, and to George Skalkogiannis and Johanne Vézina for their invaluable advice and assistance.

Last but not least, my thanks go to John, Anne, Tom, Pat, Michael and Jamie for their unfailing support and encouragement along the way.

Dedicated to

Michael, Nicolas, Lukas
Chloé and Leeland

I'm thinking. Will I be perceived as heroic in these pages, a creature of exalted spirit who, in some unbidden moment, perhaps at twilight or before dawn, breaks through the confines of human expectation to rise to untold heights, leaving behind a bewildered trail of smart alecks shaking their heads? Given my aspiring heart and, should I say, mild tendency toward conceit, it would please me no end if I were. But it is not my intention. I simply want to render in true and touching detail the account of a cocker spaniel's short stay and untimely death on planet Earth, now ruled, not by wooly mammoths or Cro-Magnons or Neanderthals, but by self-regarding humans, leaving it to you the reader to decide who the hero is, if indeed there is one.

Allow me to introduce myself. At the moment, my name is *Carmel.* I say at the moment, for I was quick to realize that circumstances on Earth are unpredictable, if not capricious, therefore prone to change, both necessary and unnecessary. I also realize that I've been blessed by the gods. In the beginning by a high birth, me being a direct descendant of the distinguished and decorated *My Own Brucie*, winner of consecutive "best-in-show" ribbons at Westminster in 1940 and 1941. To boot, I've inherited *My Own Brucie's* beauty, its *pièce de résistance* being a magnificent coat the colour of a fully ripened yellow plum, its texture lustrous as silk and wavy as the Atlantic Ocean—according to Jean-Marc, my present owner, that is. And if beauty were not blessing enough, I have an *élan vital* rarely seen, even in humans, he says, and certainly not in his dance class. While my ancestry is British, I've been Americanized, which means a smaller head—no offense intended—but still an overabundance of dog in a small body.

An overabundance of dog who has braved an overabundance of *Sturm und Drang*, to use a German expression, including the close experience of loss, not to mention the grief attending it. First, the pitiless separation from my mother and five siblings at a mere seven weeks. There I was, experiencing an early foretaste of the canine kingdom of heaven, if there is one, bathing in my mother's wet warmth, drowning in her milk, drenched in the smell of her glandular secretions, buried in a blissful pile of siblings, falling all over them one day, and brutally seized from them the next. Happy as the grass is green one minute, and cast into hell in the next. And words will forever fail to aptly describe the tumultuous weeks that followed. With my present owner, that is, Jean-Marc Labonté. And, of course, his friend Clarke who had moved in six months earlier. How could I not mention him, who is anything but a piece of cake and who drilled a hole straight through my heart, as you will see.

First came the perils of trying to maintain my balance on the parquet floor, so treacherous and slippery underfoot that, the very day of my arrival, my four legs capsized, catapulting me into the potted rubber plant, gargantuan at the entrance to the living room, overturning it and spilling most of its black soil onto the white shag carpet, the carpet Clarke brought with him when he moved in. Then came the banishment to the crate, heretofore used for housebreaking purposes only. That is, getting my bowels and bladder to run on schedule like the trains. *My cup runneth over*, the scriptures say, as mine sometimes did in the literal sense and, had it not been for Jean-Marc's positive reinforcement, not to mention compassion, when its solids and liquids were deposited on the parquet, I would have curled into a ball of despondency and died in those first months of my living. Then again, consider Leviathan: goad him, stir him up, fill his snout with harpoons, and fire streams from his mouth, smoke pours from his nostrils, and even the mighty are terrified and retreat before his thrashing. Such is the force of nature. Of canine nature, too. And it can be hell for all concerned.

My owner Jean-Marc Labonté, by the way, is a French-speaking Montréaler, a gentle, upright soul, slight of build, with celestial blue eyes, a close-cut curly black beard sprinkled with gray, the air of benevolence about him so real that I can smell it when he holds my head in his two hands, as he does in the morning when he puts me in my crate before leaving for work. He works as a translator for the Québec government. He also writes speeches for politicians in and out of government. But upon reaching the age of forty, a door flung open, rattling on its hinges, rapping against the wall housing his

Canine Confessions

brain. And a feeling of fatigue with life — *ennui* he called it — walked through, insinuating itself into every corner of his life. He needed something more. Something more than futile words, words, words. 'Oh the tyranny of words, empty shells of words, lying useless on the page,' he said. And sentient being that he was, that *je ne sais quoi* would have to be a living thing. A sensuous, alive thing he could hold and nuzzle and wrestle, and *I* was it. An *extravagance* to himself on his fortieth birthday, he announced to his friend Clarke.

Why not a Royal Doulton figurine of a cocker spaniel, Clarke had suggested. His mother had an entire collection of Royal Doultons she'd bought at Birks and Sons on Philips Square. But no, a Royal Doulton figurine wouldn't do. Jean-Marc had made up his mind. He wanted a warm-blooded, living, breathing, life-sized sculpture in the round.

And what name would he give to his sculpture in the round? His *extravagance*? Clarke, who sports a Clarke Gable mustache, but who'd been named after a street in Montréal, suggested *Victoria*. But Jean-Marc found it far too *brittiche* and decided on *Carmel*.

"And who's *Carmel?*" Clarke asked, suddenly suspicious.

Carmel was a long deceased aunt, an extra-large woman with almighty arms that almost crushed him when he came to visit. She lived on a farm in Saint-Georges-de-Beauce, and Jean-Marc had loved her as dearly as his own mother. *Matante Carmel* worshipped dogs. In fact, she'd rescued her own mongrel *Angèle* from sure extinction after her husband ran over her hind leg with the tractor in a hayfield. And when he raced into the kitchen, come to get his hunting rifle off the rack on the far wall, ready to shoot *Angèle* right then and there in the hayfield, *Matante Carmel* stationed her truck of a body between him and the rifle rack, the flat of one hand pressed hard against his rickety sternum, the other ready to reach up and wring his neck if need be.

Attends'n'minute là, espèce de sans-coeur, she commanded, her eyes bright as headlights, *la carabine reste au mur.* So the rifle never left the rack. And *Angèle* not only lived, but herded the cows for five more years - on three legs.

A true story in all likelihood. Consider the fish whose heart went right on beating, beating, beating, long after its removal from its body. Good heavens! Who would do such a thing…?

I've been living in this lower duplex on Hampton Avenue for almost three months now, and the smell of my mother and her manifold secretions—and my overly abrupt removal from them—is still painfully impressed upon my senses. Especially during the long procession of nine-to-five days when Jean-Marc is at work, and I am left to fend for myself, alone in my crate. I am not a clock, content to mark the minutes and hours. I am not a church organ, happy to come alive on a Sunday morning. I am not a fern with nothing better to do than paint the forest floor green. I am a social animal, unfit to live alone. In fact, when the young girl from upstairs comes in at mid-day and after school to walk me, I am overcome, reassured of my existence, like a prisoner manacled and suddenly released into the world. But she is sixteen and caught up in an adolescent world, a recent human invention apparently, and her walks are perfunctory at best, leaving me little time to empty my bladder and bowels and no time to imbibe the intoxicating smells encircling tree trunks and poles and fire hydrants. But I digress.

Despite the imposed isolation, my love for Jean-Marc has grown in leaps and bounds in these few short months. And so has his love for me. Upon his return from work, he stretches out on the floor beside me, nuzzling and wrestling me, the whole while nattering on to me in French, and the rippling rise and fall of his voice, the exuberance in it, the *joie de vivre*, the noisy intimacy of the two earthly bodies, sweep like a fresh wind through my belly and limbs and right to the very tip of my tail.

But Clarke is another story altogether. To him, I am an irritant. An intrusion. My fatal attraction to the smell and taste of deer-hide in his moccasins, decorated with porcupine quills and owl feathers, bought straight from the Mohawks in Kanesatake, was the proverbial straw that broke the camel's back. Since the chewing of the moccasins, Clarke refuses to address me directly. Now, I am simply "the dog" or just plain "she."

"She should be punished for that, those moccasins were hand-stitched by Mohawks, what's more, they cost a small fortune," Clarke said, on his hands and knees, now a quadruped himself, picking up the minute pieces of bead scattered over the bedroom floor like multi-coloured confetti after a wedding.

"Puppies like to chew, Clarke. She's teething. Just put your moccasins away, out of sight, it's that simple," Jean-Marc said with that dismissive wave of his hand that says I don't give a damn, like Clarke Gable.

But since that seemingly unforgettable incident, things have gone from bad to worse with Clarke. I get on his nerves, he tells Jean-Marc. Here he is, an interior decorator, in charge of the window and departmental displays at Ogilvy's, who's tried his darnedest since his arrival to create an aesthetic ambience here in the house. And here I am, ruining it, he says. Making mincemeat of his moccasins. Peeing on the white shag carpet. Scratching up the parquet. Drooling on the brocade upholstery. Exotic orchids on a window sill, angelfish in an aquarium — their vivid tropical colours would have made much more sense — and still provided the loose connection with nature Jean-Marc craved, says Clarke. And in recent weeks, this has made mincemeat of Jean-Marc's enthusiasm, like me with the moccasins. In fact, I've watched him, slowly but surely consigning me to the periphery of his life, especially when Clarke is home.

December 1969

One of my darkest hours occurred last week. A heavy snow had fallen on the city, the temperature had abruptly dropped to below zero, and there I lay, shivering and whining on the icy cold parquet, feeling the burden of an indefinable anguish, missing my birth mother terribly, when Jean-Marc, sensing my plight, hauled me up into his king-sized bed and swaddled me in his blankets. I had barely stopped whining when Clarke entered the room. Seeing me there, he immediately snapped to attention at the foot of the bed, the shaggy blond hair on his chest puffed up like an angry goose, his fists dug into the crests of his naked hips.

"Okay, Jean-Marc Labonté," he began, "that's it. I've had it. Choose." The ring of finality in his tone, a tremolo adding to the effect, "it's either *her* (pointing an index finger stretched to a curve in my direction) or *me* (jabbing the same index finger into the puffed-up hair on his chest). Make up your mind." And with that he spun on his bare heels and stomped down the hall to his sleeping quarters.

Mind you, I would have been perfectly content to sleep alone in Clarke's platform bed down the hall, but no, he said, I would ruin the black satin bedspread just mail-ordered from Haiku Designs in New York and for which he'd also paid a small fortune, even more than Jean-Marc paid for *me,* he said.

"Send it to the dry cleaner's every so often," Jean-Marc said, with that dismissive flourish of the fingers he uses for everything.

"Black satin?" Clarke said, furiously close to tears. "Black satin never looks the same after it's dry cleaned. And besides, the tiger appliqué is made of felt and couldn't be dry-cleaned, it would shrink."

Given the latest turn of events, I've been sleeping on the shag rug in the living room, and an uneasy peace presides, which, as the ruler of the British Empire said, is no peace at all.

January 1970

In the end, this was not the release from *ennui,* was not the grand, inclusive, new lease on life Jean-Marc had contemplated. Tensions rose to such a pitch that after another two weeks of fitful dithering, he decided to keep Clarke and get rid of me. He placed an advertisement in the Saturday *Montreal Gazette.* Sensing the immensity of my owner's distress, I would gladly have placed the advertisement myself, had I the wherewithal.

Things moved quickly enough and, on December 24, Christmas Eve, a young woman in a beige coat with a leopard-skin collar and cuffs came, looked me over as one would an expensive piece of merchandise. With Clarke out doing his last-minute Christmas shopping, Jean-Marc knelt on the floor, wrapped both arms around me and wept a flood of tears into my coat before delivering me into my new captivity. The woman settled with Jean-Marc, and bore me away in her arms, certificates and all.

Once settled in the back seat of my new owner's car, I rolled into a ball, out of my senses, hoping nature would come and take me back into herself, wretched dog that I was. For in those few brief months, I had thrown myself at Jean-Marc. Made far too much of the ecstatic moments. And in my folly, I had believed that quiet endurance and pliancy and other social graces would make a compelling argument in my favour with Clarke. But no. To him, I had been nothing but an over-eager pest, beautiful to look at, mind you, a beautiful nuisance, but a nuisance nonetheless.

January 15, 1970

Life is one bewilderment after another, for there I was, thrown to the lions, wallowing in rejection one moment, and in the next, received, I daresay hailed, as a long-awaited canine version of the Messiah, a large red satin ribbon decorating me as it had my ancestors, transforming me into the Christmas gift most coveted. The children kneeling before me on all sides, held my ears in the palm of their hands, threading their fingers through my coat, peering adoringly into my eyes, inspecting my under-parts, then leading me by the collar into the kitchen, filling my feeding bowl with dog food, my water dish with water, and watching me partake. Bewilderment did not let go of me until the next week, when my wounded psyche dared itself to think, good heavens, perhaps there *is* a balm in Gilead, enough to temper the sorrows of rejection and make me whole again.

The next thing my new owner did was change my name. Like Clarke, the family members hated the name *Carmel*.

"It's French," said the younger boy Matthew.

"It sounds like *camel*," said the older boy Mark.

"It's too much like a *Caramilk* chocolate bar," said five-year-old Kathleen.

Hence my name was promptly changed to Daisy, after Blondie and Dagwood Bumstead's dog in the funnies, apparently. It confused me initially. I'm *not* short-haired and gray. I'm flaxen-haired and full-feathered, with pendulous ears—more like the falls of a noble iris than the petals of a common field daisy—framing sorrowful eyes; mine sorrowful unto death, they say in this house. Daisy doesn't suit my temperament either. But that's the nonsensical way of humans, naming creatures before knowing a blessed thing about their inner life. To reinforce my argument, the dog next door, the shrill white miniature poodle terrified of his own shadow is named Hercules. Imagine. Hercules, who throttled the Nemean lion with his bare hands, captured the mad Cretan bull, vanquished the Amazons, slew Hippolyte and took her girdle, to mention but a few of his labours. Good heavens!

Given my blood lines and my beauty, a name such as Elizabeth, after one of the British queens, or Helen, after Helen of Troy—whose beauty launched a thousand ships and attracted a long list of suitors, enough to start the Trojan War—would have been more of an inspiration to me embarking on the ship of life, so to speak.

June 1970

Finally, after a pillar-to-post existence and all of the searing separation anxiety attending it, I now lead a sheltered life in a rambling two-storey brick house with wrap-around verandah on Kensington Avenue in the Notre-Dame-de-Grâce district of Montréal. Sheltered, meaning there have been no cataclysmic events or seismic upheavals. I know where the next meal is coming from. It's the same fare every day - Dr. Ballard's in cans, with table scraps thrown in. And except for Tigah the cat, I don't have the existential stresses of living with predators — not that I blame them for preying — predation is the only way to make a living. Time has also put things back in their place. Time relieves wounds just as food soothes the stomach. A sense of aliveness again rushes through me like a fast river. Oh, I still grieve for my mother and siblings. And for Jean-Marc. And as I grow in strength and age, bursts of longing for the working life of my ancestors sweep through me. They flushed woodcocks out of thicket for a living. But there's no thicket here. No woodcocks either. Our avenue is lined with tired old elms clinging to the pavement, and swishing, clicking maples waving their arms like ancient Qi Gong practitioners. Still, I leave my calling card at their feet, even if it serves no useful purpose. But useful is not all there is, the philosophers say.

Speaking of useful, I was brought here as a pet for the two boys, Matthew and Mark. Nonsensically named after the first two evangelists in the New Testament, no doubt. Matthew is twelve, and Mark is fourteen. (I don't belong to Kathleen, who is five, because she already owns a cat). Pets on planet Earth, where humans are superior, and males even more superior, are pieces of property, possessions, bought and sold on a whim, as I was. Thus far, the mother in this family is my master, the one who cares for me; feeding me, housebreaking me all over again, batting me with yesterday's newspaper, for I regressed to an earlier stage of development in my first grief-stricken weeks here and temporarily lost control of my excretory functions.

Monique, the mother, is in her mid-thirties. She is tall, has long jet-black straight hair. Straight because she irons all the curl out of it to create the Joan Baez look. But unlike Joan Baez, she is fair-skinned and skinny as a grayhound, with the same skittish eyes and skittish ways. Monique is a full-time homemaker. Not only does she cook, bake, shop and sew, but she cleans, cleans, cleans, polishing the kitchen appliances, dusting the wood furniture with lemon oil, vacuuming, washing and ironing everything, including the underwear and bed sheets, sweeping the wrap-around verandah, washing it down.

I'm just one more thing to keep clean, for she cleans my pads after every outing in wet weather, has everyone remove their shoes in the vestibule, because she hates tracked-in dirt, hates dust balls, fingerprints on the front-door glass, clothes draped over chairs, dirty dishes lying in the kitchen sink. It's not that cleanliness is next to godliness, no, she wouldn't go that far, but grime, dirt and disorder outside leave her feeling chaotic inside, she says.

Why she has to work so hard outside to maintain order inside, I'll never know. But I do know she loves me—already—so I'll grab good fortune where I find it. What's more, Monique is a dog-fancier, her father a dog-breeder before her. In fact, he loved his dogs more than his own children, Monique says, and if he'd had his druthers, which her mother refused to let him have, the dogs would have lived in the house and the children in the kennel. Indeed, it confounds her that she, of all people, who would not give a nickel for her father—alive or dead—would turn around and love dogs as much as he does. As they say, life's path is strewn with mystery, for truly, Monique uses any occasion to dote on me. Talks *about* me at the dinner table every evening. Lavishes me with praise just for being me. Compares me to Lady in Lady and the Tramp, the Walt Disney movie. Says I'm every bit as smart as Laika, the Russian dog they fired into space on Sputnik II and killed doing it. Talks *for* me too, explaining me to the world, so to speak, which is irksome at times, for the broken English and feigned contralto voice she affects sell me far too short. If indeed I could speak the language, I would speak it correctly.

"Ise glad Ise not a *labatory* dog like Laika, or Ise be an experiment, dead long before my time," Monique said, after a news flash remembering Sputnik II.

But above all, she talks *to* me. Mostly when she brushes the tangles from my feathers and grooms me. Makes me her confidante, as it were, knowing I am empathetic, capable of following her into her feelings, which her husband Harry cannot do, she says, cannot find the way into his own either.

Harry is forty-eight, lean and tall and tanned in all seasons, with azure-blue eyes and a fair-haired brush-cut graying at the temples. He's a pilot with Air Canada, and 'in the air' or 'on layovers' for weeks at a time. Even after he returns home, he's still in the air, Monique says, or like a passenger between flights. Offhanded. Fidgety. Edgy with the boys especially, issuing orders as if still at the controls. Then little by little it sinks in. The eagle has landed. He's home. He can relax. Relax means lying supine in the La-Z-Boy in the living room, Western novel in one hand, cigarette in the other, and vanishing into his book as into a cloud. Kathleen will often climb onto his lap and lie with him as he reads, like a lap cat, because the real cat, Tigah, is no lap cat at all.

He's a ramshackle, cantankerous tom, black as tar, with one ragged ear eaten away by frost, who prowls through the night and sleeps through the day in all weathers. And like Clarke, he's made an issue of me. The very morning after my arrival, Boxing Day, with me still wearing an accolade of red ribbon, he struts in through the rubber flap in the kitchen door, tailor-made for his peregrine tendencies, espies me lying quietly on the mat at the kitchen sink, minding my own affairs, arches his back, hisses, swipes at me with his front paw, a bristling roundhouse inches from my nose, spins around, tail lashing, and stalks back out.

Such disdain, I thought. Such unwarranted indignation. Such high-handedness. And should I be surprised by a species defamed and derided as malicious, associated with bad luck, depicted as lustful and cruel incarnations of the devil himself. To date, Tigah has done nothing to change that perception. Where is Bastet when we need him, the Egyptian cat goddess, guardian and benefactress of human beings, immortalized in bronze glory in the Musée du Louvre. No wonder my kind distrusts cats. Some to a point of hatred even.

But Monique, who admires cats, their cleverness and clairvoyance, thinks Tigah will adjust to my presence, although nothing is certain with cats, she says. You can't really *own* one. They'll move out, bunk in with another family, go wild even, at the slightest provocation.

Truth is I envy them more than I hate them. I envy their independence, their libertine ways, the respect and admiration they garner in resisting domestication. But for dogs there is no going back. So I worry. Will Monique be forced to 'choose', keep Tigah and get rid of me…perish the thought.

Now that I'm thoroughly housebroken, I've been given free rein in the house at night. But it falls far short of a deliverance, for most nights, I am coerced into sharing a bed with Matthew or Mark. Last night, however, after being wrenched and snared and snatched and wrested from one bed to the other as the two brothers fought over possession of me, I finally broke away, seeking refuge in Harry and Monique's bedroom, where I slept on the scatter rug next to Monique's side of the bed. Slept in a manner of speaking only, because Harry and Monique kept me awake well into the darkest hours, arguing under their breaths, Monique smothered in blankets up to her chin, Harry hopping in and out of bed, sitting hunched over on the side, elbows on his thighs, smoking his Export A cigarettes, spewing rings at the ceiling, then rising to his feet, removing his boxers, stepping back into them, threatening to leave and get some fresh air, finally crawling back into bed, as far away as possible from Monique without falling out onto the floor and waking everybody up. It all came to a halt when a heartbroken voice sailed straight into the melee. Sounds like my mother's yowl, my instinct told me, a fit of longing taking hold, but given the sorry state of affairs between the two complainants in the bed, it had to be one of them, but no, it was five-year-old Kathleen sending distress signals from the next room.

Monique rose and went to her, me following along behind. She'd soaked the bed again. Monique changed the sodden sheets and wet pajamas while Kathleen wailed. The wet pair was her favourite pair, the only pair she liked, she hated the dry pair, she said, crying and clutching the urine-soaked pair she loved, the scene reminiscent of an opera I once watched on television with Jean-Marc, where the heroine clutches her lost lover's blood-soaked cloak and sings non-stop for a full ten minutes as the lover bleeds to death right there on the television screen, even before the aria ends. As to which aroused the most sorrow and pity, the real-life scene or the staged scene, I would be hard-pressed to say. Fortunately for dogs, when left to our own devices, we don't wear clothes.

Another point, there is Kathleen, five years old and still not housebroken. What takes them so long if they're so superior…?

And what had Harry and Monique argued about? Well this time — I say, this time, because there have been other times — it was all about sex. It appears to be an absolute minefield for humans. In this bedroom it's more like mining for raw materials, for it is done in the pitch black under a mountain of blankets. The scenario is almost predictable: Harry comes upstairs late after finishing a Louis Lamour novel or the latest frontier paperback, which he promptly throws into the wastebasket after he's read it. (The thin ones, I've noticed, Monique salvages and uses to level electrical appliances.) He then pulls off his clothes and hops into bed buck naked, his erect sex organ pointing straight up and unceremoniously wraps himself around Monique, startling her from sleep, mostly feigned sleep.

"It's way too late," she mumbles, shrugging him away, the blankets up to her ears.

"Oh, it's always way too something," he says, agitated, pitching the pile of blankets onto her side, switching the overhead light on, his erection bobbing back and forth like a metronome, turning barber pole arterial red and venous blue as he stalks around the room, invoking the universe in loud whispers.

"A man should be entitled to make love to his wife when he feels the urge, especially when he's up in the air half the time."

Monique rises to her own defence. She is not his all-willing servant. She is not an electric light bulb you turn on and off with the flick of a switch. She is not one of the beauties in his Louis Lamour novels, who live in saloons and never sleep. And that's the way it ends, not with a bang, not even with a whimper, but with sleep, that merciful sleep that reconciles all anomalies, as the wise man said, if only through the black-faced night.

Monique joined the Voice of Women a year ago. She's also attended a number of second-wave feminist peace rallies downtown with her friend Marina. All are leave-your-dog-at-home affairs. And by her own confession, she's not been the same with Harry since. Especially in bed. Although there never was much "zing or oomph" in their lovemaking, she admits. And Harry's not the same with her either. He's testy. He's fighting back. He who hardly ever raises his voice, except to the boys.

"Don't tar all men with the same brush," he says. He didn't start World War II, he hates war, hates 'the bomb', as everyone calls it, as if there were only one. And believe it or not, he loves all women, a beautiful woman is a beautiful woman, liberated or not, and he can't tell the difference just by looking.

Then he retreats into himself, his terrestrial non-combative self. Hoping his rational arguments have settled the issue once and for all. He tries to stay out of the line of fire, be nonchalant, like a cowboy riding into town on a stolen horse, Monique says, reading more Westerns late into the evening. Smoking more cigarettes.

In the meantime, the earth keeps right on turning, the sun also rises, the new day dawns, and off they go, ignoring the bad patches, Monique says, like the crack in the living room ceiling she keeps hounding Harry about, growing wider by the day, if only he would notice.

October 12, 1970

This morning, with Harry off on flight duty, the children in school, Monique washed the breakfast dishes, scoured the sink, scrubbed the kitchen floor, then brushed me and talked for hours while I listened.

"I hope Harry's plane doesn't crash on this run, 'cause I didn't even say goodbye to him this morning, mind you, he didn't say goodbye to me either. (She's brushing the tangles out of my ears.) I don't know what it is, but when he comes up to bed after reading one of his Westerns with that huge erection and no preliminary introductions I freeze right over, it's like he's in a movie that I'm not in, like a cowboy who walks into a saloon and acts like he owns the place." (She's brushing the feathers on my hind quarters.) Monique wishes she'd known more about sex and erections when she got married at twenty-one, fresh out of O'Sullivan's Business College, which was all business of course, and back then decent girls were greenhorns, they didn't let boys have their way with them, they saved themselves, at least she did. Harry had to wait.

In fact, she'd only seen one real-life erection before she saw Harry's, and that was when she was six and didn't know such a thing existed, she was playing by herself in a pile of snow in front of her house on a city street when a man she'd never seen before smiled at her then led her quietly by the hand and into the fenced alleyway right next to her father's dog kennel, and with the dogs barking and clawing at the fence, he took this big pink stiff thing out of his pants. One look at it and she let go with this bloodcurdling shriek and he took off like a racehorse, stuffing it back in as he went. She buried the incident right there in the snow in the alleyway, never told a soul, because it shames her, even to this day, why would she go into an alleyway with a stranger, even after her mother had warned her, how stupid was that, she says.

And when she met Harry at nineteen, she stuffed the thought of his having one into the farthest corner of her mind, where it lay like a nagging detail, everything else about Harry, his social station above hers, his father a bank manager and his mother a collector of antiques, the confident curve in his smile, the aviator blue eyes, the sure, clear, polished look of his flying officer's uniform, she loved, and he was all chivalry, holding her coat as she put it on, helping her with a chair in a restaurant, opening doors for her, how considerate, she thought, surely, he would bring that same chivalry to presenting her with his erection when the time came, because like it or lump it, she knew it would come, and she'd have to make the best of it, because what a catch he was, her friends at O'Sullivan's said, seeing his photo, "he'll fly you all over the world, the Bahamas, the Pyramids, the Taj Mahal." (She's finishing up with my tail.) Now she stops dead, as if she's walked into one of those tree trunks on the front lawn, sweeps up the hair on the kitchen floor and goes out, leaving me to ponder the imponderable, stretch the mind beyond the limits of understanding, and me unschooled in the reasonings and cerebrations of humans, all still a puzzlement to me.

For one thing, why does Monique lead me across the street at the prospect of a male dog approaching me, an encounter I would relish, if only for the casual intimacy involved in his inspecting and smelling my private parts. What would be wrong with that? I fear my initiation to sex will resemble hers: nothing at all, then gates full open and hell for leather…

October 20, 1970

Last evening, despite concerns about kidnappings by the *Front de libération du Québec*, Monique attended her Voice of Women meeting with her friend Marina, who lives on the next avenue. Marina is ten years older than Monique and came to Canada from Norway some twenty-five years ago, as a war bride. The two create an odd spectacle. Monique so fair-skinned and spare and lithe, Marina ruddy and dense and square-shouldered, with peering eagle eyes and an eagle's nest of graying hair, tufts of it sticking out hopelessly in all directions like twigs. And if her hair is a shambles, Monique says, so is her house with its mess of plants, magazines, newspapers, posters pinned up everywhere plus two white Australian cockatoos with green and yellow up-curving crests, flying in and out of their cages *ad libitum* says Marina, who loves Latin and wants to resurrect it. Marina is also teaching the cockatoos to sing like passerines, for she loves birds ever since the war because no matter what happened, airplanes roaring in the sky, battleships exploding on the sea, guns rattling on the battlefield, the birds continued to sing and go about their business.

Monique worships Marina. Sure she's big and bold as a Nordic invasion, but she could sell sand to the Egyptians, Monique says. Just from chatting over the back fence, she talked Monique into joining the Voice of Women and more recently the Elgar Choir, where the two sing alto, practicing their parts together at the piano in Marina's living room. And she's a doer. When she's not locked in or locked out, she's marching or demonstrating for something larger and loftier than herself.

Canine Confessions

The purpose of this Voice of Women meeting was to make placards and banners for the delegation going to Toronto for Saturday's demonstration against the Vietnam War. And with Harry on flight duty, Marina's sixteen-year-old daughter Kirsten came to babysit. Except for the long straight blond hair and braces on her teeth, Kirsten is a carbon copy of Marina. Broad, brash and unapologetic. Tonight as usual, she brought her guitar. Always the guitar. With DEATH MAKES LIFE TRANSIENT written in bold block letters on a strip of white adhesive taped to its black case, like a profession of faith, or perhaps a kindly reminder to celebrate the evanescent, what does not last.

Kirsten has been taking flamenco guitar lessons for five years and plans to travel to the cradle of flamenco in Andalusia, Spain, next summer after she graduates from high school. She wants to absorb flamenco's Arab, Gypsy and Jewish roots to better feel its melancholy and desolation.

After Kathleen went to bed, Kirsten flicked on the television in the den, muted the sound and practised *picado* scale passages, the mournful rhythmic roll of the *rasquedo*, the *alzapua* and *tremolo non-stop* until Monique came home.

Matthew and Mark don't like having Kirsten over. Her legs are too fat to wear a mini-skirt, they say. Besides, they hate flamenco. They don't need a babysitter anyway, and when Kirsten appears, the boys disappear. Upstairs and into the bedroom. Last evening, they collared me into going up with them—against my will—for with Monique gone and the bedroom door closed, the place is suddenly transformed into a battlefield, the boys like natural-born belligerents, enough to incite fear and trembling in any quadruped. To begin with, they fire darts—not at the usual cork target of multi-coloured circles—but at a life-sized colour poster of a monumental bull moose Harry brought home to them from Vancouver. They tack it to the wall and make the moose's eye their target. When all is done, the moose looks more like Sebastien the Roman martyr in his final pitiable hour than a majestic Canadian moose. They then play the national sport: hockey. On a miniature rink with miniature metal players manipulated into action by knobs and levers at both ends. When the score reaches 10-0 for Mark, Matthew seizes both pucks and hurls them at Mark's head, causing Mark to vault over the rink, grip

Matthew by the yellow hair and pin him to the mat, so to speak, knee jammed into his Adam's apple until he says, "I'm a puny little jerk" twenty times.

Matthew, who *is* spindly and thread-like for his twelve years, complies, rattles off "I'm a puny little jerk" twenty times, then crawls into bed with a Hardy Boys book. Left to his own devices, he is a bookworm. He is also good at math and science and a member of the chess club at school.

Mark is another story altogether. He's dark-haired, dark-eyed, tall for his age, broad-shouldered and thick through the chest. Thick through the head too, his father says to Monique. Why? Because Mark has no patience with books or homework or written assignments. So much so that Harry is threatening to put him in boarding at Loyola High School, where he will *have* to buckle down and learn something if he doesn't want to be a garbage collector, or worse yet, deliver advertising flyers door-to-door. Yet Mark is irrepressible and full of talk. Words pour from him like steam from a geyser. And the heat and energy behind the words conspire to make an instant, if not always lasting, impression.

Has he made an impression on me? Well, he's more than tried to, fixed as he is on teaching me tricks, everything from shake a paw, to sit up and beg, walk on my hind legs, roll back and forth like a rolling pin. All to impress his friends, Matthew says. I hate tricks. They make my legs twitch. And they fly in the face of my very nature. No self-respecting cocker spaniel wants to be a trickster or an entertainer, much less stoop to the vulgarities of a circus.

Fortunately, Mark also has a meagre supply of patience. I am a slow learner, he says, and with darkness falling last evening, he walks me to the football field for my final outing. The usual four buddies are there, one, minuscule for his age, with thick eye glasses and a polo-shirt two sizes too big for him, making him the object of derision from the overgrown triumvirate as we arrive.

"What a squirt like you needs is a step stool to carry with you everywhere," the most overgrown one is saying, as Mark ties me to a tree.

"Shut your trap, leave the guy alone, one of these days he'll have a growth spurt, and when he does, he'll beat the shit outta you guys," Mark adds half-jokingly. "And I'll be there to give him a hand." (This from Mark, who less than an hour ago, pinned his spindly brother's Adam's apple to the floor with his knee and had him say twenty times "I'm a puny little jerk.") Ah, that sly selectiveness of humans leaves an uncertain feeling in the pit of my stomach.

But the offhanded prediction and tacked on warning seems to settle it, at least for now, and the five close ranks, huddling in a loose circle under the immense and aging oak tree at the field's edge, in a sort of preordained religious ritual. And what do they do? They smoke. Cigarettes usually. But tonight, one of the boys produces another substance, more pungent and sweet-smelling, as it travels around the circle, each in turn inhaling and exhaling, studying the glowing cinders and flicking the ashes, all of them hunched over, kicking at the grass, as if silently marking a sacred rite of passage. With all of them wrapped in a cloud of smoke, chemistry and mysticism, Mark suddenly breaks through the silence. He can now prove the existence of God in five different ways. If they're interested. They're more interested in the existence of girls, they say, but the smoking has made them compliant and contemplative, and they listen. His first proof is from causality.

"Nothing comes from nothing, everything comes from something," he begins, "and everything leads back to a more original form, and that form is God."

Mark then pauses, as if struck through by a flashing blade of insight. More likely, he has forgotten the other four proofs, because he hates studying, hates school, and theology is way too ethereal for his carnal, corporeal self. So he quickly looks to his wristwatch.

"Oh shit, time to go, see you guys," he says, a *laissez-faire* tone to his voice, as if the other enumerations could easily wait. He unties me from the tree and we leave the other four still smoking under the oak tree, still in the dark about the other four proofs.

Once home, Mark hauls me up the stairs, into his bed and under the blankets, wrapping a powerful arm tight around me, chokingly tight, as if he's trying to squeeze the remainders of a substance from a tube. I struggle to pry myself loose. Will I die of suffocation, I wonder. Yet he holds on in a kind of mute, under-the-covers desperation. One of my strengths is to lie still and allow a trying situation to slowly render its secrets, so I grudgingly acquiesce. But once Mark is asleep, I extricate myself, go downstairs and lie at the front door, listening to the flamenco drifting in from the den like a wind moving over the waters, the deep desolation of its rolling repetitive chords connecting me to old griefs interred in my Spanish origins, as I watch and wait for Monique to appear miraculously through the front door.

November 1, 1970

Last evening I went trick-or-treating with Kathleen. She dressed as a witch and I supposedly as a pumpkin with an orange towel wrapped around my middle and held in place with Velcro. Lately, Kathleen has been pestering Monique to let me have puppies, a useless exercise. Like pestering God for rain. For Monique continues to say no. Yet, the mere contemplation of gestation fills me with joy and expectation. The urge to propagate throbs in canine genes as well. Consider this. When God ordered Noah in the Old Testament to go forth from the ark and increase and multiply, he went out of his way to be specific, listing fowls and beasts and cattle and creeping things, as well as Noah and his wife and their sons and their sons' wives, each according to their kind. That explains our courting and mating intelligence. Matching that of many humans, from what I see around me. Still, I have not been permitted to use that intelligence. At least not to date. In fact, during my first estrous cycle, it was as if a pestilence had struck the land. Monique lifted me up into the van and to Benny Park for my walks. Why? Because the two males in the immediate *environs* would smell my pheromones, she said. One is the deluded Shih-Tzu who fancies himself a guard dog for the imperial palace in China, judging by his belligerence. The other, of course, is Hercules, the feckless, pluckless poodle next door, who, according to Monique, would certainly play the brave hero during my receptive season and jump the fence, hoping my senses would be stirred enough to allow intimacies I would consider unthinkable otherwise.

Perish the unthinkable. Hope leaps eternal in the canine breast.

November 25, 1970

Alas and alack, so much of my existence has been dictated. Not by me, but to me! Earlier this month, I was shackled and escorted to a veterinarian, who anesthetized me and removed my reproductive organs. Having puppies was too much responsibility. Too much responsibility for Monique, that is. My juices will now stop running. I will be denied the innate joys of nurturing my offspring. An impoverishment to say the least. But I will adapt. As they say, no impoverishment is entirely without prospects. For one, my surrogate family has chosen to keep me — or so it would seem. And their mere presence, particularly following an absence, short-lived as it may be, fills me with a strenuous and profound joy.

January 1971

Like most dogs, I dream. About what is painful, for the most part. However, in yesterday's dream, I was one of those mystical hounds with an all-white coat, living in a Northumberland sanctuary near Hadrian's Wall, an otherworldly place, with catkins hanging from hazel-trees, cauldrons spilling over with food and drink, other dogs in milk-white coats, and as assistant to the spring-goddess in charge of the sanctuary, I had magical healing powers, licking and miraculously healing, not only my own wounds, but those of the pilgrims who came to be restored. My state of exhilaration and dismay at being conferred with these powers was such that I lost my way in a maze of hedges, and my agitation in trying to paw my way out awakened me with a jolt, only to stir the fires of longing in me, longing to be more than a piece of property, for I was not born to be a mere decoration.

"Oh, Daisy's part of the family," I hear my owners say.

Yes, the inferior part. We, who once were forces of nature, who have had constellations of stars and celestial bodies named after us, no longer influence the affairs of this world. Sadly, our voices are no longer heard in the halls of power. Like trees and rivers and mountains, we've been degraded to sub-human status. Who are we now? Useless quadrupeds. Freaks. Bought and sold, captured and forced into dog shows, circuses, laboratory experiments, dog-fighting, movie-making, police work and the endless wars between humans. Our diminishment reaches right into human language.

Consider this:

> to be *dog-faced* is a gross insult;
> to go *to the dogs* is to lose the good qualities you once had;
> *doggerel* is mean, trivial, undignified verse;
> *dog days* are days when malignant influences prevail;
> even Shakespeare offends, calling the stupid, ignorant constable in *Much Ado About Nothing* 'Dogberry'.

And yet the term *dog* is but a slight variation on *God* himself. Indeed, in my over two years of existence, Monique is the only one to ever mention my soul. Is she alone in thinking I have one? I cannot help but wonder.

February 1971

Monique and I walked for hours this evening through the falling snow, she marveling at the profound gentleness with which it touches down on all things alike: window ledges, door frames, the outstretched arms of trees, the flattened heads of cedar hedges — and on my own flaxen-haired coat — the snow's whiteness pressing us ever more deeply into the cold reality of winter. Our own house, with the light of the street lamp streaming down upon it, appeared placid and untroubled on our return. But as Monique says, things are rarely as they seem, for it has been a tumultuous year in this house.

To begin with, Tigah the cat moved out in late July. Moved in with a childless couple just beyond the bend in the road. Then one sadness followed another. And another. It all began in mid-August when Harry announced to Mark, at the Sunday dinner table, that he would be attending boarding school in September — at Loyola High School — a mere stone's throw from this house. Mark immediately pushed away from the table, poured his roast beef dinner into my bowl on the kitchen floor (it was delicious) and drove his foot through the kitchen door, just above the rubber flap where Tigah once entered and exited the premises. He then stormed out himself.

With the hole in the door then sizeable enough for me to exit, Harry hammered a plank of plywood over the opening. A final wooden curtain had now come down on Tigah. He would never return now.

Mark, however, did return around midnight, but Harry had bolted all the doors by then, leaving Mark to spend the night pacing up and down the wrap-around verandah.

Monique spent half the night pacing up and down in the bedroom, peering through the window in a vain attempt to see Mark, repeatedly forgetting that the verandah roof obliterated her view. And through it all, she and Harry argued under their breaths again.

"People send their kids to boarding school to get rid of them, because they have no time for them, because they're too busy with other things," she contended, flipping through her sewing magazines, fidgeting with the framed snapshots on her dresser.

But Harry wouldn't budge.

Monique shot back.

"You're destroying his self-esteem," she disputed.

"Never mind the psychology," he returned. Mark was almost sixteen, and she was babying him, pampering him, preparing him to live with *her* all his life when she should be preparing him to live with people who don't give a damn about him. What's more, Mark would have to foot the bill for the kitchen door.

"How can he do that?" Monique said.

He'd have to *find* a way, Harry insisted. At sixteen he was working weekends at the hobby shop on Sherbrooke Street. At eighteen he had joined the Air Force, and at nineteen he was flying solo over the Atlantic Ocean.

And so it ended. With a closing soliloquy, which apparently doesn't require a listener. Or an answer for that matter, since Harry promptly did an about face in the reclining position, pulled the blankets up over his head and deliberately fell into a deep and peaceful sleep, while Monique continued to pace back and forth through a blinding storm of tears and frustration. She finally did lie down and with me close on the floor beside her, she stroked my coat, kneading it like dough, pressing and rubbing her helplessness into me, as it were, and all my bones felt out of joint.

May 1972

After a long layover in Vancouver, Harry finally did fly back home. Just in the nick of time to attend the Rotary Club Public Speaking Competition where Mark would deliver a speech. His first as a contestant representing Loyola High School.

Mark has been in boarding school for almost nine months now. And making a mark in public speaking, under Father Quinlan's instruction. When he comes home on weekends, he works for Marina, doing springtime jobs her husband Desmond refuses to do. Painting, cleaning windows, cutting the grass, digging new beds in the garden and tilling the soil in the old ones. And in the evening, he closes the door to his bedroom and practises speeches by the likes of Demosthenes, Chief Joseph, and John Kennedy.

"Never before in history has there been a greater need for men of integrity and courage in the public service," he begins again and again, attempting to mimic the cadence of John Kennedy's delivery, even the Boston accent.

Indeed, earlier this very month, Mark won the Rotary Club Competition—and five hundred dollars—with a speech by Maximilian Robespierre on the Festival of the Supreme Being, a section of which hurts me to the quick...

> "...He did not create kings to devour the human race.
> He did not create priests to harness us, like vile animals,
> to the chariots of kings and to give the world examples of
> baseness, pride, perfidy, avarice, debauchery and falsehood.
> He created the universe to proclaim his power..."

Vile animals indeed...

As for Harry, he was genuinely surprised by Mark's oratorical skills. Proud even. Secretly proud of himself, I daresay, who'd sent Mark to boarding school in the first place, a decision made under duress.

"I *told* you," he said to Monique in bed that night, "I told you, didn't I?"

But now it was *she* who wouldn't budge.

The beneficence of May may well be upon us, the time of the singing of birds might well have come, but up here in the master bedroom, it is glacial. The Siberian boreal forest would be more hospitable. Harry has gone on to pulp novels, and Monique's feelings have hardened into a block of ice.

To make matters worse, Harry's layovers in Vancouver are growing immoderately long.

"What *are* you doing out there?" Monique asks Harry one night, peering out from under the mound of blankets.

"Why do you keep asking?" Harry says testily. "I've already told you, I'm training student pilots, making a bit of extra money to pay for Mark's boarding school."

But Monique doesn't buy it. For one thing, he's growing a moustache. And letting his hair grow. And buying presents for the children. A brand new bicycle for Kathleen. Hockey nets for Matthew and Mark. Even playing street hockey with them in the evenings, instead of reading his paperbacks. More importantly, he's stopped fighting with her about sex. They still do it on the rare occasion, but from where I lie, it's a listless, lacklustre affair, dull as ditch water. The mountain of blankets barely moves.

"Why don't you just relax and enjoy it?" he says to her. "It's not that complicated."

But it *is* that complicated, she says to me. Sex doesn't come naturally to her. It's like a wild thing she doesn't trust, get too close to it and it might eat you, swallow you whole like a snake. And she can't separate it from everything else she feels about Harry, the latest being the humiliation she feels. Why? Because she thinks Harry is having an affair in Vancouver. But she won't press him on it. She doesn't really *want* to know in the official sense. If it were true, how could she blame him? And what would she do?

There has to be another woman, Monique thinks.

And there I am, a cocker spaniel deprived of the intensities and delights of sexual love, untrained in the art of appeasement, forced to listen, like a poor deprived Greek peasant forced to attend the performance of a Greek tragedy.

October 1972

This morning, I accompanied Monique to Marina's house where the two rehearsed the alto part in George Frederich Handel's *As the Hart Longs for Flowing Streams*, one of three Chandos anthems on the Elgar Choir's pre-Christmas concert program. Once they had practised all sections, Marina played a recording of the anthems sung by a British choir, and the two stood side by side facing the turntable and sang along, just to make sure they could keep on tempo. It was a raucous affair, for in the section, *Tears Have Been My Daily Bread,* the two cockatoos joined in with a descant of their own making, but with none of the dignity and pathos the composer intended. Two dim-witted partridges would not have done worse. And in Section 5, *With Glad Shouts of Joy and Thanksgiving*, the two cockatoos overpowered all of the assembled forces, British choir and baroque orchestra included, with a slap-happy succession of hit-and-miss shrieks that extended well beyond the coda and finale, which in itself was more than long enough.

"So much for singing like passerines," Marina said, after the final chord had sounded. If she were St. Francis, she would say shut up and the birds would listen, but she was not St. Francis and Modesta and Minerva had their own ornery minds anyway. And so the rehearsal ended. We then repaired to the kitchen for lunch.

Marina's kitchen is a jungle of overgrown plants hanging from the ceiling among pots and pans also hanging from chains hooked to the ceiling. More geranium and oxalis spill over the window sill, and all the available wall space is covered with Norwegian bric-a-brac and posters bearing protest slogans against the war in Vietnam. On the fridge door are photos of Kirsten taken on all seventeen birthdays, and on the table, a jumble of newspapers and magazines. Unlike Monique, Marina does not mind clutter and dust. There'll be plenty of dust when we turn into it, she says, so why not get used to it. Her husband Desmond doesn't mind the clutter and dust either. He's not here to mind it ... He's on the road. All week. As a salesman for Caterpillar Tractor. When he returns home on weekends, the moving parts of his jaw are locked in neutral from too much talking about machinery, he claims, and he locks himself away in the den over the garage, tying flies for his fishing expeditions in spring and fall.

Desmond is not the garrulous soldier she met in Amsterdam in 1945, Marina says. She's not the woman she was then either, the two of them so easily swept away, deliriously devil-may-care after the war ended. Yes, the war ended. Yes, they crossed the ocean. But dragging the war behind them. That's why he holes himself up in the den, Marina thinks. That's why she marches and protests and carries placards for this group and that group and the other group. That's why she joined the Voice of Women.

March 1973

At this morning's grooming session, stabs of pleasure bored into my body with each stroke of the brush. Particularly today, when Monique praised me to the skies, compared me to the sun, that most steadfast and luminous of celestial bodies.

"You are like the sun, always there, always the same," she said, "and I can tell you anything, and you won't bite me." Then she rambled on nonstop. Had she had *me* when she was growing up in Québec City she would not have moped so much, she wouldn't have been such a miserable stick-in-the-mud.

Sure she lived in a flat with her parents and two brothers, but not really *with* them, because her brothers were three and four years older and stuck together like glue, playing street hockey in winter and soft ball in summer and when they *were* around, at mealtime mostly, she seemed to disappear, disappear into her chair at the table, like a knee-jerk reflex.

She never hung out with the girls and boys at school either, never hung around the shopping mall, chewing bubble gum and smoking and fake wrestling, as they did. In fact, at twelve and thirteen she was shopping for groceries, helping with meals, doing dishes, sweeping and vacuuming the floors because her mother, a tiny, wiry woman with insomnia was slaving away in a side-room off the kitchen crammed with wig blocks, straw and felt hat bodies, rolls of lace and ribbons and netting and dried flowers and hackles and needles and a treadle Singer sewing machine, making hats for milliners and hat shops in Montréal. Later on, she made wigs and toupées for shops in New York.

When she had deadlines to meet, hats to ship out in a hurry, Monique had to pitch in, and when her mother's eyes got tired she lay down on a narrow army cot shoved against the far wall of that little side-room. It was her bedroom, her "shop", everything, it paid the bills because Monique's father who worked full-time as a machinist at Anglo Pulp and Paper fed his money to the dogs for food and worming and inoculations and veterinarian fees and stud fees, all to breed a Springer spaniel or Brittany spaniel he could one day show.

And when he ran out of money, he sold a dog or gave one away to save on expenses. Oh how he loved his dogs, spent all his spare time in the kennel, grooming them, talking to them—like she was talking to me right now—and when her mother had a massive stroke at fifty-one and died in that little side-room buried in hats and wigs, the dogs moved in and the children moved out, her brothers enlisted in the army and went to Valcartier Camp and she, who'd just finished high school, packed her bags and boarded the train to Montréal and to Aunt Irène, her mother's twin sister, the one with grit and gall and gumption enough for two, everyone said.

There she was, an orphan, standing at the door of Aunt Irène's apartment in Montréal, and there was Aunt Irène, small and wiry and ropy like her mother, but oh so worldly in comparison with her silver cigarette holder, her eye shadow and mascara and copper-red Afro and long purple fingernails and earrings swinging and clicking every which way, and oh so lavish in her flood of emotion, wrapping Monique in her arms, crying out in a loud voice that it was *ma soeur Yvonne* finally returned to her in more youthful form, her outpourings so physical, so new as to be almost too much, but in the weeks that followed, the two had wept, one over losing a mother, the other a sister—only to find her again, *tout un miracle,* Aunt Irène said, as if she'd never died at all.

Moving in with Aunt Irène was an act of faith, a leap in the dark, like opening a door and seeing a stranger looming, tall and wide as the door-frame itself, staring down at you, Monique said. She was scared stiff and grinding her teeth in her sleep as never before. Perhaps she should never have come, she thought to herself, never. Especially when she didn't know a living soul in Montréal except Aunt Irène, who was a whole new strange world in itself. But beware of those two words, never and always, Aunt Irène had said, one as unreliable as the other, if you leave the door open, who knows what will come in, and in no time at all—in return for room and board—she was working at *Tête-Folle,* Aunt Irène's hairdressing and beauty salon on Côte-des-Neiges Road, sweeping up the hair, booking appointments and operating the cash.

But Monique had had her fill of wigs and heads and human hair long before *Tête-Folle*, and Aunt Irène knew it.

"Why not go to O'Sullivan's College?" Aunt Irène said to her one evening, leafing through the classifieds in *La Presse* with her long purple fingernails, "take a secretarial course, study office management." Aunt Irène would pay for the two-year course, if Monique would work at *Tête-Folle* on Saturdays—anything but go back to Walter and the dogs.

Had Aunt Irène not pushed and prodded, she might well have gone back to her father and the dogs, she was that much of a wimp, a wallflower. Yet she'd grown to love living with Aunt Irène, she loved her loudness, her bravado, her earrings trailing on her shoulders, her rattling bracelets, the way she changed her hairstyle almost every week, her verve so contagious that Monique finally screwed up the courage and registered for a two-year course in secretarial work and bookkeeping at O'Sullivan's College. Not only did she make friends there, but a year and a half later she had met Harry. In a café close to O'Sullivan's. She'd dropped her books, sending papers flying through the air and scattering all over the floor around her table, and Harry had put down the newspaper he was reading at the very next table and helped her pick them up.

"Can I buy you a coffee, something to eat?" he said, still arranging the papers for her on the table. It was that simple, and before the splotches of red on her neck and face had gone away, before she could say yes or no, he had attracted the attention of the waitress and she was taking their orders. Not only was Harry courteous and attentive, but he seemed so dead sure of himself and of everything around him, even answering his own questions, his eyes, blue as blue can be, looking so straight at her. It unnerved her at first. Who was this guy, she thought, so quick to rescue her, so in charge of the situation. To be honest, she felt flattered. No guy, certainly no man so composed, so self-assured, had ever given her a moment's notice. A second look even. To the boys at school, she'd been next to invisible, too tall, too skinny, too plain with her black ponytail and her glasses. And here was Harry, seeing her. She was visible. Was it her new Audrey Hepburn hairstyle, her newly-plucked and shaped eyebrows, why not make the most of your skinnyness, look even *more* like an *orpheline*, Aunt Irène had said, preparing her for what she called the *ambience parisienne un peu outrée* she cultivated at *Tête-Folle*. So Harry became her first real boyfriend. A boyfriend in a hurry. Within months he was pressing her to get married, even if Aunt Irène was dead set against it and said so in her loudest voice, earrings swinging, bracelets jangling. It wasn't Harry, she said, she liked Harry. It was her.

"*T'es ben trop pressée à dix-neuf ans, ma belle,*" she said, "you're only nineteen, take your time, get a job, rent an apartment, earn your own money, travel, count the stars in the sky; above all, learn about you."

But Harry couldn't wait, wouldn't wait, how could he, he was thirty-three and already had a house for them to live in. Before she had time to think, he popped the question. On a Sunday afternoon in mid-May. With the city exploding into full-blown spring and she, fresh from finishing her course at O'Sullivan's, Harry picked her up in his station wagon and wearing his flight captain's uniform—making it even more official— drove her to his house on Kensington Avenue. And there it was, the prize she'd done nothing to win. The house was red-brick, two storeys, white trim and a white-roofed verandah, so cozy and snug-looking, like arms wrapped around the entire front and sides, up to the entrance to the garage. The same old elm trees stood at the edge of the sidewalk, their roots exposed, growing into the sidewalk, their branches in bud, arching half-way across the avenue.

Harry pulled into the driveway, stopped, opened her car door, and with one old-fashioned sweep of his arm, led the way up the steps to the wrap-around verandah and into the house—so formal, like a real estate agent showing a house to a client, she remembers— guiding her through the rooms: the spacious kitchen, so clean as to look unused, with pine table and chairs, matching avocado appliances, and door leading out into the garden, then the fully furnished dining room with crystal chandelier, mahogany table and upholstered chairs, china cabinet and buffet, and in the corner by the bay window, a tea wagon holding a silver tea set, which badly needed polishing, she noticed, and at the opposite end the open French doors with beveled glass panes leading to the living room, the red Oriental carpet, plush olive green sofa and black leather La-Z-Boy, table lamps and floor lamps, and past the front entrance, the den, with hide-a-bed and television with twenty-four-inch screen, and up the stairs to the three bedrooms, also fully furnished, with beds that looked un-slept-in.

And as if to leave no stone unturned, Harry pointed to the metal ladder flush against the upstairs wall, did she want to see the attic, he asked, only used for storage, remnants from the days when his mother and father lived here. No, she didn't, why would she, she said to herself, imagining him climbing up behind her, looking straight up her skirt. Then as if he'd rehearsed it, he ushered her down the stairs and into the dining room, where he opened a bottle of red wine sitting on the mahogany table, took two wine glasses from the china cabinet and half-filled them, offering one to her and picking up the other. With another sweep of his arm, he led her to the plush sofa in the living room.

"This is the house I've lived in all my life," he told her in his usual deliberate way, "as you can see, it's big," his eyes scanning the walls and the ceiling. But it was way too big for him, especially when he came home from sitting all cramped up in a cockpit for hours, but if she liked it, it could be home for the two of them, she could fix it up, make it look lived-in again, give it the feminine touch, the curtains hadn't been changed since before his mother died, he said.

Monique hadn't taken a first sip of wine, much less opened her mouth to speak. "This is the pilot speaking," he seemed to say, then taking off and gathering speed. He could get airplane tickets almost anytime, they could fly to Banff, she would see the Rockies, Banff Springs, Lake Louise, beautiful from the air *and* from the ground, they could get married right there in Banff, without all the fuss and bother of a wedding here and, besides, he couldn't think of anyone he'd rather spend his life with, have children with. And with that, he reached into his uniform vest pocket, pulled out a small box of blue velvet and presented it to her.

Monique felt her heart racing full speed out of control, Aunt Irène's words racing crazily through her mind. This could only be a mistake, she thought, Harry wanting to marry *her* of all people. But what words, what new arguments could she use to make Harry wait? How much longer would he wait? How much longer could she save herself? And how could she say no to Harry, give the ring back, humiliate him, when she'd been leading him on, allowing him to neck with her all this time, touch her breasts even—at the Westmount lookout, on patches of grass around Beaver Lake, besides, who else would present her with a ready-made house and wrap-around verandah, a cake on a platter, she could fix it up, make a real home, like the ones she'd imagined in her head or seen in the prefab home catalogues that came in the mail in Québec City, she could travel, see the world—all things Aunt Irène wanted her to do anyway.

And she felt safe with Harry but did she love him the way she was supposed to? Did she love anyone the way she was supposed to? She wasn't sure. What *should* it feel like exactly, she wondered. And where did you feel it? In your body? In your mind? In your soul? In all three? Yet Harry's love for her was plain to see in a hundred roundabout ways. Even if she'd never slept with him. She'd never slept with anyone else either for that matter. Sex remained a large and looming question. And that complicated state of unknowing about Harry, his naked body, his erection and its penetration into her body, lay in the back of her mind like an unexplored continent, large and mysterious. And frightening.

But with everything happening so lightning fast, she accepted the ring. They flew to Banff in June, got married in a private civil ceremony with two witnesses—all prearranged by Harry—and booked into the Banff Springs Hotel.

For the first twenty-four hours in the hotel, she was a bundle of nerves. Even if Harry was chivalry itself, holding her chair as she sat down to dine, opening doors for her to pass through, helping her into her sweater in the cool of evening. But then came bedtime. Having never undressed in front of anyone before, she changed into her nightgown in the bathroom, out of sight, tiptoed in, quiet as a mouse, slipped in under the covers and sat there—solemn, like a hen on a clutch of eggs, she said, but all pins and needles inside.

And what did Harry do? He stood by the picture window for the longest time, smoking his cigarettes and staring out at the sky, which was midnight blue, a huge field of it all fenced in by the mountains, stars cropping up everywhere like flowers, and the moon just a slit of silver in the distance, but enough to light the tips of the mountains. When the moon finally disappeared behind a curtain of cloud, Harry came over to the bed. He removed every last stitch right there in front of her and crawled in. To a sitting position beside her. She expected him to say, "This is the captain speaking," but no, after a moment that felt like a week, he pulled her down to lie beside him. With reverence almost, as if he were handling a piece of fine bone china. That was fine. But in no time she could feel his erection pressing into her hip and growing harder and longer by the second and the unexpected sticky fluid oozing from the end of his penis onto her brand new nightgown. That was it. She knew she should have rented an apartment, travelled, counted the stars in the night sky, as Aunt Irène said.

"You know I've never done this before, Harry," she blurted out, pleading with him to go easy, take his time, wait.

And Harry did wait. And wait. They visited Jasper National Park, Moraine Lake, the Columbia Icefield, and still Harry waited. The day after they flew back to Montréal, Harry left on flight duty to Toronto and Vancouver.

Home alone, Monique talked to herself.

"Okay Monique, face it. You're married now. And married couples have sex. That's why they *get* married in the first place. Those are the bare facts. Harry can't wait forever, won't wait forever, he's already sitting up in the bed buff naked, eyes round and shiny as blue marbles, till well past midnight, and smoking his Export A's, the bedroom choked with smoke. So get over it. Harry's a gentleman. And who knows? You might get to like it, once you get the hang of it, you might learn to love him back."

So she made up her mind. And when Harry came home from Vancouver, she let him in. It hurt like the dickens the first few times, she said, because she wasn't slippery enough, too sticky, the canal had no stretch to it, no give, and how would she ever push a baby through that cramped passageway if she got pregnant, she wondered, and the thought of that alone terrified her, what in heaven was God thinking when he made it such a torture for women—and such a picnic for men, because here was Harry, spilling his semen into her and proclaiming his love in a flood of words, like a flock of birds let loose from a cage, she said —everything so free and easy and all of one piece. God had to be a man. But, what astounded her most about Harry was the tone of voice when he delivered the load of sperm. He didn't yell or shout. There were no whoops or battle cries, as some of the girls at O'Sullivan's had reported. No. Harry was so soft-spoken she had to strain to hear him, and all tenderness, and it seemed to come from the soles of his feet. The Harry she never knew. But true as it was, it came — and it went — like a spark rising from a fire or a bright idea flashing through your mind. Harry was back to his usual self.

But to her it was also a fly-by-night affair. A flash in the pan. Unreliable. You couldn't trust it. Like a wild animal, it was safest in its cage. Her first impulse was to avoid it. Or at least put it off as long as possible. Impossible to do when Harry was addicted to it. He came home from flying, and it was the first thing on his mind.

"The children are sick, the stove is not working, I have my period," none of these dampened his desire. She couldn't keep up with him. It was like eating food when you weren't hungry.

"Why do you have to do it so often?" she said.

"Because I like it," Harry said. "Everybody likes it, everybody except you."

So she wasn't like everybody, and marrying Harry was like trying to build a house starting at the top.

Monique's long monologue ends suddenly, and she pitches the grooming materials into the drawer, slams it shut, and she's gone, all of her lamentations hanging in mid-air, a sharp reminder that the delectable mountain peak of sexual satisfaction is a pipedream for others as well as me.

July 1973

Mark is again a full-time resident of this house after graduating from high school in June. Indeed, when Harry, Monique, Matthew and Kathleen flew to Newfoundland to climb Gros Morne Mountain in the National Park, part of a two-week vacation in early July, Mark stayed behind to look after me. And to work for Marina. Washing all the windows and applying a fresh coat of white paint on the outdoor window frames and doors. To assuage my loneliness for those away, he takes me with him when he goes to work in the morning. I say work in a manner of speaking only, for in the second week, he spent much of the afternoon in the house. In the house alone with Marina — discounting me, that is — and Modesta and Minerva, who could never be discounted. As always, Marina's husband Desmond is on the road and visiting farms and talking machinery with farmers Monday to Friday for Caterpillar Tractor. And Kirsten and her guitar are off on a six-week sojourn in Andalusia, the Mecca of flamenco in Spain. On these afternoons with the house all to herself, Marina is using the time to instruct Mark in the ways of human intimacy.

On Monday afternoon, they sat on the living room floor, he in a white T-shirt and shorts, she in a hot pink halter top and forest-green pedal pushers, the colour combination not unlike an azalea in full bloom. With their backs braced against the couch, they leafed through art books from the Helsinki City Art Museum, its glossy pages spread open on their laps, displaying erotic wood-block prints called *shunga*, from the "floating world" of the Japanese Edo period, Marina explained.

I can see that sex is a complexity for the Japanese as well — and exceedingly exacting, judging by the images displayed in this book. More than that. One would have to be a contortionist, at least a master of yoga, or at least have the strength and husk of a Sumo wrestler to assume some of the sexual positions depicted in these books.

The afternoon whiled away, and the two sat there, Marina pointing to the different positions, lingering on some more than others.

"Do you like this one?" she'd ask, "or this one better?" or "Which one would you like to try yourself?" their fingers, Mark's and hers, grazing one another, touching as they glossed over the images.

Tuesday afternoon brought more of the same. More art books, these explicitly erotic, with drawings and water colours of women and men by Austrian painter Egon Schiele, who saw his works as a "vessel for enlightenment" Marina said, coming-of-age works he created while on the road to sexual discovery, according to the books' authors.

Study of the art books was followed by back massages on the carpet, with T-shirt off and halter undone, followed by leg massages with grapeseed oil to "slacken the constrictor muscles and tendons used that morning in the garden," Marina massaging Mark's upper thighs and lower legs, his body taut and outstretched to full length, first in the prone position, then in the supine position, all on the living room carpet, Mark in turn massaging Marina's thighs and lower legs, also in the prone and supine positions on the living room carpet.

The regimen on Wednesday included more art books and more extensive massaging, this time for the flexor muscles as well as the extensors, these followed by lessons in the "art of kissing" Marina called it, so crucial to the process, now with the two sitting on the living room couch.

"Try this," Marina said, teacherly as an Eastern guru, patient as Job, as she demonstrated the use of the lips and tongue, over and over, again and again — until he got it right, which seemed to take a lifetime.

The afternoon of Thursday brought a change of venue. With me tagging along behind and, of course, Modesta and Minerva, the lessons moved upstairs to Marina's bedroom, where Marina brazenly removed her hot pink halter top and forest-green pedal pushers with matching under panties and displayed her strapping, solidly packed naked body to Mark, all the while instructing him about the Samurai, for whom sex was life-affirming and a safeguard against misfortune, then inviting him to touch her naked body *ad libitum,* (Again, Marina loves Latin, loves the way it rolls off the tongue.). The *ad libitum* could easily have led to *in aeternum* had Minerva not landed on Mark's head and Modesta shrieked like an outraged screech-owl, the minute Mark began the "touching" component of the program. Ah, those detestable cockatoos, becoming a little more human every day.

On Friday, Mark did no work at all. The two spent the entire day reviewing the lessons learned throughout the week. As a further enrichment, Marina retrieved a book from her bird-book collection on the overloaded floor-to-ceiling bookshelf in the living room and read to him a vivid description of the courtship of the Canada goose by John James Audubon:

> "He advances gallantly towards the object of contention, his head scarcely raised an inch from the ground, his bill open to its full stretch, his fleshy tongue elevated, his eyes darting fiery glances, and as he moves he hisses loudly, while the emotion

which he experiences causes his quills to shake, and his feathers to rustle. Now he is close to her who in his eyes is all loveliness; his neck bending gracefully in all directions, passes all around her and occasionally touches her body; and as she congratulates him on his victory and acknowledges his affection, they move their necks in a hundred curious ways; he then caresses his mate and the mating begins, his cries filling the air with exultation."

"We have so much to learn from animals," Marina said, closing the book, a prelude to the culmination, or shall I say consummation, of the week's activities, for the two then slowly and ceremoniously removed every last scrap of clothing, Marina first removing Mark's shoes and socks, T-shirt, shorts and underwear, then inviting Mark to strip her down to nothing, and when it was done, they wound themselves around one another before collapsing on the couch, Mark's erection in a state of exultation greater than the Canada goose, greater than I'd ever seen with Harry, Marina entering more deeply into the experience with each passing moment.

In my brief tenure on earth, I had not seen such a display of human learning. Marina the instructor, yielding her secrets slowly, Mark malleable as clay.

December 1973

Monique brushed my coat today in preparation for the hallowed traditions of Christmas. Twelve days during which every one and every thing must appear perfect as a Christmas card, Monique says, and I am no exception.

Aunt Irène is coming to Christmas dinner. So is Harry's father, Ned, who is seventy-five and lived in this house until he retired. He then signed it over to Harry. It was way too big and way too lonely for one person sitting home all day, he said, and he rented a small apartment in an aging but still-elegant building on Sherbrooke Street in Westmount, close to the stores.

Ned is a remote man, sartorial in his elegance—three-piece suit, gold pocket watch and chain, white shirt and cuff links, silk tie and tie-pin—and not an ounce of fat on his tall frame. Not surprising, says Monique, since he eats no fat, like Jack Spratt (which is more than okay with me). I've been introduced to him, and Monique is right, he is taciturn. As if all the melancholy thoughts of the world were stored inside his body for him to guard. And tight-lipped, probably from holding his pipe in his mouth all those years. For when he comes to dinner on a Sunday, he spends most of his time sitting on the stuffed chair close to the window, fiddling with his pipe as if it were something alive and breathing, commanding his care and attention—running pipe cleaners through the stem, filling the bowl, tamping down the tobacco, lighting it, puffing on it, the bowl cradled in the cup of his hand—and staring out the window. Monique thinks Ned left a large chunk of himself at the Bank of Montréal when he retired—the only place he'd ever worked. From teller at age eighteen, he rose and rose, all the way up to bank manager of its downtown branch at age sixty. His silence should come as no surprise either since he's lived alone so much—in this very house. Alone with six-year-old Harry after his wife Ella died—and completely alone after Harry left to join the air force at age eighteen. Ella died at thirty-two, right there in the flower garden out back. She was digging two new beds for two *grandiflora* hydrangeas she'd just bought from the nursery, when she fell in a heap on top of the newly dug-out pile of topsoil. This is where Harry found her when he came home from school. The doctor called it undiagnosed, genetic arrhythmia of the heart.

Ned rarely mentions Ella. And neither does Harry, claiming there's little to mention since he hardly remembers anything about his life way back then. But Monique thinks they put their grief away, like people do, like items put in a safety deposit box or sealed envelope to be opened later or never at all. In the meantime, they toughened up. They went to rugby games, hockey games at the Montreal Forum, they listened to Friday Night Boxing from Madison Square Garden on the radio and they fiddled with Ned's car, their heads hidden inside the hood, their bodies sprawled underneath the chassis, replacing its broken parts, repairing its body, changing the tires, keeping it on the road.

And through it all, Harry dreamed of flying. He collected action photos of airplanes and pasted them into scrapbooks—the Flying Fortress, the British Spitfire, the Peashooter, the Sparrow Hawk. He made airplane models and hung them from the ceiling in his room. He worked weekends at the model shop, And at eighteen, he joined the Royal Canadian Air Force—over Ned's objections.

"Hold your horses," said Ned, "the war won't last, what you need is an education for right down here on earth."

But Harry's mind was made up. He went to the RCAF recruitment centre, then on to Victoriaville, Windsor Mills, and Trenton, where he flew Tiger Moths and Fleet Finches. How he loved the Tiger Moth, he'd told Monique early on, the way it could soar, belly up, loop over, swoop, dive, the feeling of freedom in it, everything else evaporating into thin air.

Later, with Squadron 125 in Torbay, Newfoundland, he flew Hawker Hurricanes as air cover for allied convoys crossing the Atlantic. The war ended, Harry left the air force and became a pilot with Trans-Canada Air Lines.

After the brushing, I'm left again to ponder the mighty occurrence of losing a mother, a sorrow I know so well, a sorrow that never seems to completely exhaust itself. No wonder Harry wanted to fly, soar like a bird. Look for her in the heavens. So do I. So do other earthbound creatures. Think of the Persian poet and what *he* said:

> *"Oh that I could be a bird and fly,*
> *I would rush to the Beloved."*

December 26, 1973

Aunt Irène and Ned did come to Christmas dinner. Monique roasted a turkey, boiled the giblets and, instead of adding them to the stuffing, poured them into my dish, a delicacy for me on Christmas

Day, she said. Like other dogs, I don't have the discriminating palate of an epicurean, and I wolfed them down in one swallow, before Monique could change her mind.

The seating at the dinner table was prearranged. Aunt Irène sat next to Monique at one end, because Harry says she talks too loud, laughs too loud, and he can't hear himself think. But Aunt Irène was unstoppable. Even from the end of the table her exuberance spread through the room like a contagion. There she was, calling out in a loud voice to Ned seated at the other end, telling him how she'd converted *Tête-Folle* into a unisex salon and inviting him to come for a haircut—don't bother with the appointment, she said, just walk right in, I'll make a special case. (Never mind that the hairs on Ned's head would not add up to fifty, if you could count them.)

Except for Kathleen upsetting her milk onto Matthew's lap, and me being called in to lick up the spillage, the dinner proceeded without incident. The turkey itself was on the dry side, Monique thought. The carrots and peas slightly overcooked, but I don't know, I eat everything that's put in front of me, cooked and uncooked and all of the infinite gradations in between.

Marina and Desmond and Kirsten dropped in for plum pudding and Christmas drinks after dinner. Mark and Marina were overly formal with one another, acting like almost perfect strangers, masters of concealment that they are.

After the plum pudding, Marina brought out Christmas carol sheets for everyone. And while everyone sang the tune, Marina and Monique sang the alto part. Ragged and amateurish as the singing was, choirs of angels could not have matched it for sweetness. And with its reverberations falling down upon us like bloated snowflakes, Aunt Irène volunteered *Quelle est cette odeur agréable* in a thin, bird-like, out-of-character voice that seemed to come from the ends of the earth. Imagine, I thought to myself, one entire carol dedicated to the "odeur agréable," in and around the stable—surely coming from the animals in attendance at the event. And on that same train of thought, imagine a prophet of that stature electing, or so it would seem, to be born in a stable and warmed by the breaths of cattle and sheep, how could humans still possibly think of us as inferior after all of that…?

Kirsten then unearthed her guitar from its black case, strapped it on and played a pastiche of flamenco pieces she'd learned in

Andalusia last summer. But timing is everything. In music especially. And before we knew it, the solid, sad, disconsolate chords had cast a dark spell over the pure and innocent carols still magically suspended in mid-air. In the lull that followed, the children drifted off, Kirsten put her guitar away, and the guests began to stir in their seats. Harry soon drove Ned and Aunt Irène home, leaving Monique and me to sit in the glow of the Christmas tree, hanging on to the ends of the day.

March 19TH

Blame it on the Voice of Women. Blame it on the Women's Liberation Movement. Blame it on Marina. Monique is now a feminist she tells me, and taking courses at the new Concordia University. Marina lent her *The Feminine Mystique* by Betty Friedan and she saw herself jumping off every page. She's not a radical, crusading feminist—leaving home or going on strike or burning her bra in Dominion Square. No, she's more like the sleeping beauty, more sleeping than beauty, who awakens after forty years, sits up, looks down at herself sitting there and wonders who and where she is. She is taking two courses—one in Canadian history, the other in French literature, learning for learning's sake, because she knows nothing except office work and sewing. Sure, she's made all the curtains and drapes in the house, all the cushions and bedspreads and placemats, but how could she be forty-two and know so little? How could she forget almost all her French when her mother and Aunt Irène were born in the French language stronghold of the Saguenay, when she grew up in Québec City, how could she have lived all these years and not heard the choral masterpieces she's been singing in the Elgar Choir, like the Brahms *Requiem* they're rehearsing now?

At the risk of sounding tedious and repetitive, I know how she feels. My sheltered existence does not allow me to be lured by my own curiosities either. Even for canines, there is more to life than hunger and thirst and a roof over one's head. Just thinking about it, that crushing feeling of confinement returns again, like a numbing bitter-cold spell in winter or a subterranean disturbance, and impulses that seem to have vanished appear in the clear pool of my instinctive memory, upset the placid order of my being. Without realizing it, Monique too is disturbing the placid order of her being as well. I can tell by the pitching and tossing and thrashing in her sleep, and the bluntness in her brushstrokes when she grooms me.

June 19th

An ill-wind blows through the house. Aunt Irène has had a stroke. She's moved in with us, and is occupying the den, this too disturbing the placid order of things. For even after her stroke, she's like the proverbial parade of bugles passing by, and you have to pay attention. But she's not here forever, she says. *Non, monsieur.* She'll be leaving soon enough, for she still has *Tête-Folle* to run, and her assistants have no ambition, no drive, no push. Between customers, they do their nails, pluck their eyebrows, wax their legs and talk about their boyfriends. So having a stroke has been an immense frustration. As she says herself, she's never had the *"patience immense"* you need to wait for things. For recovery has been slow and unsteady. On the bright side, as if by a miracle, she's rediscovered her mother tongue, almost completely lost after being stored away in mothballs when she went to Chicago. Out of the soupy fog of semi-consciousness came whole clusters of French words, like sunken islands appearing in the Saguenay river, she said. Another comforting thought, she was not killed instantly, like her sister Yvonne. Yes, the stroke was *"intempestif"*, coming in the mad rush before Easter, and *"grossier"*, coming as she was giving a young man a Ringo Starr haircut, causing her to collapse and fall smack on top of him, her assistants said, leaving him pinned to the chair and staring into the mirror in disbelief, the tufts of hair on one whole side of his head still up in clips.

A flashing ambulance, its siren wailing, came and sped her to St. Mary's Hospital close by.

"She'd had a cerebrovascular accident," the emergency doctor said, "with partial paralysis down the left side of her body."

After a three-week stay in hospital, the doctor ordered a stay in a convalescent home, given the flaccid muscles and persisting weakness down her left side—not to mention the danger of further strokes—unpredictable as aftershocks after an earthquake, the doctor said. But a convalescent home was not a real home, Monique said, and brought her here, where she sleeps on the hide-a-bed in the den, where the TV is, and Aunt Irène has a mania for movies on TV.

Aunt Irène is also a night owl. There'll be time enough for sleep later, she claims, and sits up well past midnight, watching movies. And smoking like she did in Chicago. Yet she's up poking around the kitchen in her aluminum walker before seven, although she hates the aluminum walker, it makes her look like *"la Tour Eiffel,"* she says. In fact lately, she's been carrying the walker out in front of her like a tray or a birthday cake, as if *it* needed *her,* a sign that she may soon be ready to throw it off and use a cane.

Since being here, she's told the children story upon story. About her and her twin sister Yvonne—their maternal grandmother—the second grandmother they never had a chance to know. And shouldn't they know where they come from.

Irène and Yvonne were born on a pig farm north of Saint-Honoré in the Saguenay and lost their mother when they were three. Two weeks after pushing their brother Emmanuel out into the stubbornly cold world of January. Her death was a *grand mystère*—and still is for Aunt Irène. So they'd brought each other up, mostly Irène taking care of Yvonne who would have stayed in their mother's womb if given a choice. But at twelve, they were cleaning houses in Chicoutimi after school and on weekends. At fourteen, they were working in hair salons in Chicoutimi and saving their money. On the morning they turned eighteen, they rose from their three-quarter bed, came downstairs dragging two black suitcases *en carton* behind them, one stashed with clothes, the other stashed with hair-dressing equipment they'd collected over the years and used to practise on each other.

They didn't even eat breakfast. They just pulled on their winter coats, hats, scarves and mitts, and each picked up a suitcase.

"Vous partez en voyage, vous autres-là?" their father said, standing at the half-open door with Emmanuel, on his way out to feed the pigs.

But it was a miserable morning, the March wind whipping through the open door, and he didn't wait for an answer. And before the pigs had been fed and watered, Yvonne and Irène had walked off the farm and all the way to the bus station in Chicoutimi. Once aboard, they rode bus after bus until they reached Chicago. Chicago, because their cousin Étienne Coulombe had gone there to work at eighteen and had come home five years later, wearing a smile as wide as Lac Saint-Jean itself, and sporting a gold front tooth—signs of the prosperity and worldliness he'd met there.

In Chicago, Yvonne and Irène worked in beauty salons, learned to smoke, learned to speak English and, of course, the latest in hair styles—the permanent wave, the poodle cut, the page boy, the bobbed *gamine* cut, everything—and four years later opened their own salon, calling it *Paris à Chicago.* Because after the war, beauty and fashion rose like cream to the top of people's minds. Business boomed in *Paris à Chicago.* Until out of nowhere, Irène fell head over heels for a GI turned real estate agent called Curt, married him on a reckless long Easter weekend and moved to the other side of town, leaving Yvonne alone in *Paris à Chicago* and at sixes and sevens, because the twins had never really been *divisées en deux.* Even in Chicago, they'd slept in the same bed. Six months later, Yvonne had had enough of her aloneness. She sold *Paris à Chicago,* closed the door on Irène and Curt, and took bus after bus until she reached Québec City. There, she rented a room on Côte-de-la-Montagne, just below the Dufferin Terrace, and found work as a saleslady in the hat department of Holt Renfrew on Buade Street. Within weeks she'd met Walter. He was walking with two dogs on the Dufferin Terrace. And in another reckless fit of loneliness, she married him. Like Irène, she had no patience. Had she only waited, Irène said, one more week. For by another accident of fate, she, Irène, would throw her real estate agent overboard and board the bus to Montréal.

"Ah le fameux diable du destin," she exclaimed and shook her head.

Once back in Montréal, Irène worked in a beauty parlour on Park Avenue. Two years later, she opened *Salon Tête-Folle* on Côte-des-

Neiges Road. The business was an almost overnight success and in no time she had to hire one, two and then three, *coiffeuses,* and now when she least expected it, *misère noire,* the stroke.

September 1971

Aunt Irène is also slowly getting to know me. I say slowly, since I am the only dog she has ever really known, although she does remember the dog on the pig farm in *Saint-Honoré.* But he was *solitaire,* had no name and lived outdoors. He was probably part wolf, she thinks, with his ragged gray coat and pale cream-coloured eyes and a howl—*comme un gros chagrin*—that swept through the two of them lying all of one piece in the bed at night. The dog was not part of the family. Not even part of the assembly of pigs and geese and hens outdoors. In fact, just talking about the farm, she says, and picturing the dog lying there among the drying cords of wood, brings back her own *gros chagrin.* Because there was no family left, not after their mother had gone. All the *désir* and *passion* and *savoir-être* and *minutie* needed to make a family had gone with her.

Their grandmother, who was *corpulent,* with most of the fat assembled around the middle, plodded up the road every morning, through slush and snow and storm surges of every kind, from the farm next door, tied her apron *autour de l'équateur,* scoured the house and cooked the meals and fed Emmanuel goat's milk from her very own goats, *parce qu'Émmanuel, c'était le divin messie venu à Saint-Honoré.* And their father? He gave himself over to the predictable outdoors and its even more predictable pigs.

"Did you miss your mother when she died? Kathleen asked, full of curiosity and questions.

"*Ah mon Dieu oui,*" Aunt Irene said. In fact, they couldn't believe she had really died. Because one day she was there, and the next day she was gone, like one snap of the fingers with nothing in between to prepare them. And when they were old enough to walk to school, maybe nine or ten, they took a notion one day, on their way home, to sneak into the cemetery next to the church and look for the tombstone with their mother's name *Edwidge Coulombe* written on it, but they couldn't find it. That night before going upstairs to bed, Irène brought it up with their father at the kitchen table.

"Qu'est-ce que t'as à t'fourrer l'nez partout?" he fired back, sticking her nose in where she had no business. Their mother was buried in Roberval with her own people, he said, stepping into his rubber boots, stomping out the door and slamming it. But later that night, with Yvonne asleep, Irène crept from their bed and halfway down the staircase, because she'd heard human noises in the kitchen. And through the rungs she saw someone sitting at the table in the dark. It might be their mother come back, or the ghost of her, she dared to think, but no, it was their father, his head in his two hands, talking to himself, *sa voix pleine de rage et de chagrin.* And before his rage and grief could race up the stairs and straight into her, she crept back up and into her bed and clung to Yvonne, *les deux cramponnées une sur l'autre.*

From that moment on, she knew. Their mother would not be back. From that moment on, she and Yvonne became survivors, with their own built-in society of two, their little hearts growing braver by the minute. And harder. And colder. *Comme deux cubes de glace, un collé sur l'autre,* she said.

"Mine's harder than Yvonne's," she told Kathleen. "Your grandmother's more *argileuse,* more like shale, more brittle."

Aunt Irène tells Kathleen and Matthew these stories, and they grow quiet, as if the cold and hard realities they contain, so dangerously close to home, are being impressed upon them for a first time, and they are turning them over, trying to find room for them in their minds. Even Mark, who is nineteen now, has taken to Aunt Irène and is watching TV movies with her into the early hours of the morning.

It's as if a night visitor has stolen into our house, causing it to move and stretch and bend in new ways to accommodate a verbose and illuminating presence.

Mark continues to work for Marina, painting all of the upstairs, except the den over the garage where Desmond ties his flies. Nobody goes there but Desmond. Not even Marina. Not since he posted the NO TRESPASSING sign on the door.

As always, Mark takes me with him when he goes to "work." It seems I have a tranquilizing effect on Modesta and Minerva, confined to the cage during the painting and agitated as a result. Confinement within their skin and feathers was one thing, but confinement within the cage was an insult. To add to it, Mark and Marina have been confined to the living room couch for their sexual activities, since the whole upstairs is shrouded in white sheets because of the painting, and they too are agitated as a result. Especially since the lessons have exploded into full-blown copulation and all the foreplay attending it. It's the first item on the agenda upon our arrival. I lie beneath the cage, forepaws stretched out before me like a sphinx, calming the cockatoos, and watch. In this realm of learned and sensuous activity for humans, Mark is a model student.

This morning, with Marina in a flowered cotton housecoat, he pours her a cup of coffee and joins her on the couch as she sips it, one hand surreptitiously brushing her thigh with the tips of his fingers, as they talk about undercoats and second coats and thinner and turpentine, he slowly but surely works the housecoat open, revealing her fleshy thighs, her thicket of pubic hair, now talking about the colour scheme for Kirsten's bedroom, three walls in flesh tones, the fourth in black as she requested, ever so deftly removing the housecoat completely once she takes the last sip from her cup. And with the couch squeaking and creaking under the strain, Marina stretches out full-length, her bulk and heft spilling over the edge. She then watches and waits as he removes his jeans and boxer shorts and T-shirt, reaches up and pulls him down to bury his face in her two immense breasts, smooth and white and round as full moons, also spread out and spilling over the edge of her torso, their huge protruding nipples pointing optimistically toward the ceiling. He sucks on both equally, first one, then the other, running his tongue over their smooth white surfaces, his head then slowly and deliberately moving down, kissing her belly, then her shins and feet. Not until she invites him in does he enter, and then, with the meticulousness and ritual of a Japanese tea ceremony, waiting for her to ask again and again, to beseech him even.

I can see why the sexual act is such a minefield for humans. Why they need lessons. For the male sexual organ when erect, with that growth of disheveled hair encircling it and those two bag-like contrivances sagging beneath, red as the caruncles on a turkey gobbler, is anything but beautiful, and when approaching the object of its desire —from the front as humans do—is nothing short of menacing once it reaches it full height. So timing is of the essence if it ever hopes to inspire awe and by some miracle be welcomed into the Taj Mahal, so to speak.

As I sat there taking in the entire spectacle, the sight of it, the smell of it, the sheer fervour of it, that longing for intimacy with my own species returned again full force, and yes, the miracle of it, the divineness, does indeed surpass all understanding.

October 1971

Mark now has a girlfriend named Antonia. He met her at Dawson College where both are studying business administration. Unlike Marina, Antonia is tall and sleek, with long, straight black hair, a long Modigliani neck and nose, skin the colour of liquid honey, and the inquisitive look of one trying to understand something. Everyone thinks she is Mark's first girlfriend, but I know better. I was a spectator when he broke the news to Marina one evening last week. It all began with copulation on the couch. But it was a distracted affair, hasty, and the minute the act was consummated, Mark pulled on his clothes, stretched up to full height and became oratorical, as if he were about to prove the existence of God from a podium, to an audience in a darkened room. He began by thanking Marina. She had taught him how to love a woman. She had made him feel alive again. All well and good, but he needed someone his own age, he said, pacing now, jingling the loose change in his pockets, and he had met a girl at Dawson College.

Marina broke in.

"Don't worry your head," she began, slipping into her white terrycloth housecoat and tying the belt tightly round her waist in business-like fashion. "I'm very happy for you. And for the girl. You're a young man, and you're alive. When trees grow, they branch out in different directions," she said. But sex was not mathematics, not addition or subtraction or even division, he could still come from time to time. Brush up on things. Get a refresher. Learn something new, because sex was alive, always in a state of flux, it had a body, you could touch it, smell it and taste it, Marina said.

But Mark was resolute. He'd made up his mind, no ifs, ands, or buts. Like a grateful student, he politely and complacently thanked Marina again for what he called "everything," and with me in tow, promptly left. And left her standing there, naked underneath her white terrycloth housecoat, like I might leave a bone after sucking all the marrow from it. In one same minute their sexual intimacy had been "everything" and "nothing." A pilgrimage to the brink of wonder one minute, a short taxi ride around the block in the next.

October 1971

On her way to courses at Concordia University, Monique stops by *Salon Tête-Folle* and spends some hours doing bookkeeping, purchasing and other administrative chores, making sure it's business as usual. Because roadblocks—two trans-ischemic attacks, as the doctor calls them—and frequent spikes in blood pressure have obstructed Aunt Irène's path to recovery. So she continues to live with us. And to smoke. And to watch late-night movies.

As for Monique and Marina, they continue to sing in the Elgar Choir, a nest of singing birds, Marina calls it. And to practise their parts together in Marina's living room, the two sitting side by side on the piano bench, as Marina hammers out the alto part on the keyboard. Marina took piano lessons as a child and can read music. Yesterday, they rehearsed the *Vesperae Solennes de Confessore,* a work for choir and orchestra by Wolfgang Amadeus Mozart. He wrote it after the woman he'd fallen head over heels for dropped him like a hot Austrian sausage, Marina says, which might explain the first in-your-face declamations in the *Dixit Dominus,* like a volley of boulders delivered in quick succession, and nothing to prepare you for them. They also got a head start on selections for the gala concert in March, among them the *Five Mystical Songs* by Ralph Vaughan Williams for Baritone, Chorus and Orchestra. In the *Third Mystical Song,* they took turns, one singing the *pianissimo* hummed unison, while the other sang the baritone solo:

> *"You must sit down, my Love, and*
> *taste my meat,*
> *So I did sit and eat."*

all of its carnality coming to a hushed conclusion on a satiated "Ah-h-h."

In the final antiphon,

> *"Let all the world in every corner sing*
> *My God and king*
> *The heavens are not too high*
> *His praise may thither fly"*

the cockatoos hollered and squealed *fortissimo* the whole way through, showing no regard for the primacy of contrast in the music, paying no heed whatever to the *dolce* at,

> *"The earth is not too low*
> *His praises there may grow"*

their screeching rising to hysterical at

"The Church with Psalms must shout
No door will keep them out
Let all the world in every corner sing
My God and king."

All as if to say there are countless ways to sing God's praises in this fathomless universe. The British way is not the only way. Never mind cockatoos, humans themselves have devised fathomless ways to do everything—thirty-two ways to wash dishes, fifty ways to leave a lover, six hundred and eighty-five ways to dress an egg, not to mention the many ways to skin a cat … or an innocent lamb … what for? … parchment … imagine … parchment …

And while we're imagining parchment, imagine Monique, innocent as a lamb herself, when it comes to Marina, that is. Innocent of Marina's instruction in the rudiments of carnal knowledge to her son. In fact, when she announced to Marina that Mark now had a girlfriend, "an Italian beauty called Antonia, tall and imposing as a Roman statue," reaching one long arm to the ceiling for emphasis, Marina pretended not to hear. She carelessly threw the music scores into the piano bench and promptly changed the subject.

March 1975

March has been another tumultuous month in this house, all the more so for being so unexpected—like yesterday's blistering snowstorm scattering everything in its path—incredulous even, since an almost monastic quiet had settled on the place after Christmas, like a winter consolation of sorts. A procession of days, one resembling another, their events equally unspectacular…Monique had enrolled in yet more courses at Concordia University, including one on twentieth century plays and playwrights, and was attending classes regularly, Harry had flown in and out as usual, Mathew had been fundraising to subsidize a trip to Florence, Italy, with his history class, and Kathleen had been patiently waiting for March break and a promised trip to Disney World with Harry and Monique.

In fact, winter had not stirred in its February sleep, the twilight gleam of lengthening days had barely shown its face, when Aunt Irène, in a sudden fit of *impatience* and insubordination, threw her aluminum walker overboard—as she had Curt in Chicago. Enough was enough, she said, *chu rendue au boutte*. The cane would have to do.

One overpowering impulse inspired another, for the very next day, Mark dropped out of his studies at Dawson College. Days later he had found work selling sporting goods and body-building equipment in a specialty store on St. Catherine Street downtown, all of which made Harry more adamant than ever. Mark should move out. Rent an apartment. Experience life in the real world if he didn't want to learn anything in school. These were Harry's parting words before taking off to Vancouver, scarcely audible in the barrage of clanging and banging as Mark transformed the garage—a receptacle for all things thrown into disuse, "a scrap heap," as Monique called it—into a body-building room, a miniature gymnasium, with skipping ropes, barbells, a weight bench press and pull-up bar for chin-ups. And when he wasn't at work or with Antonia, he was in the "gym, working out, pumping iron, building body mass and muscle strength."

"What about your mind?" Monique chided him, adding that even Arnold Schwarzenegger had gone to university and wasn't content with just being Mr. Universe.

But to Mark the body was everything. He couldn't see, smell, taste, hear, talk or even think without his body, and neither could she, he reminded her.

The axe fell in late February.

Out of nowhere, Mark said, Antonia stopped taking his calls. Evening after evening, he paced back and forth like a prizefighter waiting for the starting bell to ring, from the gymnasium to the den where Aunt Irène was watching sitcoms and movies, waiting for Antonia to return his calls. In a fit of desperation, he finally went to

Dawson College. In fact, he bumped into her in a corridor. Unexpectedly, he told Aunt Irène. And when he pinned her down, she fessed up. She'd met someone else. It was so serendipitous, Antonia said, so very "happening," she'd literally stumbled across this guy getting into an elevator. And she hadn't phoned because she'd hardly had time to think, it happened so fast, and she wanted to tell Mark about it without hurting him.

A lame excuse, Mark said to Aunt Irène. But she needn't bother filling his parents in on all the tiresome details, they wouldn't understand. They'd blame *him*…if he hadn't quit school, if he'd stuck with it, and on and on.

March break came, Mathew flew to Florence, and Kathleen flew to Disney World with Monique and Harry, only to leave me, as well as Mark, bereft, our emotions in a state of disarray, a feeling of abandonment most prominent among them. With nothing to concentrate the mind, boredom soon set in. Like most dogs, I thrive in the midst of great commotion and do not suffer solitude well. And a room with a view does not relieve the pangs of separation. I spent the days moping, trailing Aunt Irène around the house like a shameless gumshoe, becoming even more of a nuisance on the third day when I stupidly interposed myself between her and her cane, causing her to lose her balance, then her patience as she ferreted me out from underneath with the pointed tip of her cane, an embarrassment to say the least.

The interminable evenings I spent in the gymnasium with Mark, as he worked out like a man possessed, grunting and grimacing with every exertion, the beads of sweat pouring like tears down his neck and onto his chest.

On Wednesday evening, after going through a punishing ninety-minute ritual of exercise, Mark pushed the weight bench press out from under the pull-up bar and replaced it with an old discarded kitchen chair. He then stood on the chair, looped one end of a jump-rope around the pull-up bar, looped the other end twice around his neck and tied it. The sight of him standing there on that chair, large and intimidating as a piece of statuary, his body limp as one crushed by an elephant, staring down at his new Adidas, his lips a grim, thin line like Ned's when he holds his pipe — the glow and smell of his sweat — all of these conspired to spread terror through me, then canine courage, and like Hyrcanus leaping onto his master's funeral pyre, I leapt onto the chair and held it fast with my almighty forelegs, barking as I had never barked before—more than enough to terrify Aunt Irène, who threw open the door to the gymnasium, her hair half in rollers, only to see Mark standing there helpless, an inert mass, the skipping rope limp around his neck, its red handle resting on his chest like an amulet used in sacred rites of passage, the kitchen chair immovable under the supernatural weight of my immovable upper body.

"*Pour l'amour du Bon Dieu, qu'est-ce que tu fais là?*" Aunt Irène shouted, now throwing her cane overboard and hobbling over, locking her arms around Mark's calf muscles. Then locking her eyes on me. Seeing me for the first time, as it were, like Saul of Tarsus struck from his horse by a light from heaven, my faith and courage under pressure, hitherto concealed from view, now miraculously revealed.

Mark quickly turned shamefaced. He removed the rope, jumped down off the chair, and the procession of three stumbled out of the gymnasium, filed past the clock in the hallway steadily intoning 11 p.m. and into the TV room. In the flicker of light from the TV screen, the two sat staring. Both seemingly at a loss for words. I lay on the floor beneath them, desperately wishing Monique would walk through the front door, deliver all three of us from the chaotic flashes of light coming non-stop from the television.

Mark finally broke through the silence.

"It was just an experiment," he said, he wasn't really planning to hang himself, he was simply seeing if it was possible, and he begged Aunt Irène not to tell his parents, because they'd send him to a shrink and he didn't *need* a shrink. Aunt Irène said she'd have to think about it. She knew more than a little about shrinks because some of her customers came straight to *Tête-Folle* from their shrink and, *still,* even after an hour with the shrink, they talked non-stop about their problems, as if the shrink hadn't heard them, and sometimes shrinks themselves were the problem, one woman even fell in love with her shrink and that was an extra problem to add to the pile.

But she wanted to know, did Mark have a death wish. Naw, he said, he just liked swimming in whirlpools, driving through hairpin turns, anything on the danger list, he like to feel the fear rushing through his body.

"But do you want to die?" she asked point blank.

"No, I want to feel alive."

"Alive, dead, I don't know, never mind the shrink, now we need a philosopher," she said, but alive or dead, he should stay out of the *gymnase*. He should drop in on her when he came home from work — and if he ever thinks of doing more experiments — ever — he should notify her first, hint at it at least, she'd had enough of here today and gone somewhere else tomorrow, she wanted a promise.

"Promise," he said.

"First love, *mon garçon*, is like the first snow, it comes, it's beautiful, it transforms the world, but sometimes the heat of the sun is too much and it melts away," she went on, "but who can escape it, only hearts of ice and stone — like *this* one," she said, almost shouting again and jabbing the purple fingernail on her thumb into the dark hollow between her breasts.

"And you never know," she added, "you too might do it one day too, abandon someone, leave someone standing there, someone who wants *you*, and that would be *sans pitié* for the other one."

Again I, the ever faithful one, am left to ponder the perfidy of humans. The hard stone inside the peach. They want and they don't want, and they don't know what they want.

March 1975

Since that fateful night and every night thereafter, I have been sleeping in Mark's bed, under the covers, abiding the feverish heat of his boiling muscled body, allowing my quiet forbearance and resignation to flow into him like a brook into a river.

As for Aunt Irène, she is like the goddess Coventina in my dreams, her den a sanctuary where Mark comes, her tacked-on artifice affecting an other-worldly aura, her bubbling cauldron of words endlessly spilling over and being replenished.

Such was the ecstasy at my surrogate family's return from Disney World that drops of urine fell like tears from my overburdened bladder, filling me with shame for having stained the new ersatz oriental area rug in the front hall. Nothing was made of it. Just as nothing was made of my heroic exploits in the gymnasium days before. For nobody knows what prompted them. Nobody but Aunt Irène. And Mark is a good actor. As always, he talks. Like a radio announcer over static. And Aunt Irène keeps asking him who he thinks he is, mostly when they watch late-night movies together. If he can't learn from books, maybe he can learn from movies.

"Are you like that character?" she'll say, "or are you more like this other one?"

And more often than not, Mark is at a loss for words, and him so great at public speaking, so glib when he wants to be.

"You don't say, that's fine," Aunt Irène says, "only fools know everything for sure."

But Harry knows something for sure. Since returning from Disney World, he's been pushing hard. Pushing Mark to move out, learn the ropes, find out what it's like to fend for himself.

In bed at night, Monique objects.

"Mark needs time," she argues, "did you see the garage? It doesn't look like a junkyard anymore, he's cleaned it up, besides he's way too unsettled to be thrown out of the house, eighteen or not, he's just not ready for the big heartless world out there."

To bolster her arguments, she brought everything back to herself. What would have happened to *her* at eighteen if she hadn't had Aunt Irène to turn to, to watch out for *her*, she said.

Harry argued back. "This is not Disney World, this *is the big heartless world*." And at Mark's age he was out in that world—more than that, he was thousands of feet above it, flying airplanes, and flying them solo.

The arguments rage, and Mark continues to work at the sporting goods store downtown. On Thursday and Friday he begins his shift at 1 p.m. and works till closing time at 9 p.m. And of late on these mornings, he takes me for a run in the park and then to Marina's. She has welcomed him back like a prodigal son, so to speak, and this time around, there is a scorching intensity, an astonishing wildness, to their lovemaking on the couch. As if the preservation of the world depended on it. The sights and smells and sounds of the secretions and exudates provide a veritable feast for the dog senses as well.

April 1975

The choral repertoire for the spring concert is a "heavy lift," according to Marina, a "big sing," with dozens of vocal hurdles to cross. So Monique and Marina have increased the number of practice sessions in Marina's living room. I of course tag along to calm the cockatoos. Like most animals, I was born with a love of music, a language far older and deeper than human words. If words separate me from humans, music reconnects me to them. I also love the scent the two singers unwittingly secrete from their pores when they sing, a sweet scent akin to mother's milk. Yesterday, they rehearsed the *Ein Deutches Requiem* by Johannes Brahms, which, unlike other Requiems, is sung in German. Marina fortunately has more than a scattering of German and is helping Monique with the pronunciation and phonetics of the language — the soft and hard "s", the "sh" sound as in "Fleisch", the "v" sound as in "Wohnungen." They also read through an English translation of the text.

For how can they sing with feeling hearts and the "elastic tempo" and *rubato* the conductor demands if they don't know what they're singing about? Once they'd learned the notes, they sat, English translation in hand, and listened to a recording by Otto Klemperer conducting the Philharmonia Chorus and Orchestra. First, the opening dialogue with orchestra, *Selig sind, die da Leid tragen*, (Blessed are they that mourn, for they shall be comforted), so care-worn and full of sorrow—not the grief-stricken kind—but the serene sorrow I know so well, introspective and calm as a lake.

Oddly enough, Modesta and Minerva showed no interest, wanted nothing to do with *Blessed are they who mourn, for they shall be comforted.*

"Is it too northern?" Monique wondered, "too severe, are they too tropical?"

Marina had her own explanation.

"Why should they think about death and mourning, much less sing about it, when they're famous for living a very long life, especially in captivity, and will probably outlive all of us here," she said.

Notwithstanding, to everyone's astonishment, during the *Denn alles Fleisch* (All flesh is grass) and its formidable, slow-moving crescendo, Minerva and Modesta slowly began to dance on their perch, probably mistaking it for a slow and stately sarabande. But good heavens! Their body language was lewd with nothing stately in it. Had their genitalia been external, they would have come in full view of anyone who cared to look, for the two fanned and flared their tail-feathers, exhibiting more and more of their under regions as the crescendo mounted to its climactic moment.

We also listened to the transcendent *Wie lieblich sinde deine Wohnungen* (How Lovely Are Thy Dwellings), Marina reminiscing about first hearing it sung when she was only six. It was in the Cathedral in Trondheim, Norway, with its vaulted ceilings and massive Corinthian columns standing in clusters and its stained glass windows, the shafts of coloured light streaming through them, and she trying to snare them in her fingers, everything so big and she so small, and how pangs of pleasure had entered her body upon hearing it, so that she herself felt like a lovely dwelling place, and she'd felt those same pangs of pleasure, those same physical feelings, listening to it today.

When Monique got up to leave, she noticed Mark's pullover sweater lying on the arm of the sofa where she'd been sitting.

"What's *that* doing here," she asked Marina, "has Mark been over here working?"   "No, not working," Marina said, he sometimes dropped in after walking the dog, nodding her head toward me, the innocent bystander.

Monique brought Mark's sweater home. Once in the door, she held it up by the shoulders, arms hanging limp on both sides, as if taking a new measure of the person who owned it. She then hung it on the clothes tree in the entrance hall and headed for the kitchen where Aunt Irène was already preparing dinner.

May 1975

Lately, I've been watching late-night movies with Aunt Irène and Mark. Last night, it was *The Graduate* with Dustin Hoffman and Anne Bancroft. As the credits rolled by at the end, the two were full of talk. About Mrs. Robinson and Benjamin Braddock. Mark thought Benjamin Braddock would have been wiser to go off somewhere on his own, to do something less fairytale—something more adventurous, more daring, on the edge, instead of chasing down that girl and settling down to the exact same kind of life his parents had.

As for Aunt Irène, she thought Mrs. Robinson was lonely, bored even, stuck in a *cul-de-sac*, and Benjamin Braddock made her feel alive inside and sensually connected to someone or something real.

But still, Aunt Irène could not identify with Mrs. Robinson, because she herself had never been sensually connected to anyone except Yvonne—not even to Curt in Chicago, now that she thought about it. How could she have walked out on him the way she did, if she had felt that connection. And unlike Mrs. Robinson, Jesus had never loved her, and she'd never been prosperous, so prosperous that you're bored, because you're never bored when you're *dans l'adversité*, fighting to survive as she had on the farm, in Chicago, at *Tête-Folle*, and now here, recovering from her stroke.

While I am the repository for Mark's secret affair with Marina, I suspect Aunt Irène knows where Mark goes on Thursday and Friday mornings. But she doesn't let on.

I hate cats. No, I do not hate cats. But I do hate Ebony, the black female cat who lives across the street and appears in television commercials for cat food and thinks she's a feline deity for all of it. The memory, ever fresh, of my first unnerving encounter with Tigah upon coming here doesn't help. If anything, it intensifies my feelings of antipathy toward the feline species in general.

Are we natural-born enemies? Perhaps. But Monique likes to think that we can learn to live together, that interspecies relations can be harmonious, that Tigah was just too old and set in her ways to make the required modifications.

"Cats are from Mars," she says, "and dogs from Venus."

Good heavens! Venus! Who sprang fully grown from the white foam arising from the severed genitals of the castrated Uranos and who took many lovers and bore many sons. Really! What kind of utopian thinking could compare me—reduced to a life of complete celibacy and no offspring—to Venus?

As for Ebony, she is an elitist. Worse still, a tormentor. Which may explain my behaviour last Friday morning, walking home from Marina's with Mark—off the leash—and all the glorious release of repressed energy attending it. I smelled Ebony from a distance. Then I spotted her. Stretched out like an indulgent film star on the front lawn, in her sleek black coat. Learned behaviour be damned, I said to myself, the promptings of my instinctive self taking over. I charged across the street in a paroxysm of unbridled passion, prepared to grab her by the red florescent collar she wears, and with her necklace of bells clanging, shake every last ounce of feline arrogance out of her. But she is nimble. She is quick. And before I knew it, she'd climbed the closest tree. And from its branches, hissed and spat at me in her disparaging way. How humiliating, I thought, as Mark collared me and led me helplessly away, chastising me all the way up the stairs and into the house.

In the innermost chambers of my dog's heart, I do not hate Ebony. I envy Ebony. I envy her self-possession and refusal to be human in any way. I envy her freedom. Freedom from the impediments imposed on me by the diabolical leash, the worst human invention since gunpowder.

September 1975

Mark moved out of the house the Tuesday after Labour Day and into a second-floor flat on Saint Urbain Street. He took with him the bench press and barbells, pull-up bars and assorted body-building paraphernalia, as well as pieces of furniture Monique had been collecting for him at garage sales all summer.

"He should take his bed and dresser too," Harry said, again over Monique's objections.

"What if things don't work out?" she said, "what if he has to come back home, where will he sleep then?"

"There you go again," said Harry, "making it easy for him."

In the end Mark *did* take his bed, plus mattress, sheets and blankets. And his dresser.

Sharing the flat with Mark is Chuck, a buddy who works part-time at a sporting goods store. Chuck is a weight-lifter, training to qualify for the Canadian team at the Summer Olympics in Moscow in 1980 no less.

Did he have a family, Monique wanted to know.

"Yes, of course he does," said Mark, "everybody has a family." His mother worked for a dry cleaner on Park Avenue. His father, who'd been a freestyle wrestler in his twenties, had made a living moving pianos. Up until five years ago, that is, when he lost his concentration in the middle of a move and sent the piano barreling down two flights of stairs, through a plate-glass door and out into the traffic. Now, he was superintendent of a luxury apartment in Outremont. In fact, Chuck's father had given them appliances and all kinds of furniture for their flat, perfectly good discards relegated to the basement by apartment dwellers.

Canine Confessions

I was introduced to Chuck on moving day, and he bears a striking resemblance to the British bulldog, with whom I share ancestry, in fact. He's short, wide and compact, with a massive head set squarely on a bull neck with folds in it, and legs thick as fire hydrants beneath him—all of which was initially intimidating, especially when he picked me up off the floor and held me to his chest for a moment. Good heavens! Had he mistaken me for a barbell, I wondered, terrified he would hoist me high above his head in one frightful gesture of triumph. But no. He eased me down to the floor again with uncommon respect, as he would surely do with a barbell.

After handshakes all around, the two filled the van with Mark's possessions and they were gone.

Harry of course was tickled to see Mark go. Monique was torn. Matthew and Kathleen registered no feeling. And Aunt Irène was cautiously optimistic. He wasn't going to Chicago or crossing the ocean, and Saint Urbain Street had as many possibilities as anywhere else. Because she'd rented a room there, not much bigger than a clothes closet, when she first came to Montréal from Chicago.

As for me, I suffered an acute attack of separation anxiety, for I had been watching movies with Mark and Aunt Irène, sharing a bed with Mark every night since the terrorizing event on the Ides of March that had made me a hero in Aunt Irène's eyes. Indeed, on our last night together, Mark thanked me for being there and made a lengthy whispered speech into my coat. While impossible to describe, the intimacy of that moment, the communion, was real to the senses for both of us. The hotness, the sound and smell of our breathing, the concord, all taking me back to that blissful pile of siblings from which I'd come.

October 1975

The poet said it best. "With rue my heart is laden." For Ebony, the black cat across the street, the object of my green envy, was run over and killed by a hit-and-run taxi as she scampered home shortly after dusk last evening. Aching with remorse, I watched from the window as the neighbours stood around like trees in the aftermath, commiserating in whispers, the taxi driver long gone, Ebony's family shattered, the small children's faces buried in the folds of their mother's skirt.

"Get another cat," the feckless ones will say, as if Ebony were replaceable. Cold comfort to some, I know, but Ebony will continue to arch her back and eat Purina Friskies in her TV commercials, even as her remains lie two feet under. Good heavens!

February 28, 1976

We are still reeling from the effects of February, rocked by one earth-shaking event after another.

The first happened on a quiet and innocent Sunday morning. Harry was away on flight duty, the children still asleep. Monique, Aunt Irène and I were in the kitchen having breakfast, when the plaster ceiling in the living room came hurtling down in immense chunks, shattering into thousands of pieces as they struck the floor, the chesterfield, Harry's La-Z-Boy, the lamps — everything — throwing up a cloud of white dust, like smoke from a battlefield, insinuating itself into every nook and cranny of the house, downstairs and up. As Monique said, a flock of wild turkeys let loose in the house, an infestation of wild locusts, could not have created more pandemonium. And there she was in its midst. Staring at the ruins in disbelief. Searching for words. Inhaling its dust.

"Why are we so surprised? It was bound to happen," she said finally, groping her way through the debris. The crack in the ceiling had been there for months. And growing imperceptibly longer and wider by the day. And it wasn't going to repair itself. But they'd put it off and put it off, like they did everything else.

Yet she thanked her lucky stars. The living room was deserted at the time. Had it come crashing down the day before, Monique's insurance broker, an innocent civilian, sitting in the living room with her discussing her coverage, would have been covered with pieces of plaster, if not crushed or maimed or killed. And her with him. Before she'd even bought and paid for the extra coverage.

Misfortunes rarely come singly, for the plaster dust had barely settled when in came the equally jarring phone call from Harry's boss at Air Canada. Harry had suffered a life-threatening heart attack. Not at the controls. Not at the airport. In a hotel room in Vancouver. At three o'clock in the morning. Harry's boss then "stood on his head, bent over backwards" Monique said, to heap praise after praise on the flight attendant who just *happened* by some miracle or act of divine Providence to be close by and, like Harry, wide awake at 3 a.m., "on high alert," so to say. She'd moved with lightning speed, he assured Monique, being expertly trained in emergency procedures, because — and the doctor had confirmed as much — with nobody there to help, Harry may not have survived the episode.

But to Monique, that little extra dose of confirmation from the doctor, about Harry having had somebody there to help, was cold comfort at best.

"Had Harry been *alone*, had he been *asleep*, he may not have *had* the heart attack," she railed to me from her bed late that night. In any case, she could not imagine the flight attendant waiting in the wings to save the dying Harry. No, it was as she'd suspected. And he'd made it official. Harry *was* having an affair in Vancouver, and he'd been caught *in flagrante delicto* (another Latin expression picked up from Marina) and couldn't she just picture the two of them going at it full tilt on top of the bedclothes, Harry crash-landing on her nude body, and her then worming out from underneath the wreckage, scrambling into her clothes, calling the ambulance, and now all of Air Canada, in the air and on the ground across the country, would know about it. It was all too humiliating. Of course, she would spare Aunt Irène the crude details. And Marina. And Mark. And Matthew and Kathleen, who thought their father was perfect.

Two days after Harry's heart attack, Monique flew to Vancouver, leaving Aunt Irène, now almost back to her former self, to "hold the fort," so to speak. And one week later, Harry and Monique arrived home.

Wild horses could not contain my unbridled joy upon seeing them cross the threshold, Harry now leaner, less sure of himself, a certain laxity in his look, a certain trembling hesitation in his hands. Once I'd lavished them with kisses, Kathleen, who is now twelve, rushed in and wrapped her arms around Harry's waist and held on, as if Harry were a tree trunk. She didn't let go, and Harry buried his face in her mop of curls. Matthew, now a glum and distant seventeen, was next in line. He shook Harry's hand in that formal way of greeting a visiting dignitary. Aunt Irène brought her usual *élan* to the moment and threw her arms around Harry's neck, her bracelets and bangles jangling down to her elbows. She was an expert in convalescence, she assured him, and he would recover as she had, because, believe it or not, every wound heals sooner or later.

But once the excitement spilling over into jubilation had died down, a formal feeling came, descending upon the entire household, like a spell of freezing rain after a winter thaw, weighing down on all of its members. And there has been no break in the weather. No relief. Monique and Harry now move past one another like icebergs, their bodies stiff, their language and gesture ceremonious at best. Yet they continue to share the same connubial bed. Why? Because Monique wants to be in the room, at the ready like that flight attendant, she tells me, in case Harry has another heart attack. She doesn't want Matthew and Kathleen worrying for nothing either. Or asking questions. Even if Harry's heart attack leaves a trail of questions behind it. Who will bring home the bacon if Harry can't, is one nagging question. So Monique continues to attend her classes at the university. And to run the business end of operations at *Tête-Folle*. For much as Aunt Irène has recovered her vitality, her days of fiddling in people's heads, talking to people in mirrors, pampering them, are over. The very thought of going back saps her strength, and her legs buckle beneath her, she claims.

Harry's strength is also sapped. His doctor has ordered an indefinite period of convalescence. And no flying for six months—time to recover and stabilize the atrial fibrillation that precipitated the "cardiac event," as he called it.

During Harry's afternoon naps, I keep silent vigil at his bedside, breathing my body warmth into his slippers. And when he wakens in the dimming light of late afternoon, he, who has largely ignored me since my arrival here, now reaches down and threads his fingers, sometimes trembling, through the golden fleece covering my touch spots, oh so gently, as if something has given way inside of him. The gesture is so unprecedented, it disarms me, overwhelms me, compels me to roll over onto my back, legs reaching up, pawing the air, exposing my private parts in that overeager way of canines that strains the nerve of most humans and pushes them away, Harry included, for who among them understands the subtle language of quadrupeds?

April 1976

With Harry in convalescence, my daily outings have taken a favourable turn, especially now that winter is past. On a sun-drenched morning this week, for instance, Harry, dressed in jeans and a roll-neck sweater, looked down at me.

"We're going to Mount Royal," he announced.

We hopped into the van, drove along Queen Mary past St. Joseph's Oratory, along Côte-des-Neiges and up past the orderly rows of tombstones in the cemetery—a would-be paradise for dogs, with its rich smells, not only of bones but of resurrection in every clump of soil and blade of grass. We parked at Beaver Lake, and walked and walked and walked. Around the lake now returned to liquid, placidly awaiting the return from exile of ducks and geese and itinerant seagulls, up a rising slope through fresh new patches of green and clusters of budding trees, their branches bent low from having borne the brunt of winter. Indeed, the youth and exuberance of spring exploded around us at every turn, its alchemy at once new and old as Egypt.

Half way up the long slope, Harry sat on a park bench to catch his breath and watch the tireless birds, flitting in and out of trees, convening on branches, wasting no time, scrambling to get things done, calling out to one another, announcing the dimensions of their space, flashing signals, *cris de coeur,* and colours. As for me, I longingly watched the squirrels and chipmunks, so full of grace, racing up and down tree trunks, tracking down materials, scouring for scraps in the ground detritus left over from last year, chattering as they went about their business—the sheer sight of them filling me with wistfulness, and yes, grudging admiration for their profound desire to survive in the adulterated wilds of a hard-bitten northern city.

We also encountered a number of dogs being paraded by their owners, chattels like me, the most pathetic of all a beautiful Brindle Boxer with accoutrements—a red felt coat and rhinestone clothespins adorning his ears, but clearly a low achiever in every other way, leaping like a jackrabbit at the mere sight of me passing by. Looks are not everything.

To my great joy, Harry also takes me for play sessions at the dog run in Trenholme Park. Upon arriving, he greets the other dog owners, makes the required small talk, but most of all he stands at the chain-link fence, like someone visiting a zoo, and watches the dogs as they play, I central among them—racing, wrestling, rough-housing, falling over one another, taking, giving, nosing into a trusting pile, playing for playing's sake, the shared blissfulness of it reaching deep into our hearts.

On the walk home afterward, the excess gusto continues to gush through me, as evidenced in my gait, the wag of my tail, the sweat dripping from my tongue. And it always manages to make Harry smile—a certain accomplishment, because Harry is not a smiler. He's a pilot. Most at home with itinerant clouds and aloof skies and distant rims and edges and standoffish runways you touch down upon and depart from.

March 1976

After the late-night walk, Harry and I frequently join Aunt Irène in the den. She comes alive under cover of darkness and craves company, begs us to stay a while, maybe even watch the late-night movie. And occasionally we do. Harry goes to the dining room, pours a rye and ginger ale for her and for himself, settles into the stuffed chair next to the hide-a-bed, and the three of us watch whatever is offered. Aunt Irène doesn't discriminate, "English, French, kiss kiss, bang bang", it doesn't matter, she watches it anyway. Last Saturday it was East of Eden, with James Dean, Julie Christie and Raymond Massey.

"*Un film tout à fait frappant,*" Aunt Irène exclaimed afterward. She saw *herself* in this movie and hasn't stopped talking about it since. She is like the son Cal, James Dean's character. She had craved her father's love just as he had. She'd been jealous of her brother, Emmanuel, just as he'd been, especially when her grandmother fed him goat's milk. Most of all, she too had never completely believed her mother had died—and *Dieu sait*—perhaps she was alive and running a brothel somewhere, like Cal's mother.

Harry doesn't get it. A movie's a movie. It takes things to extremes to make you keep watching, he tells her. Besides, the past is the past, and there's no use crying over spilt milk.

But Aunt Irène doesn't hear him. The mystery of her mother has taken possession of her, a ghost she cannot exorcise. What's more, she's taken a great notion to go to the Saguenay and to Roberval and to visit the cemetery where her mother is supposed to have been buried. She wants to see the tombstone. She wants to read her mother's name on it, *Edwidge Coulombe*. And the dates. Once and for all. Just to make sure. For her own sake—and for Yvonne's. And if her mother is not *dans la terre à Roberval*, she wants to know where she is. She'll kill two birds with one stone, and visit the pig farm in Saint-Honoré while she's in the general vicinity. Because she's never gone back home, never seen her brother Emmanuel, never uttered a word to him, since that miserable day in March when they walked all those miles to the bus terminal in Chicoutimi.

Harry thinks it's a harebrained idea, but now that he has time on his hands, the two of them twiddling their thumbs day after day, he'll take her. He'll take her to the ends of the earth if that's where she wants to go. Besides, he's hardly travelled anywhere on the ground, except to the airport and back. And he would love to see the flora and fauna of the Saguenay from down below for a change, especially in May when the snow is off the ground and its lakes and rivers swollen from the freshet. And with nobody home to walk me during the day, I, Daisy, will travel with them.

May 1976

We left on the twenty-fifth of May, in early afternoon, Harry at the wheel, Aunt Irène in the passenger seat, and me in the middle seat behind them. Aunt Irène served as map-reader, calling out every place by name in a megaphone voice, every geographic location, every change in direction, almost like a tour guide. By early evening we had turned north at Trois-Rivières and were snaking along the precipitous bank of the Saint-Maurice River, past Shawinigan and Shawinigan Falls. By nightfall, we had reached La Tuque, a pulp-and-paper mill town.

Once past La Tuque, Aunt Irène folded her map and put it into the car door's pocket. Since she is a night owl, and Harry accustomed to long treks, we drove and drove through the darkness now inhabited by trees and bushes and boulders. And animals, Harry said. Fixing his attention on the road, watching for moose and deer attempting to cross his path. Once past La Tuque, the two also lapsed into silence, as if observing a certain undeclared decorum upon entering the wilderness.

At 1 a.m., we pulled into a small motel nestled in a clearing close to the side of the road. After I'd relieved myself, Harry and I walked over to the door underneath the lonely red and yellow neon sign. A bell tinkled as Harry opened the door, and a man appeared behind a counter. We had obviously roused him from a deep sleep, for he was disheveled, unshaven, and still in his white undershirt, not quite long enough to conceal his hairy pot-belly. He lit a cigarette, sucked on it and left it hanging from the corner of his mouth, as Harry told him what he wanted—two units, one for his aunt, and one for him (and me, of course). With the cigarette still stuck to his lower lip, the man looked down at me, the third member of the traveling party, and scratched the hairs on his belly.

"*Pas d'chiens icite,*" he said in a smoker's monotone, "*pas dans les chambres.*"

Harry rented the rooms anyway. I would sleep in the car, he said. Once he'd settled Aunt Irène into her room, he walked me to the black edge of the world of evergreens surrounding the motel one last time, then led me back to the van.

The van was still warm. So I soon fell asleep, only to be harshly wakened moments later by walls of rain pelting down on the roof and windows and crackling claps of thunder. Good heavens, I muttered to myself, a state of abject terror upon me. I hated thunder and lightning. They paralyzed me. And there I lay, trapped in the van with nowhere to hide. Afraid to even take a deep breath. My fear had reached an almost intolerable peak when through the pours came Harry, opening the hatchback and lowering the back seat, lugging the bedding from the motel room rolled up in his raincoat. Spreading it out on the lowered seats, then climbing in himself, pulling on his dry pyjamas, lying down, pulling me down beside him and cradling my trembling body in his. And that is how we lay till morning broke. Wrapped together against the cold and wet and clapping thunder—the two of us an almost replica of that Galilean man recently unearthed by archeologists. Marina had heard about him on the news. In the Hula Valley they found him, dead since 10,000 B.C., his dog still cradled in the bones of his arm.

To our astonishment next morning, the car and motel were drenched in a downpour of sun, and the wall of forest surrounding the motel was swishing and clicking in the breezes. Harry was also astonished to find Aunt Irène already up and dressed and sitting in a metal chair painted glossy turquoise outside her motel room, her made-up face upturned, her eyes closed, soaking up the morning sun. Aunt Irène was equally astonished to see Harry crawl out the back door of the van and lug the rumpled clump of bedclothes into his motel room. She studied Harry, then quickly put two and two together.

"*Quelle nuit pour toi, Daisy, toi qui a si peur du tonnerre,*" she said. For she'd seen me slink into the depths of the hall clothes closet when thunder struck at home. She massaged my two ears, garbling on in French about how she too had been terrified of thunder as a child on the farm.

"But as somebody said, no fear, no courage," she said, insistently kneading my head with her two bejeweled hands, as if the fear and courage were ingredients stored together inside my head, and she was kneading them into a proper mix.

Once back in the van, we drove to Chambord, stopped for breakfast, then headed farther north again, skirting the rim of Lac Saint-Jean, a massive inland sea thirty-five kilometers in diameter, all the way to Roberval, where Aunt Irène's mother was said to be buried.

Riding along the main street in Roberval, Aunt Irène put her map down and began to fidget in her seat. She lowered the mirror on the sun visor and ran her fingers through her hair, lately in a *bouffant* page-boy and strawberry blond. She licked her fourth finger and ran it along her eyebrows. She recovered her lipstick from her black patent leather purse and applied a fresh coat, mashing and smacking her lips together, then moving her head back to capture an overall view in the mirror. We pulled up to the church and cemetery, and Harry glanced at Aunt Irène.

"Who are we looking for here, what name?" he asked, glancing left and right, scouting around for a parking spot.

"*Coulombe, Edwidge Coulombe,*" she said, fiddling with her hair again, pulling at her ear lobes hung with silver loops that looked more like bracelets.

Harry parked the van, leashed me and took me for a walk along the lakeside. He didn't want me urinating or defecating on the tombstones, certainly not on *Edwidge Coulombe's* tombstone. We then entered the graveyard, the pungent smell of purple and white lilac sifting down from freshly sprung blooms by the wrought iron gateway. The tombstones, large and small, some time-worn and listing to one side, others polished and untouched by weather, were lined up helter-skelter throughout. Harry and Aunt Irène pored over each one, studying the names and the dates. Many named *Coulombe* had been laid to rest here, but *Edwidge Coulombe* was not among them.

"Let's go knock on the door of the presbytery and ask to look at the register," Harry said finally.

But by then, Aunt Irène had taken her reading glasses off and rammed them into her patent leather purse.

"*Je l'savais,*" she began, "I knew it," shouting, shattering the quiet decorum of the cemetery, pulling Harry by the sleeve of his windbreaker toward the entrance, "*je l'savais ben qu'trop ben, je l'savais depuis longtemps.*"

Over Aunt Irène's objections, they *did* go to the *presbytère*.

"We've come this far," Harry said, "and you don't want to turn around and go home again without knowing for sure."

I watched from the van as they emerged from the *presbytère* and made their way back, Aunt Irène wild, shouting and waving her arms at Harry, Harry pulling her back when she walked headlong into the way of an oncoming dump truck.

"*Je l'savais, je l'savais, j'lai toujours su,* she continued to shout once inside the van. For *Edwidge Coulombe's* death was not listed in the register either, and Monsieur le Curé's assistant seemed to know more than she was willing to say, Aunt Irène thought.

"So what do we do now?" Harry said, once she had regained a modicum of composure.

"We'll go to Saint-Honoré," she said, "we'll go to the farm. We'll ask Emmanuel, he will know."

Harry turned the ignition key, started the engine and we were on our way.

We backtracked along the great lake, a mystical white mist rising from it in the early afternoon sun. We then veered inland through a mix of forested areas and vast open fields where wild blueberries would grow *à profusion* in late summer, Aunt Irène said. We rode past farmers' fields where cows stood feeding at troughs. After stopping for lunch at a small road side restaurant, Harry took me for a long walk on the road's shoulder, past a farm house and its outbuildings and herd of cows, some with heifers nuzzling them.

I am not a herding dog, but this was my first encounter with cows and the smell of manure and cow dung intoxicated me, stirred ancient memories alive in my cells. I wanted to eat it, roll my body in it, I wanted to chase those cows as my ancestors had chased badgers, and I would have, had the despotic leash not held me back. The cows themselves — those feeding at the trough heaped with hay — ignored me completely. Others turned and stared at me with that vacant look of creatures who've forgotten who they are, who they once were — sacred cows garlanded with flowers and led through streets in celebratory processions with dancing and music, worshipped for their cosmic, generative power, the personification of Mother Earth herself — all of that past grandeur now lost, for as some poet said, we've seen the future and it's murder.

By mid-afternoon, we had reached *Concession 6*, the side road leading to Emmanuel and the farm. It was a narrow gravel road, muddied and heaving from spring thaw. Harry slowed down, winding cautiously around puddles and piled up stones. Aunt Irène again brought down the mirror on the sun visor, applied fresh lipstick and rouge and patted her *bouffant* page-boy with both hands.

"Emmanuel, he won't know me, and I'm sure I won't know him," Aunt Irène said, fidgeting in her seat. But she was sure she would know the house — weather-beaten wooden boards, two storeys, with a slanted shingled roof, two small vertical windows in the front, each with four panes, and the door on the far side — the woodshed close beside it. And by now, 1976, for sure there would be a mailbox at the road, with *Emmanuel Tremblay* written on it.

And sure enough, further along the road, there it was. The mailbox with *Emmanuel Tremblay* written on it in black paint, the two-storeyed house now painted white, the woodshed still standing.

Harry pulled into the yard and parked next to a stand of spruce trees much taller than the house, growing just beyond the shed half-filled with wood. But the pig pens and pig sheds with tin roofs in the field behind were gone. And in their place, a field full of wooden freestanding sculptures, some larger than life people, others mechanical contraptions in a variety of vivid colours and angular shapes.

As we emerged from the van into the cool and glare of the late afternoon sun, a woman wearing a large cardigan over a dress and apron appeared from around the side entrance to the house.

"Vous cherchez quelqu'un?" she called out, *"Êtes-vous perdus?"* walking toward us, pulling her sweater around her with one hand, and shielding her eyes from the last blinding beams of sun with the other.

Aunt Irène said no, she wasn't lost. She was looking for Emmanuel Tremblay. Emmanuel was away, the woman replied, working at *Chute-des-Passes*. And he would not be back until sometime in the summer. When pressed for more answers, the woman introduced herself. She was *Marthe Tremblay*, Emmanuel's wife, and what business did they have with Emmanuel, she asked.

What business did she have with Emmanuel? she repeated, in the same local patois, no business. She was Irène, Emmanuel's sister, Yvonne's twin, and she'd come to pay him a visit.

"Ah ben j'ai mon voyage," Marthe said, pulling her sweater around her, as if a sudden unexpected chill had run right through her body, her eyes flitting from Aunt Irène, to Harry, to me, to the van, to the house, and back to Aunt Irène, seemingly at a loss as to what to do or say next.

Aunt Irène, seeing her disarray, immediately invited us all into the house and began herding us toward the side door.

We stepped through two doors and were immediately in the kitchen. The floor was a patchwork of forest green and white linoleum tiles, and in its centre a bright red table top and four red vinyl-covered chairs, all with chrome legs. And there indeed were the two small front windows with white lace curtains held back by forest-green ribbons tied in modest bows. And seated in a rocking chair by the far window, a tiny, hawk-eyed woman wrapped in a black shawl, endlessly rocking—and endlessly talking to herself, ever so softly, as if to some intimate presence inside her, her two hands all knuckles, restlessly moving, pressing and kneading one another.

Marthe hastily ushered us into the parlour off the kitchen, sat Aunt Irène and Harry down on two stuffed chairs and offered them a cup of coffee.

But Aunt Irène was way too agitated and had no time to waste on preliminaries. Who was that woman, she wanted to know, jabbing her index finger directly at her, and where did she come from, she wanted to know, as if the woman were an intruder, a *persona non grata*, someone who had thrust herself upon the scene without being invited.

Marthe wasted no time either and immediately carried in one of the chrome-legged chairs from the kitchen, set it down close beside Aunt Irène, sat herself down on it, and began. She could call Emmanuel at *Chute-des-Passes,* she had his number in case of emergency.

But by now, Aunt Irène was back on her feet and itching to have words with the old woman still endlessly rocking. And then it was Marthe back on her feet, laying a mollifying hand on Aunt Irène's forearm, trying to hold back any advance she might make, then rushing to say that *Edwidge* did not know her family, not even Emmanuel.

And so it was, the two standing up and sitting down, heads swiveling, eyes darting back and forth, from the old woman rocking, to one another, both seemingly bowled over by the events thrust upon them so unexpectedly.

Yet Marthe seemed resolute. Bent on setting things straight. She could tell Irène everything, *l'histoire au complet* – if she wanted to know it.

Yes, she did.

Fine, because she'd heard *l'histoire au complet* from Emmanuel.

Yes, she wanted *l'histoire au complet.*

From the beginning?

The beginning, the end, the middle – *toute la patente.*

And so Marthe began.

Edwidge Coulombe c'était pas n'importe qui, non, non, she began. Edwidge Coulombe was somebody, with her long neck and high cheek-bones and straw-coloured hair stacked loosely on top of her head, and her fitted bodices buttoned up to her haughty chin, and that high-flown air about her, reaching right down to her fingertips, and her teaching diploma from *l'École normale de Roberval,* in fact, she was a teacher at the school in Roberval when their father met her, he was visiting his brother who had a butcher shop in Roberval, delivering his pork to sell, and coming from one of the best families, Edwidge came into the butcher shop, because the Coulombe's *bought* their meat, her mother *une hautaine,* educated at the Ursulines convent in Québec City, writing everybody's letters for them, Edwidge's father, was the mayor of Roberval, her uncle, *le curé de la paroisse,* and the very thought of Edwidge throwing over her teaching job to live on a pig farm, *dans les concessions de Saint-Honoré à part d'ça,* was the height of madness, so when the two ran off, the minute school was out for the summer, got married in a *presbytère* in Chicoutimi, and moved to the pig farm, Edwidge's father said, *que'l'diable l'emporte,* you made your bed, now lie in it, and she lay in it for three years—three years almost to the day, as if she'd marked the days on the calendar, and two weeks after giving birth to Emmanuel, she didn't die as people said, she simply walked to the bus stop in her Sunday clothes and took the bus to Roberval, to her parents' home and to the school where she'd been teaching—as if she'd never left—and demanded her classroom back, her pupils, taken from her, she said, she burst in on her father in his mayor's office, her uncle in his *presbytère*, kicking at their doors at all hours of the day and night, banging with her fists, hollering, demanding that they do this and that, go to the principal of the school, and her father, her mother, the relatives so ashamed, so scandalized, that they lumped her into the back seat of a car before daybreak one morning, sandwiched between her father and uncle and, with a hired driver at the wheel, delivered her to Saint-Michel-Archange asylum in Beauport near Québec City, so when the story spread that she had died in Roberval, nothing was done to change it, the neighbours in Saint-Honoré scarcely knew Edwidge, she never went to church, and when she went to the general store, she wore her fancy hats and flouncy dresses and never spoke to anyone, so nobody cared that she was dead because nobody liked her, even if they *did* know her, and for Emmanuel's father, it covered up the shame.

In the beginning, Marthe went on, once a year in the fall, their father left his cousin in charge of the pigs, put on his navy blue serge suit, the one he'd bought in Chicoutimi when he got married, his white shirt and tie, and took the bus to Beauport to see Edwidge. But, she claimed she didn't know him or mistook him for the school janitor or the groundskeeper at the church, sometimes accusing him of robbing her money and her books and her jewellery. When he returned to Saint-Honoré late the following evening, he sat in a chair at the kitchen table in the pitch dark and talked to Edwidge—as if she were at the table with him—holding on to his hope, promising her this and that, pleading with her not to go, Emmanuel said, because he heard him from his bed, talking, talking far into the night, sometimes even weeping, sometimes *en colère,* but with the years he seemed to lose all hope and stopped going altogether.

Then five years ago, with high summer everywhere and the hot sun beating down even at suppertime, Emmanuel found his father in the pigsty, lying in the straw among the pigs, the pigs frantically whisking their tails to keep the flies off him. The pigs loved him, Marthe said. In fact, the last of the pigs had just been slaughtered and trimmed and trucked to Roberval when the phone call came from the mother superior at *Saint-Michel-Archange* asylum in Beauport. Edwidge Coulombe had improved *de façon remarquable,* the new drugs had worked miracles. In fact, she was so calm, so manageable, she could go home.

"Home?" Emmanuel said, on his high horse, this was never home to Edwidge Coulombe, he said, let her go to Roberval where she belongs. He ranted and raved until Marthe grabbed him by the buttons of his shirt and forced him to look straight into her eyes, "if your father was still alive, what would he do, would he bring her here?" Marthe demanded, gripping his shirt front until she got an answer.

Of course his father would bring her home, Emmanuel railed, he worshipped her, she was like the statue of *Notre-Dame-du-Salut* in front of the church, her up there, him down here, Emmanuel went on. So that settled it for Marthe, she had no children, she would take care of Edwidge Coulombe.

"Imagine she's a boarder," Marthe said to him, so before the snow came, they drove to Beauport and brought her home. She didn't know Emmanuel of course, how could she, he was two weeks old when she walked out, she couldn't. The two were perfect strangers. Edwidge didn't remember the house either, most of the time she thinks she's in Roberval, living in her father's house or in her classroom teaching her students, and when Marthe sees the rosary beads moving through her fingers, she thinks she's back in *Saint-Michel-Archange*, praying with the nuns. But, she gives no trouble, and demands nothing, she swallows her pills, sleeps, eats, and rocks and talks and prays. If you didn't know she was there, you might think it was a radio playing quietly in the next room.

And what happened to the pigs, Aunt Irène wanted to know.

After his father died, Emmanuel sold the pigs and landed a job *à Chute–des-Passes* as a watchman for the power station. And because it's hundreds of miles away, he works for three months, then comes home for three months, and when he's home, he builds things.

"*Emmanuel, c'est un patenteu, quand y'est icite y passe son temps à construire ses patentes dans sa shoppe,*" Marthe said, from logs he cuts down, he carves monument-sized people he calls his family and paints them every colour in the rainbow, and from old car parts and farm machinery, he creates never-before-seen contraptions, some useful, most not.

And where was his *shoppe*, Aunt Irène inquired.

His *shoppe* was back there in the woods, behind his *patentes,* Marthe said with a vague gesture of her hand, for she'd never been there herself.

Aunt Irène listens, her eyes still fixed on her mother rocking, the garbled litany of the old woman's words indecipherable from the parlour.

Now more at ease with the impromptu visitors and back in charge, not only of her own premises, but its unvarnished history, Marthe invites her guests to stay for supper.

But Aunt Irène doesn't seem to hear, for she is on her feet and moving deliberately toward the door.

Will she leave her telephone number, Marthe asks, following along behind, will she keep in touch now that she knows, will she come back when Emmanuel is home?

Aunt Irène is noncommittal, preoccupied, rethinking her place in the larger scheme of things, perhaps, since there is no place for her here, given the naked little truths she heard today. No, she needs time to think, she says, quickening her step as she moves past the old woman rocking.

And so we take our leave. With darkness falling around us, Harry pauses on the porch to take one last look at Emmanuel's *patentes* in the field behind, now spectral and haunting figures in vibrant carnivalesque colours peering eerily through the indistinct half-light of evening.

Once in the van, we drive slowly away, the clouds whipping up from the horizon, heaping overhead, wrapping us in premature darkness. For once, Aunt Irène is speechless. In a silent rage, I suspect.

Harry has nothing to say either. I lie on the back seat, my snout resting on my front paws, my tail wrapped snugly around it, pondering the significance and weight of loss and lies and, again, my limbs feel dislocated and all my bones out of joint.

Just this side of Chambord, Harry pulls in to a motel and dining room. This evening, with the wind bending the treetops and the occasional blast sideswiping the van itself, not to mention the crackling thunder in the distance, he rents one motel room with two double beds and smuggles me in, slung over his arm, disguised as a garment bag.

As Aunt Irène settles in, Harry goes to the dining room and returns with hamburgers and French fries and soft drinks. He then opens a can of Doctor Ballard's and scoops it into my dog dish. I wolf it down in seconds, then lap up the water poured into my bowl from the bathroom sink, for what delectation can compare to a bowl of cold, clear, fresh water after miles of travelling over land. Hence the jubilant slurping. I know, grossly unsuited to the occasion. For the two eat in crushing silence. All I hear is chewing and swallowing and the metal clink of utensils. Once they finish eating, Harry takes me out. We slink around the end of the motel and halfway down a brambly slope, just far enough away for me to conduct my affairs without being seen. Harry is particularly nervous this evening, because the stench of skunk is strong, potent enough to make his eyes smart and to intoxicate me, give me ideas, obliterate all my desire to please humans and transform me into a predator—and then where would we be, Harry says, stinking up, not only our room, but all fourteen rooms in the motel, including the office, which would be the icing on the cake for Aunt Irène and fourteen stations of the cross for the chambermaid tomorrow. Harry, like me, can smell things from far off.

When we return, Aunt Irène is sitting ramrod straight in the loveseat in a flannelette nightgown the same vibrant purple as her fingernails, a whitish wool blanket draped over her shoulders, looking grim as an Indian chief, arms folded, eyes locked in position, almost catatonic. Harry reaches down into his leather overnight bag and salvages a flask of rye whisky.

"I'm going to pour myself a nightcap, a good stiff rye on the rocks," he announces. "Would you like one?"

"Why not?" she says.

Harry disappears and reappears with a bucket of ice, pours the drinks and sits down on the loveseat beside her. But no sooner have they taken a first sip than Aunt Irène has thrown off the blanket and is back on her feet, pacing back and forth in her nightgown, the words pouring from her. But the usual fire and exuberance is gone.

"You know, Harry, Yvonne and me, we left the Saguenay, and me — not Yvonne — I brought the Saguenay with me, the hard and the cold and the brutal parts. I carried them like a block of ice buried inside my body, like those blocks of ice the men carved from the river and buried in the sawdust, and I could feel it there today with that old woman, *la mère manquée,* big and frozen and cold. I wanted to grab her by the two shoulders and stand her up on her two feet and shake her and say wake up, look at me, *ta fille Irène, que tu as laissée là pour crever.*"

Aunt Irène is back to hollering again, and Harry has to remind her that we are in a motel room and it's way past 11:00 at night and I, Daisy, am in the room against the motel's rules. But there is no holding Aunt Irène back now, she continues to pace back and forth like a courtroom lawyer, the loops in her ears swinging, her bracelets clanging up and down her arms with every new flare-up ...

"You saw me today, you saw me walk away from her, well that's what I do, I walk away. I walked away from the farm, I walked away from Yvonne in Chicago, I walked away from Curt in Chicago too — just like that," she said, snapping her fingers. "Why did I walk away from Curt in Chicago? Because he cried, he yelled, he killed people in his sleep, shooting, stabbing, cursing, choking, every night the same, as if he was still in the war, every night, I couldn't listen anymore, I couldn't sleep, and so I left him there — *pour crever, lui aussi.* One morning after he went to work, I packed my bags and left, took the bus to Montréal. That's what I do, that's what we do in the Saguenay."

I lie there quietly, listening to Aunt Irène so racked with remorse and self-loathing, cursing the climate of her birthplace, and streams of empathy run through me, the climate of my birthplace buried deep within my being also, and that feeling of our fates being sealed by worlds and weathers not of our making rises to meet me once again.

As for Harry, he is like a sponge, soaking up Aunt Irène's revelations, his gaze pointed at the ceiling, as if her outpourings were being congealed and suspended in mid-air like drops of light from a hanging fixture.

By midnight, Aunt Irène has unburdened herself, run out of words. And she is dead tired. And there being no questions and no answers, they both go to bed. I lie in the space between the two beds, my limbs like jelly, Aunt Irène's desolation entering into me, cleaving to my flesh and bones.

On our trip south and homeward the next day, the sky has cleared, and intimations of a new season appear at every twist and turn in the road, the buds swelling on the branches of trees, carpets of green grass rolling out in the fields, birds appearing like angels descended from heaven, the bark of birch trees shining silver in the early afternoon sun, tender twigs sprouting their newborn shoots. For as the poet said, life urges and pushes forward—despite Aunt Irène's mounting rage now shaped into questions being hurled at Harry, like bitter blasts of unseasonably cold wind.

"Why did Edwidge Coulombe have children if she couldn't take care of them?" she rails.

"Why didn't she stay a school teacher in Roberval if she didn't like the pig farm?" "Why did our father and everyone else lie to us the way they did?"

"And Emmanuel, why was he fed goat's milk and not me and Yvonne?"

"Your mother had a mental illness. She *couldn't* take care of you," Harry says, a hint of impatience sharpening his tone too, "and your father was probably ashamed of himself and wanted to put her out of his mind, forget about her, hoping *you'd* forget about her as well. Besides, it all happened sixty-five years ago, and you're still here, you don't really *need* your mother after all these years, do you?"

Aunt Irène throws a murderous look at Harry, and he changes the subject to Emmanuel.

"Too bad you didn't get to meet Emmanuel," he says, "too bad we didn't get a closer look at his inventions."

"To hell with his inventions, who wants a family made of pieces of wood?" Aunt Irène shouts, *"qu'il aille chez l'diable avec ses patentes,* let him live with his inventions." She never wants to have a closer look at them—or at Emmanuel. And the conversation ends there.

During the rest of the drive home, Harry bends over backwards to mollify Aunt Irène, as if his efforts to pacify her had been a lapse in etiquette. But her passions are not to be mollified. At least not on this evening.

Darkness comes early, and with it gathering clouds followed by a series of rain showers, putting Harry on high alert for moose and deer, moose especially, he says, since their eyes do not reflect the light from oncoming cars. But by the time we reach La Tuque, the showers have stopped, and the heavy curtain of cloud has parted, and spread out before us in the open space created, a consoling tapestry of stars with their tiny radiant hearts, and a half-moon appearing and disappearing from view as we wind our way along the Saint-Maurice River.

When we reach home it is way past midnight. Once I've relieved myself, we steal into the house like thieves and retire for the night. Tonight I sleep in the den with Aunt Irène. And tonight, in one last spontaneous gesture, she invites me up onto the hide-a-bed to sleep at her feet, establishing a precedent.

May 15, 1976

In recent nights, I've dreamt repeatedly about the cows I encountered while travelling to and from the Saguenay. In one dream, they are milling around in a holding pen, waiting to be shipped to the slaughterhouse, when one among them, as if supernaturally invested with a newfound power, leaps over the fence. The others all leap fast behind her, caught in the high fever of contagion and emulation, the entire herd then stamping and snorting and galloping like wild horses down the middle of a country road, their udders lit up and glittering like stars or upside-down sparkles on a birthday cake, milk falling like torrents of rain from them, flooding the road, bringing all the cars and trucks to a complete stop.

Bernadette Griffin

The humans emerge from their vehicles, wading through the flood of milk, waving their arms, confounded by the phenomenon, as by a force of nature, and at a loss as to what to do next, and there I am in their midst, everyone's attention fixed on yours truly, looking to me to herd the cows back into the holding pen. But, the cows are unstoppable, for they soon become airborne like winged horses, new incarnations of life itself, flying above the heads of people, while I paddle around helplessly in the milk rising like flood-waters around the chaos.

That feeling of captivity and its ensuing helplessness is a recurring one with me lately and has muscled its way into my dreams.

June 3, 1976

Marina and Monique presented their last choral concert of the season on Friday evening last. Even as the warmth and solace of summer were upon us, the *pièce de résistance* on the program, I am told, was "Frostiana", six choral settings of poems by Robert Frost, with piano accompaniment.

Of course, I did not attend, as dogs are also barred from the concert hall. But Monique told me all about it the next day. Aunt Irène went. And so did Harry. To Monique's total and utter astonishment, there he was, in line with the well-wishers back-stage after the concert, he too seemingly astonished at her state of being, always so euphoric, so radiant, after a concert. Even the two Healy Willan motets, especially,

> "Rise up my love, my fair one, and come away
> For lo, the winter is past
> The rain is over and gone
> The flowers appear upon the earth
> The time of the singing of birds is come…"

with its outpouring of love words culled from the Canticle of Canticles, its three-against-two rhythms, had come off beautifully, the melodic lines fluid as silk, the conductor had said afterward.

In the lingering euphoria of the living room, where everyone had gathered after the concert, Aunt Irène recalled *Choose Something Like a Star* from the Frostiana, and how the sopranos had held that long sustained note, oh so high up there, like a star shining in the heavens, and the other voices singing down on earth below it. Harry liked *Stopping by Woods on a Snowy Evening* sung by the men; he remembered the poem from his school days,

> *"The woods are lovely, dark, and deep,*
> *And I have promises to keep,*
> *And miles to go before I sleep,*
> *And miles to go before I sleep."*

And Kirsten heard the tinkle of the horse's harness bells in the piano accompaniment against the bass voices gliding like a horse-drawn sleigh through the snow.

With the euphoria only half spent, the love words from the Canticle of Canticles still swimming in their heads, the visitors went home, and everyone retired for the night. Monique and Harry soon fell fast asleep, while I lay awake beside them, caught in my own thoughts. I know Harry lacks the eloquence of Solomon in the Canticle of Canticles, would never compare his love to a company of horses in Pharaoh's chariot, and would never liken her stature to a pine tree, her breasts to clusters of grapes. I know the two will not go leaping over the mountains of myrrh or skipping over the hills of frankincense in one fell swoop. But with Harry going to Monique's concert, do I see a fault line appearing in that formal feeling grown between them like a brick wall, ever since Harry's heart attack in Vancouver, even as he prepares to return to work after his six-month sick leave? Who knows? In the story of the world, the human characters are among the most unpredictable. Besides, one swallow hardly makes a spring.

May 15, 1976

Congratulate me! I finally did it. Like the cows in my dream, I leapt over the back yard fence. With Monique gone to a Status of Women convention in Ottawa with Marina, Harry back at work, the children at school, and no one to walk me, I seized the moment. Aunt Irène had just put me out into the back yard to attend to my daily eliminations, when I was gripped by an overwhelming impulse to gain my freedom. Like the cows. In seconds, there I was, strutting down the street with that same placidity and air of dignity I'd seen in the cows — free at last, the sun streaming down on me, signs of summer visible at every corner. For hours I walked, stopping as I pleased to smell the trunks of trees and fire hydrants and detritus and litter in all of its forms. I walked past houses and stores, past pots of daffodil, tulip and lily sitting on bleachers, flashing their colours in the sharp sun of late afternoon. I walked past outdoor terraces, where customers sat, baring their limbs and sipping *cappuccino* and *caffè latte.* I ploughed through puddles. I stopped to let children pet me as they dawdled home from school.

By nightfall, the euphoria of freedom slowly gave way to the daily and necessary compulsion to eat and drink. And I soon found myself overwhelmingly attracted to the smells filling the air around a certain place of commerce with a large aluminum door. I lingered there in hope and expectation until an older gentleman with glasses and hair like John Lennon, only gray and unkempt, emerged from behind the aluminum door. He was thin and wore tight black bluejeans and a black jean-jacket with streaks of silver studs down both sleeves, more like a country and western singer. He looked down at me sniffing around for food and, as if reading my body language, engaged me in conversation.

"What's a beautiful high-falutin' dog like you doin' hangin' round the Monkland Tavern at eleven o'clock at night, eh girl?" he said, losing his equilibrium when he reached down to pat my head and read the metal name tag on my collar. Once he'd steadied himself, he began to scuff unevenly along the sidewalk. I instinctively followed along behind, for the smell from the establishment seemed to have rubbed off on him. Not only was it pleasant, it was promising. He walked slowly, stopping to grope through his pockets for cigarettes, stopping to look for a lighter, stopping to light up a cigarette, talking to me non-stop until we reached his apartment, a brownstone building well past its prime, as he was, with peaked gabled windows betraying an earlier grandeur, just a few blocks away. With one hand on the door handle, he paused, looked down at me, threw his half-smoked cigarette out onto the street, and promptly invited me in.

"Come on in, girl," he said, "I know what it's like to get lost and get hungry and to have nowhere to go, I been there, so c'mon in, girl, I'll fix ye up with somethin'."

He grasped the railing with one hand, sometimes two, and we stumbled up the stairs to his apartment. It took him an eternity to locate the keys in his pocket. And even longer to find the keyhole in the lock. But once inside, he switched on the light, paying no attention to the thumping pulsations of music coming from the apartment overhead. The light revealed one small nondescript room with a kitchenette in one corner and a toilet and shower in the other.

"You'll have to excuse the mess," he said, "but I'm only here temporary, so there's no use fixin' it up, I'll be up and gone from here before ye know it."

He made his way into the kitchenette, pulled three slices of bread from a plastic bag on the counter, placed them in a cereal bowl from the cupboard overhead, opened the fridge and poured milk from a carton over the bread. He then stooped down to place it on the floor in front of me, lost his equilibrium and, in recovering it, spilt all of the contents onto the floor. Discounting the manner in which it was presented to me, it was delicious. I had barely finished when he ambled over to a couch under the one and only window, lay down fully clothed, beaded leather jacket and all, and fell instantly into a dead sleep, despite the infernal racket coming through the ceiling. With no way out, I stretched out on the floor beside him. In time, the insistent beat pulsing through the ceiling came to an end, and I could hear the pours of summer rain falling, pulseless and soporific, on the street beneath, and I too fell into a deep sleep.

When the gentleman wakened the next morning, he looked down at me as if I were an apparition, an unannounced guest, a party-goer from upstairs fallen through the ceiling. But in the next instant, it all returned to him.

"So you're still here, eh girl?" he said, patting my coat, "so I guess I'll have to feed you, but then you'll have to be gettin' back to where you came from, eh girl?"

He gave me three more slices of bread seeped in milk, led me by the collar down the stairs and turned me out.

"Atta girl, that's it, you go on home now, wherever that is, eh girl," he said, his voice a mix of coaxing and cajoling.

And there I was, free again. It was still drizzling rain, the gray clouds above threatening more rain, and the unfamiliarity of my surroundings had me feeling ill at ease, if not shamelessly timid. After walking several blocks through the rush of human and mechanized traffic, I came to a park, almost deserted, with grass, towering shade trees and benches. And bordering the park on one side, another main thoroughfare with its own parade of people and hum of motor traffic. On the corner stood a young man strapped to his accordion, squeezing out bittersweet French waltzes into the drizzle and cool of morning, an upturned black beret on the pavement beside him holding a sprinkling of coins. I approached him. But he was lost in his music and paid no attention to me. I wandered through the park, past choirs of chirping sparrows perched on the branches of trees. On impulse, I chased several gray squirrels and nibbled at a scattering of bread crumbs strewn on the grass near a park bench. On another fateful impulse, I stepped out to drink from a puddle of water in a gutter on the main thoroughfare and, unwittingly, into the roar of an oncoming truck. It veered, narrowly averting me, or so it would seem, when a pedestrian wearing high-heeled red sandals and carrying a large red patent leather purse promptly pulled me from the gutter and dragged me by the collar to her car, her hold so resolute, so unflinching, I felt like a condemned criminal being led to her execution. She placed me in the back seat of her Impala station wagon (another one of those vehicles with delusions of wild grandeur), jumped into the driver's seat and drove away, talking to me in the rearview mirror as she drove.

"I had a dog beautiful as you once only bigger, part German Shepherd, part Labrador, part something else I forget what, but big, and smart, I taught her to sing the "ooh-ooh-ooh's in *Indian Love Call*, the "woof-woof's" in *How Much is that Doggie in the Window*, you know, the one with Patti Page on the record but, like you, she didn't have an ounce of common sense in traffic and got loose just that once when I wasn't paying attention and got killed by a truck, just like you almost did right there now, so I decided this is crazy, and I bought two dogs, two Shi Tzus, in case something happens to one there'll be one left over, 'cause you never forgive yourself, your owner won't forgive herself either if something happens to you, so I'm taking you to the SPCA. She'll probably come looking for you there, and I'll tell them, I'll say don't put her down, she's way too beautiful, call me if the owner doesn't come looking for her, because people can be heartless, buy a dog for their kid at Christmas, like chicks at Easter, then turn it out to fend for itself when they see how much trouble it is, but you look too well cared for, too well groomed, your owner's probably beside herself searching high and low for you…" she said in one long breathless string of words as she drove, her blonde hair, wavy as an ocean, blowing in the wind from the open window.

Upon reaching the SPCA, the woman collared me again and attempted to lead me inside. But by now, my inner state of turmoil was such that I resisted with all of my crude, brute strength. A burly gentleman then appeared, leashed me and led me in, the unwholesome smell of fear assaulting my senses at every turn.

The SPCA's interior felt more like a prison than a shelter. I looked in disbelief at the rows of cells, each containing a dog or a cat, all obviously driven to their wit's end by confinement, if not by too much grief. Once placed in a cell, I felt a misery, a desolation unequalled since the separation from my earth mother. Alas, my quest for freedom had been an exercise in self-deception. Too impulsive. Too unplanned. And what manner of freedom was I seeking when my species had been living in bondage for thousands of years? I curled into a ball in the farthest corner of the cell, mindful only of the yelp of dogs, helpless murmuring of cats, and concentrated odour of animal anxiety.

Shortly after darkness fell, an attendant came with his keys, unlocked my cell, leashed me and led me back into the front lobby. And standing there, arrayed in a gleaming white T-shirt, was Mark — the valiant hero come to rescue me from my latest captors, a stubble of black beard on his face, chest muscles bulging, my leash folded in his fist. He lifted my shaking body off the floor, gathered me into his arms and held me there in that desperate way of old, an ecstasy of joy now shooting like arrows through my entrails. Once I had stopped trembling, Mark set me down, signed a few papers, thanked the gentleman for keeping me safe, and we walked away. He hailed a taxi and we were gone. To Mark's flat. Until Monique returned from her Status of Women convention in Ottawa, he said, I would be staying with him and Chuck.

Given the unpredictability and duress of the previous two days, I took one look at Mark's outdoor circular staircase and my entire body hardened into plaster, my feet bolted to the ground. Again, Mark gathered me into his arms and lifted me up the winding flight of stairs and into his flat.

It opened straight into a room filled with two bench presses and various other pieces of weight-lifting equipment. To the left was a hall lined with cases of empty bottles smelling like last night's Monkland Tavern. The hall opened onto a kitchen and two small bedrooms. Mark's roommate Chuck was sitting at the kitchen table when we entered, watching the Olympics on a small TV sitting on the kitchen counter. Upon seeing us, he rose and scooped me up as he had at our first encounter.

"So Daisy, I hear you're a helluva jumper, clearing a six-foot fence. With a bit of training, you could be a high-jumper in the Olympics for dogs," he said, nuzzling me, then lowering me back down and turning his attention back to the Olympics on TV.

I slept with Mark that night, cradled in his arms, the communion between us as unmistakable as ever, as if part of the grand design of the universe — before its blueprints were changed, that is.

On my second night there, a Friday, Mark and Chuck entertained, in a manner of speaking only, because the eight friends who came, young ladies as well as young gentlemen, brought their own beverages and drank directly from the original receptacle. No food of any kind was prepared or served. As for the seating, some sat on the two bench presses, while others sat on cases of "empties" brought in from the hall. Two more young gentlemen then strode in like performers onto a stage, carrying musical instruments in black cases. Indeed, the evening unfolded as if preordained. While the guests lit up cigarettes and began drinking from their respective bottles, the two musicians lugged the two wooden chairs in from the kitchen, unearthed an electric guitar and an electric bass from their cases, plugged their amplifiers into the wall sockets, tuned the instruments and began to play—and sing. Tunes they'd been practising together—*Love Will Keep Us Together, Lucy in the Sky with Diamonds, Don't Be Cruel, We Can Work It Out,* followed by their very own compositions, one particularly loud, grinding selection by Jake the guitarist, entitled *I Don't Wanna,* in which he cited a long list of things he did not want to do, all accompanied by robotic movements of the torso and contortion of the lower limbs. In the din, Mark produced a pipe, lit it and passed it round and round the room already choking with smoke from the cigarettes. And if one is to believe that people of few words are the best people, these were better than best, for they said nothing. And the more they smoked and drank, the more silent and remote they became. Indeed, the speechlessness created an abyss of sorts. An unexpectedly uncomfortable void. For the musicians had exhausted their repertoire rather quickly and had laid their instruments to rest in their cases.

Surely the void and darkness has not fallen upon us forever, I thought, when Chuck and the young woman named Olivia, with neck pendants reaching down to her waist and bracelets on both ankles, began to press into one another on the bench press, whisper into one another's hair, run their hands over one another's bodies. And seconds later, the girl named Deirdre with the orange Afro and orange fingernails was sitting on the table in the darkened kitchen, her legs dangling, Mark wedged in between them, his lower body pressing into the edge of the table, his fingers threading through her fiery-orange Afro.

Like a shot fired in the air at a foot race, this was the signal for the other guests to leave, for they began making their exit, some carrying cases only partially drunk, others leaving them behind—for Mark, they said. Soon everyone had left.

Everyone except Olivia and Deirdre of course. They stayed overnight. Deirdre in Mark's bed, and Olivia in Chuck's.

I sat alert on the bare hardwood floor in Mark's room and watched the two of them. Unlike Marina, whose naked body is thick as a tree trunk, Deirdre's was more like a telephone pole, her fiery-orange Afro an osprey's nest on top. While she had no breasts to speak of, she had the energy and brassiness of an electric wire. With no help from Mark, she pulled off all her clothes, pitched them into a heap at the foot of the bed, then helped Mark off with his, for he was clumsy and finding it difficult to step out of his trousers without losing his balance. Unlike Marina's slow and steady build-up, Deirdre barreled through the preliminaries, charging each advance with youthful exuberance. To her, it looked as easy as falling off a ladder. A revelation to me in this instance was the condom. At the appointed time, from her seated position on Mark's erection, Deirdre reached out an open hand and casually requested the condom. Mark reached under his pillow where it lay in readiness and handed it to her. And in the same sure-handed manner of women rolling up their pantyhose, she rolled up the condom, unfurled it onto his penis, a flagpole pointing straight up, and slithered down its length. In no time it was over and done with, and the two were fast asleep.

I, however, was kept awake by the two in the next room. One grunting and panting and yelping as if lifting weights in his sleep, the other squealing and giggling and all the subtle gradations in between.

Early the next morning, with Mark and Chuck still dead asleep, the girls rose, slipped into their clothes and threaded their way past the stacks of boxes in the hallway and, without a sound, pulled the door open and shut on the abandon of the night before.

When the doorbell rang some two hours later, Mark sprang to his feet, scrambled into his jeans and shuffled to the front door bare-chested. And there she was, Monique, come to take me home. Upon seeing her, I was over the moon, helpless to contain my exhilaration. And hungry. If humans cannot live by bread alone, dogs cannot live on a diet of Kellogg's Corn Flakes soaked in tepid water. After greeting me, her eyes scanned the premises, settling first on the beverage cases stacked in the hallway, then on Mark standing there not yet fully awake, a miniature skull and crossbones now tattooed on his belly. Immediately he came forward and kissed her on both cheeks.

"I guess I got you out of bed, sorry, I should have called first, but I was so worried about Daisy and thought you'd have to go to work today," Monique said.

"Oh that's okay," Mark said reassuringly, stepping back, yawning, scratching at his belly, and scanning the premises himself, seeing it as she'd seen it, I would think, and apologetic as a result.

"Sorry I can't show you around the place, but Chuck's still asleep, we had some friends in last night and the place is a mess, I know, in fact I was just about to tidy up."

"Maybe another time," Monique said, "but thank you for rescuing Daisy from the SPCA and taking such good care of her," she added, blissfully unaware of my hunger pangs after a three-day survival diet of Wonder Bread marinated in milk and waterlogged corn flakes. And we left. Again, Mark was forced to carry me down the spiral staircase, as he and Chuck had done time and time again throughout my stay with them.

The drive home was pure wretchedness. A long litany of chastisements coming from Monique through the rearview mirror.

"Shame on you, jumping over the fence and going off like that when Aunt Irène wasn't looking, and her not able to chase after you, shame on you, you're lucky you weren't killed by a car or run over by a bus or, worse still, stolen and sold to some stranger, shame on you, Daisy," she went on, her tone so accusatory, so berating that upon reaching home, I felt gutted, my self-esteem shrunken down to nothing, my flesh shriveled, even into the outlying regions of my body, my bones ground to dust. Wide and deep as my emotional spectrum is, I had never felt this magnitude of shame. Shame for having displeased Monique, that is. Not for the act itself. No. My freedom days had been a feast for the senses. An intoxicating four-day festival of new tastes, sounds and sights. For once I had followed my instinct, gratified my desire, even if in the end, I had become a vagabond with no fixed place in society. It was not really freedom as I had imagined it. Not the pearl of great price acquired at the deepest expense by animals in the wild. No. It was fool's gold, freedom wrapped in a bundle of contradictions. Face it, I said to myself. You are a human fabrication now. You can never be a feral dog. The wildness, the wholeness, was bred out of you thousands of years ago. Face it.

In contrast, Aunt Irene and Mathew and Kathleen greeted me like a lone soldier home from the wars. But there was no ticker tape parade. No trumpets and drums. I had wreaked too much havoc, too much panic. For appeasement's sake, I simply avoided Monique altogether. In fact, at night I've taken to sleeping on the hide-a-bed, at Aunt Irene's feet, keeping them warm, for they are cold she says — *comme deux blocs de glace* — in all weathers.

June 3, 1976

After our voyage to the Saguenay, Aunt Irène shut herself up in the den, ate by herself and didn't utter a word to anyone for a week. Not even to Harry. And when Monique tried to bring up the subject of her trip to the Saguenay, having heard the hard-bitten truth about it from Harry, Aunt Irène threw up both palms and sat up straighter on the hide-a-bed, her body rigid as a column of marble. Even my abiding presence at the foot of her bed, she barely suffered. Harry thought we should wait, show a little patience. She probably needed more time to make sense of everything she'd heard up in the Saguenay, because the truth was always hard to face dead-on, even if you already suspected it.

Then one night after our late evening walk, Harry poured two rye on the rocks, brought one in to Aunt Irène in the den, sat down in his usual stuffed chair beside the hide-a-bed, I at my station beside him, and the three of us watched the late-night movie.

In fact, Aunt Irène and I have been watching movie after movie, English or French, whatever happens to be on, she seemingly ready to lose herself in whatever world is presented to her on a given night.

If I could, with one paw, arrest the flood of grief that has spilled into every corner of every room in this house overnight, I would do it. But how can I? I too am overwhelmed by Aunt Irène's sudden and unimagined passing. She simply never woke up yesterday morning, as if she'd taken another one of her ill-considered notions to leave this place, to walk away again, go somewhere else—into one of her movies perhaps, in one last brave and defiant gesture.

In the morning, there she was, her face barely visible under the covers, her strawberry blond hair splayed over the pillow like an open fan. And there I lay, keeping her feet warm, when Monique knocked on the door of the den and, without waiting for an answer, barged in, for neither of us had stirred, and it was well past 9 a.m.. She quickly scanned the situation, me motionless as an Egyptian sphinx at Aunt Irène's feet, Aunt Irène motionless under the covers, and immediately fell to her knees beside her, lifting the blankets off Aunt Irène's face, only to fall back on her heels and cover her own face with both hands, as if she'd come upon a train wreck and couldn't bear to look. For I could see Aunt Irène now from where I sat, her skin a sickly yellow, eyes half-open, purple lips coming apart and listing to one side, one hand locked into a blue fist lying on her chest. For a long time, Monique knelt there, frozen to the scene, as it were, unable to take it in or make any sense of it. Then in her paralysis, she noticed me, Daisy, as she has often seen me, constant as the North Star at its station in the sky. She reached for me, pulled me down beside her, wound her two arms around me and wept, the hot tears seeping into my coat, taking me back to Jean-Marc and the day I was suddenly whisked away from him.

There had been no warning. No alarm bell. No thunderbolt. In fact, the night before, she and Harry and I had watched *Born Free*, about a lion named Elsa, orphaned as I was, torn from her siblings as I was, raised to maturity by humans as I was, then released into the wilds of Africa, as I had tried to release myself and failed.

"How can you be free with predators everywhere?" Aunt Irene had said afterward.

"You think she shouldn't have been separated from her sisters, don't you?" Harry said, "but she wouldn't have been free in the zoo either, stuck in a cage."

"No, but at least she'd be with her sisters," returned Aunt Irene, "anyway, nobody is born free like that movie said, the animals too, they're always running away from something, everybody runs away."

"Yeah… freedom's a bit of a pipedream, like everything else you long for," Harry said, "when I was eighteen, I couldn't wait to fly, to get away."

"Did you feel free up there flying?" Aunt Irène asked.

"Yeah, in the beginning I felt free as a bird up there."

"Up there, down here, over there, far away…freedom, is it a place where you go…?"

"Maybe it's just the place where you belong, like those lions…"

"Or maybe it's more being yourself in the place you are…you can't just keep looking always somewhere far… running away…"

With their musings hanging loose in the air, Harry rose to his feet, kissed Aunt Irène goodnight, briefly massaged my back with one hand, and left.

Aunt Irène turned off the television and sat for ages in the almost dark. She thought more clearly in the dark, I'd heard her say. Then came the nightly ritual, removing her earrings, necklaces and bracelets, washing off her makeup in the adjoining washroom, swallowing her pills, getting into her nightgown, opening the hide-a-bed, pulling the bed covers back and finally bedding down—my signal to jump up and settle at her feet.

Before flicking off the lamp, she propped herself up on her two elbows and stared straight through me.

"Daisy," she said, in a megaphone voice too loud for midnight, purple index finger nail aimed at me like a weapon, "don't jump that fence again, you hear that? You, you're like me, you have no place to go, you cannot go back anywhere, so that's it, don't jump that fence again, you stay right here with your people."

She then extinguished the lamp. And that is how the evening ended. With a strict order issued in the almost dark.

In the morning, once Monique had emptied all of her tears into my coat, I jumped back up onto the bed and lay at rigid attention, forepaws out in front, a sentinel on guard at Aunt Irène's feet now ice-cold, as Monique swung into action.

First came the ambulance and doctor who pronounced Aunt Irène dead.

Shortly afterward, two men arrived from the funeral parlour, removed her rings, her nightgown, placed a sling around her jaw and tied it at the top of her head, tied her hands together, her feet together, attaching labels to them, wrapped her in a white shroud, wheeled her from the den to the front door and out into a large black hearse-like vehicle parked at the curb, and drove her between the trees lined up on either side, as if to honour her passing—all on a splendid, sun-filled afternoon in June, the purple lilac bush next door stooped way over, weighed down by too many blooms.

June 15, 1976

As usual, no reason was given, but I—supposedly a member of the family—was not permitted to attend any of the ceremonial rites attending Aunt Irène's death. Indeed, I was left to grieve alone. Curled into a fiddlehead on the hide-a-bed. Through two long and empty days and evenings.

On the third day, the day of the burial, I was escorted to Marina's and left to spend the empty hours with her and the cockatoos. Marina sequestered me in the kitchen, however, away from the cockatoos, who are enamored with the new gymnasium she bought for them—a framework of vertical and horizontal bars hanging from the ceiling next to their cage, with ladders and swings and parallel bars and pick-apart balls made of twigs and coconut fibres and seagrass for them to pick on. Because the two had been picking at one another. Bickering and plucking one another's feathers. Modesta always getting the worst of it, and having night terrors as a result, sending earsplitting shrieks through the whole house at midnight, and Minerva sulking for hours when chastised for persecuting her one and only sister.

To be honest, I am not fond of Minerva, not since she viciously attacked me as I passed by, inoffensive, minding my own affairs that one day last winter. She's become too easily intoxicated by her own dominance, like a big fish in a small pond, and forgets she comes from an egg.

From an egg or not, Marina says, two of anything, especially two females, has its own set of problems, and these two are suffering from emotional, intellectual and sexual deprivation, she thinks, and out of sheer boredom chew the furniture, the plants, rip pages out of books, bite, puncture, everything.

While the cockatoos played in the gymnasium, I lay listless on my side on the cold kitchen linoleum, caught in a tangle of affections, wretchedness high among them, wretchedness about my lowly place in the family constellation. Marina, who thinks animals' voices should be heard in the councils of government (which they would be, I daresay, if cockatoos were elected to represent them) seemed to read the temperature of my soul and bent over backwards to comfort me.

"Look at you, so sad, so forsaken, Daisy, don't worry, it's not like you were deported to Devil's Island," she said, (wherever that is) "don't worry your head; they'll be back for you."

And knowing how I hate the cold and slippery linoleum, she fetched a blanket, folded it in four and ceremoniously spread it out like a Persian carpet for me to lie on. In the afternoon, it was two Frisbees in the park, with wild chasing and leaping and catching them on the fly, be they only inert masses made of plastic.

Yet the evening dragged. It was well past dark and raining heavily when Harry finally came to retrieve me. Once home, he rubbed me dry with a towel, a carnal reassurance more consoling than words, and led me upstairs. Matthew and Kathleen had already gone to bed. So had Monique. Still, I went to her and licked her hand outstretched to greet me even as she wept, her face buried in the pillow, me doing my darnedest to ignore the frightful drum rolls of thunder in the distance. As I sat there, I watched as Harry undressed, pulled back the blankets and lay down, the front of his body flush up against Monique's back. And in another act that seemed to reach far beyond his usual chivalry, he wrapped his arm around her body fresh with sorrow from the burial, and there they lay until morning.

June 26, 1976

Monique brushed me this morning and later washed me down with the arctic-cold water from the garden hose, a hateful procedure. I am not a plant in the garden, not a polar bear in the North Pole, I wanted to tell her, but her mind was elsewhere and paid no attention to my resistance; ah the one-sidedness of domestication. During the brushing, she talked a blue streak, flitting like a butterfly from one subject to another and another, beginning with Aunt Irène's burial.

In her will, Aunt Irène had scribbled in two add-ons at the last minute. With no mincing or explanations. The first said she didn't want anyone from the Saguenay attending her funeral. The second said she wanted to be buried next to her sister Yvonne in *Cimetière Saint-Charles* in Québec City.

Cimetière Saint-Charles itself, Monique said, was a deathly quiet place on the day of the burial, nothing moving except a few nodding dandelions and patches of bloated clouds drifting apart and merging and drifting apart again. But inside of her, things were anything but quiet. Just standing there at her mother's grave and Aunt Irène's open one right beside it was like opening a trap door to a cellar and all the old feelings crumpled up inside her appearing like new, like a huge wad of unread newspaper. And lowering Aunt Irène down to lie beside her mother again—after all these years—what did she feel? Not sorrow. Not grief. She felt the farawayness, the out of reachness, the middle of nowhere lost feeling that came with being in the company of her mother. "Here," she wanted to say to her, "here she is, take her, your twin, the brave one, the loud one, take her back, the only one you loved, the only one you felt at home with." Yes, she wanted to say that, because she knew it now, in strange and complicated ways, the two could never really be separated, divided in two as Aunt Irène had said, could not bear each other's burdens alone, could not attach themselves to anyone else. So it was not surprising that they both died half broken-hearted, without warning, like a snap decision made overnight after a strange notion taken, as they'd done everything else.

Another thing that turned her inside out during the visitation and funeral and burial, was Mark. Not only was he late for everything, but his clothes smelled of marijuana, and she could tell he'd been drinking before every event. She could smell it on his breath (startling to me when the penchant to smell one another is taboo among humans). And how could she not notice the cases of beer stacked in the hallway of his flat when she came to pick me up, and it doesn't end there, she plans to bring it up with Mark—and with Harry—when the time is right, because she doesn't think Harry noticed. The two had been too formal and polite with one another to notice anything important.

Harry may not be so polite when she brings up the subject of the flight attendant in Vancouver, the one in the room when he had the heart attack, the guardian angel who saved him, for she plans to bring that up as well. But there'll be a right moment for that too. What if he has another heart attack arguing about it, defending himself, reliving the event? Worse still, what if he takes off, flies out one day and decides not to come back. People *do* that. Aunt Irène walked away from Curt overnight. Wouldn't that be a fine stew to be in, where would she be then, because she's not self-sufficient, never *has* been, never earned any money of her own, never lived on her own, yet here she is calling herself a feminist and marching in Voice of Women demonstrations and going to Status of Women conventions in Ottawa—all Marina's doing of course—when she doesn't even know what it means to be in charge of your own body. Besides, Kathleen and Matthew are still at home and need a father, and they love Harry. Why create a disaster for them?

Monique then moved on to the subject of Aunt Irène's will. For in it, she leaves the sum of her earthly possessions to her, Monique. This includes *Tête-Folle*, the beauty parlour, her furniture and personal belongings, and a life insurance policy bought when she came back from Chicago and unexpectedly large, enough to pay off *Tête-Folle's* few debts and plenty left over. It's mind-numbing, she says, like someone giving you the sky and there it is over your head, big and blue, and you don't know what to do with it. Because it's too big. For starters, what will she do with *Tête-Folle*? Run it herself? She's never run anything in her life. Sell it? She's never sold anything either. The prospect of sitting on a load of money was another thing she wasn't prepared for, and it took her breath away.

This was a long drawn-out brushing, commensurate with the unforeseen correspondence of events, not with the tangles in my coat. And what is more insulting to a dog's raw skin than blasts of ice-cold water from the bloody-minded garden hose…

August 15, 1976

Last night, after a day of scorching heat, leaving it too hot to sleep, Monique seized the moment and brought up the subject of the flight attendant in Vancouver. Harry was reading his latest Louis Lamour novel in bed—he's been doing that again lately—when Monique, propped up on her pillows, put down *A Doll's House,* the play she's been reading for her course on plays and playwrights, and began.

"Could I talk to you about something?" she asks.

While merely introductory, her question sounds over-rehearsed.

Harry removes his reading glasses, lays them on his book and turns his attention to Monique's hands fumbling with the top sheet.

"Sure, go ahead, what's on your mind?"

Then the burning question.

"That flight attendant, the miraculous one who saved your life in Vancouver, was she in bed with you that night?"

Harry hesitates, as if wrestling with a multiple choice question.

"Yes, she was," he says finally.

"And other nights?"

"What can I say, yes she was. But that's all over now, I haven't seen her since. Oh I did talk to her once, that's true, on the phone, just to thank her for moving so fast and calling the ambulance and everything, but she knew there was no future in it, I told her as much, she knew."

"Why was there no future in it?"

"Because there wasn't."

"But why?"

"Well, first of all, I didn't love her, sure she was beautiful and full of life and available, but no, I didn't love her."

"So how do you… how do you go to bed with someone you don't love?"

"I don't know."

"You don't know?"

"No, I don't know… How do *you* do it?" Harry said, not bothering to wait for an answer. He picked up his glasses, stuffed them into their case, slammed his book shut, flung it onto the floor, turned his back on Monique, flicked off his bedside lamp, lay down and went to sleep.

And that is how it ended. With another burning question.

August 16, 1976

Harry rose just after dawn this morning and stole soundlessly out of the house and to the airport. With him gone, Monique threw off the covers, sat up, pulled on a sweat suit and walking shoes and took me out. We walked and walked in that uncertain gray divide between night and day, through a slow and steady drizzle, past houses fast asleep and trees still held in the hypnotic trance of dawn, Monique also in a daze, as if sleepwalking and, I suspect, stunned by Harry's question of the night before.

Back home, we had breakfast, and with Matthew and Kathleen still asleep, she trimmed my coat and my nails.

"That is *it*," she said, grabbing snatches of my hair and pulling them taut, my skin smarting with each pull and still tender from the last long drawn out brushing.

"That is *it*, finally it's happened," she said, "you wait and wait and wait—too long, and everything comes falling down—like the living room ceiling."

Harry had reached a flashpoint, she knew that. He didn't even say goodbye this morning. And she won't be a bit surprised if she gets another phone call from Vancouver saying he's not coming back, and then where will she be. Especially now that she's put *Tête-Folle* up for sale. And how could she blame Harry for thinking she doesn't love him? She never approaches him, and he hasn't approached her once since his heart attack. The two are like perfect strangers sharing a bed. No wonder he stopped having sex with her. No wonder he went to bed with someone in Vancouver. Someone who doesn't turn into a pumpkin when she sees an erection, who doesn't panic at the very thought of having it up against you, who knows what to do when she arrives at the ball, because she's supposed to like it, she's supposed to like erections, love them even, she'd read the covers of magazines waiting in line at the supermarket—thirty bed-rattling positions for mind-blowing orgasm, twenty secrets to supersensory lovemaking, ten naughty ways to unmask his inner ape, explore your inner sanctum, hold onto your man, make him *feel* like one—and in twenty years she hadn't tried any of them.

With Aunt Irène now gone, perhaps she *should* sleep on the hide-a-bed in the den, but who'd be there if Harry had another heart attack? And what a fine pickle they'd all be in then.

And so the nail-trimming session ended, with a series of dawning realizations.

August 20, 1976

On Wednesday morning, a tide of fresh cool air poured in, displacing the heat wave that had swept over us in early August. In the new cool, Monique helped Marina dig up sods in her lawn in preparation for a new bed of day lilies she would plant in the spring. Once the sods were dug up and the earth turned over, they sat in the sun on Marina's back deck, and sipped iced tea from tall glasses, me at their feet. But the repose and refreshment was short-lived, for in burst Marina's husband Desmond, home at last from a two-week fishing trip, clomping up onto the deck in his hiking boots and canvas hat looking like a pincushion studded with multicoloured flies he'd tied himself over the winter. He removed his hat, hugged Marina and bowed to us in gallant manner, rubbing his dense stubble of beard and apologizing for not having shaved in two weeks. He then returned to the car and began unloading equipment — tent, sleeping bag, lanterns, fishing rods and baskets and other assorted fishing gear — everything but fish.

"No fish again?' Marina called out to him.

"No, no fish," he called back, "yes, of course, oodles of fish in the rivers and streams, enough to eat some every day, but never mind the fish, they like it where they are, if you want some fish you can buy it at the fish store," and he lugged all the gear into the house.

"That's Desmond," Marina explained, "he catches the fish and puts them back, he loves fish, he loves how they leap up from the water, I think he loves fish better than humans, they're more predictable, he says, he likes farm machinery better than humans too, *it's* more predictable *too*, but he doesn't like dogs that much, Daisy," she added, looking down apologetically at me, "because he says they're too *human*."

In fact, that's why they never had any more children after Kirsten — and Kirsten was pure accident, part of the devil-may-care delirium after the war. But more after that? No, Desmond said, why more, humans should stop making more copies of themselves.

Marina understands how Desmond feels, she lived through the war too, yes to be sure, life on earth is imperfection and pain and catastrophe, but to her, it's like she read in one of her books on mythology, earth is connected to heaven by a long rope, and you have to climb that rope every day, every week, climb and climb, and at the end you're there and you just step in — that's why she marches and protests, that's why she sings. In fact lately, she's been taking singing lessons once a week and practicing her *solfège*, all in preparation for the choral season in the fall, because her vocal cords, her diaphragm, and her abdominal and intercostal muscles have no more stretch, have become stiff as a board over the summer, and she wants her whole physiology in top shape for the choir weekend in the Laurentians over Thanksgiving—an annual affair to kick off the season, integrate new members and get a head start on the coming season's repertoire.

"You could take some singing lessons too," she said to Monique, because she could benefit, *anyone* could benefit, especially with *this* teacher she's discovered, who is six feet tall and every part of her large and dignified, like the female warriors in Nordic mythology. Marina calls her Brunhilde because she *looks* like Brunhilde in Wagner's opera *Die Valkirie*, with her floor-length dresses, the hems and sleeves edged in gold braid, and wigs, a different wig for each day of the week. Brunhilde studied voice in Germany and in the United States and is a disciple of total-body singing, which uses not only the physical body, but the *feeling* body and the *awakened* body. Awakened not only to music, Brunhilde says, but to how music is contained and released from the body in an act of total surrender, because the human voice by itself, the larynx, is nothing but an organ, a few ounces of flesh. It is artless, like a rock before it becomes a sculpture, but when properly supported by a mounting column of air, it can ascend in rapture and fill a cathedral, and to prove it, this Brunhilde can sing a long *andante* phrase some sixteen bars long on one breath, at a volume that will knock you flat against the wall, and still have breath left over.

For Marina, who could sell sand to the Egyptians, this was an easy sell. Easy because Monique knows nothing about vocal technique, nothing about the *feeling* body, absolutely nothing about the *awakened* body, and how can she be "in charge of her body" as they had so strenuously advocated at the Status of Women convention in Ottawa if it wasn't even *awakened*, so she too signed up for singing lessons with Brunhilde.

Monique went to her second singing lesson with Brunhilde this evening. She returned flushed and smiling, splotches of red on her neck and face still visible, "hot, burning inside" from all the physical effort, she said.

Kathleen—who has her own turntable in her room, loves the Beatles, knows the words to all their songs, plays them over and over, singing along at the top of her voice—looked up from her homework at the kitchen table, again full of questions.

"Who is Brunhilde anyway?" she asked, "and why do you want to take singing lessons? At your age, I mean?"

But Monique seemed too preoccupied to hear the questions.

"It's interesting," she said, standing at the entrance to the kitchen, still holding her purse, her car keys and sheets of music manuscript with vocalises written on them in her hands, as if mesmerized by the overflow of information she'd received from Brunhilde.

"It's all so new, almost like learning to walk or talk," Monique went on, staring into space. Brunhilde, now notorious to everyone in the house, wants her to think of her body as an exciting stranger she is getting to know little by little, with a larynx, pharynx, rib cage, resonance cavities, network of muscles and bones—like no other. Because, all the minute deviations in anatomy, she said, all the particularities in character, add up to a *singer* like no other.

Monique then offered a short demonstration. Brunhilde had her place her hands at the bottom of her ribcage, thumbs pointing to the back, inhale, and with each breath taken in, to feel every feeling on the full compass of emotions—love, surprise, sorrow, anger, confusion, and their gradations, since singing is much more than mechanical, your heart much more than a pump.

Kathleen listened, then glumly gathered her books together, went upstairs and sent the Beatles blaring through the house.

Through the din, Monique sat alone at the kitchen table, adrift in her own leftover feelings verging on euphoria, or so it seemed, when the doorbell jolted her back to reality, and in walked Mark.

After greeting me like a long-lost relative returned from a foreign country, he strode into the kitchen, carefully, as if straddling an invisible line, pulled out a kitchen chair and sat down. Now it was Monique full of questions. Why had he come so late in the evening, unannounced also, how was Chuck, how was the job, and the most troubling question she planned to ask, the one she'd pushed to the back of her mind since Aunt Irène's funeral and burial, about his drinking.

But before she had broached the first two, Mark was back on his feet, expanding his chest, pulling himself to his full height, almost preparing to make a speech. But the tone was casual, if not the subject matter. When he least expected it, he'd been laid off his job. Business had slowed down, the boss said, the camping season was over.

Monique interrupted. Had he called in sick, had he been late for work, she inquired.

No, not at all, he'd overslept one morning, the alarm clock never went off. The boss was a jerk anyway, and he didn't want to work for a jerk.

Monique interrupted again. Had he been drinking, is that why he called in sick, had he gone to work with the smell of liquor on his breath like at Aunt Irène's funeral, she couldn't help notice it then.

No, of course not, why would she think that, sure he liked a drink or two, who didn't, but drinking wasn't a problem for him, he could hold it, and if it *was* a problem, it was *his* to deal with, not *hers*. In any case, he was looking for work. But he was late on the rent, and he owed Chuck money. So could he come back, bunk here for a while, until he was on his feet and had found another place to live?

The questionnaire continued. Where was his furniture and body-building equipment, because he couldn't cart the whole gymnasium back, not now, and he'd have to sleep in the den.

His furniture, his clothes, everything, was still at Chuck's place, at least for now, and, yes, he was thinking of putting his stuff right here in the garage, out of the way, nobody used the garage anyway.

Well, she couldn't say yes, right off the bat, she'd have to speak to his father when he came home from Vancouver

"I'll let you know," Monique said.

As easily as closing one door and opening another, Mark then turned all of his attention to me, kneeling down, wrestling me to the floor, massaging my chest with his capacious hands, that sensuous bodily language we both understood, that is part of our ancestry long before words were invented. If his wrestle with me would somehow alter the mood in the room, reduce his visit to the commonplace, he was wrong. With the Beatles still blasting from upstairs, Mark hopped to his feet, bade his mother a terse good-night and left.

Monique sat back down at the kitchen table and stared at the blank wall, her earlier euphoria now gone, like the overly festive wallpaper she'd pasted to the wall in a fit of spring fever and removed the next week. Laying her head down on her two arms, she wept.

Good heavens, I thought, and in a surge of slavish devotion equal to the jubilation she'd felt an hour before, went to her, pressing my body close against her leg, resting my head on her lap.

"Where is Harry when I need him," she lamented through her sobs, "why do I always put things off, why didn't I speak to Harry about Mark's drinking like I planned to? Because the way things are now, Harry won't want him back, and he certainly won't want all that body-building equipment back in the garage, I'm dead sure of that."

And the helplessness in her words, the isolation, felt like a burden she'd already carried a great distance.

We finally went for a late walk through solitary streets, the street lamps stoic as sentinels, our overly long shadows darkening the ground in front of us, and I too felt the heaviness one feels when everything matters.

November 1976

November has come like a bad dream unsolicited and, with it, that sorrow-laden undercurrent that seeps in when words run out. Give me the roaring fires of hell, the afflictions of Job, the torments of the garden hose—anything but this relapse into frosty silence.

Outside, the trees stand naked, the fallen leaves helpless on the lawns and sidewalks, waiting to be disposed of or buried in snow, and darkness drifts in earlier and earlier with the passage of days.

Inside this house, grief is everywhere, unspoken clusters of it blossoming in every room, for Monique is gone from it.

It all began when Harry returned from Vancouver in September. The evening after Mark had dropped in so unexpectedly. In bed that night, she tackled the subject directly. Mark's predicament, that is. Adding a certain maternal gloss to the events, all in an effort to make them more palatable to Harry, I suspect. Mark had come to visit, business was bad and he'd lost his job, had fallen behind on the rent and needed a place to stay until he got back on his feet.

Harry was quick to respond, as if he were still in the cockpit.

"Well he's not coming back *here*, he made his bed, in fact he took it with him, let him lie in it."

Monique fired back.

"It's not that simple, Harry," she said, "nothing's ever as simple as you make it, because I suspect — in fact, I've been meaning to bring it up with you for weeks — he's been drinking too much, maybe that's why he lost his job, up late drinking, then sleeping through the alarm and coming in late for work."

"Then let him learn," Harry said, "let him learn the hard way, if that's what he's up to."

"Why does he have to learn the hard way? Because *you* learned the hard way? "

Because there *is* no easy way to learn some things."

"Why can't he just come and sleep in the den until he's back on his feet?"

"There you go again, babying him, solving his problems *for* him."

And with that, Monique, in an unprecedented extravaganza of resistance, pitched her blankets onto Harry, bolted upright, swung her two feet out onto the floor, stood up, put on her housecoat and stomped downstairs. Being a slave to my instincts, and given the singularity of the moment, I was torn. Should I sleep with the despot in the bedroom? Or with the insurgent in the den? After a restless hour of traipsing upstairs and down, I slept in the den with the rebel. My species' history over many millennia with despots drove me to it. And there I've slept every night since the resistance began.

October came and Monique did not cave in.

If life's little wisdom is to wait, as the poet said, Harry waited. For the most part, he said little, like a ship's captain watching the movement of the stars over an uncertain sea.

In mid-October, with tensions high enough to crack your bones, Monique suddenly sold *Tête-Folle* for a tidy sum. She wasted no time. The minute the sale was closed, she purchased a used Chevrolet pickup truck, fire-engine red. And with me in the passenger seat, she drove to the Laurentians in her free time, hunting down properties for sale. Why the Laurentians? She'd spent a weekend with her choir at Lake McDonald and had fallen in love with the lake, the way it sparkled in the sun, and the stretched-out blue above it, and the red and gold and green like a decorative wreath surrounding it on all sides. We bumped and bounced along one dirt road after another and, in early November, we came upon it suddenly. Like an apparition, Monique said. It spoke to something deep in her being—a log cabin good for summer and winter, fully furnished, sitting in a clearing surrounded by woods thick with evergreen, maple, birch and aspen, a stream running through the entire six acres, a beaver dam at its far end—all on the northern rim of the tiny village of Lost River.

Monique rented the property with an option to buy it the following May. In another act of resistance, she immediately offered it to Mark as a place to stay. But by then it was too late. Mark had found employment as a sales clerk in the sporting goods department at Eaton's on St. Catherine Street. And he'd settled his outstanding debt and differences with Chuck.

All of her transactions Monique announced to Harry after the fact. And Harry listened without comment, as to the repeat of a newsflash on the radio.

The two children watched and listened as well. Mathew, who is eighteen and studying pure science at Dawson College, shrugged his shoulders. He loved the Chevrolet pickup truck his mother had bought and looked for any excuse to borrow it. As for Kathleen, she blasted her Beatles music at deafening volumes through the house after each transaction—*Let It Be* and *The Long and Winding Road*—singing along at full pitch, the one drowning out the other, so much so that Harry could not hear himself think and said so.

"The Beatles *have* to be played loud," Kathleen protested, "because everybody should hear what they have to say, besides, Mummy practises Brunhilde's vocalises all over the house and nobody complains about that."

Through all of the transactions, Monique faithfully attended her singing lessons with Brunhilde, as well as evening choir rehearsals, and of course practice sessions in Marina's living room.

But driving to the log cabin on her own, leaving everyone behind for a whole weekend, myself included, was like the leash suddenly pulled taut when least expected. Everyone was stung. Kathleen especially. And me. So much so that even Harry noticed and drove us to Beaver Lake on Mount Royal where we walked through the emptiness of late Saturday afternoon, no sound but the swish of dried and shriveled leaves under our feet and the trailing lamentations of birds overhead.

March 1, 1977

It has been a winter like no other, Monique holed up in the log cabin for weeks at a time. Yet we have borne our grief and carried our sorrows through the deep cold of January and February with a minimum of upheaval—thanks to Harry. In early December, he applied for a transfer to a nine-to-five position in Montréal—on the ground, in administrative work—a position offered to him after his heart attack and left in abeyance until now. Beginning in early January, he stopped flying completely.

He now goes to work at 7:00 a.m. and returns at 5:30 p.m. sharp. He and Kathleen then make supper. For all hints on cooking, he picks up the phone and calls Marina. He also does all the housekeeping. Chores he's never done before including laundry, vacuuming, helping Kathleen with her homework—math especially—and picking her up from her guitar lessons and swimming lessons at the YWCA.

And in the late evening, when Kathleen has settled into her bed, he walks me to the park, a desert in winter, flat and white as a sheet. If no one is around, he turns me loose and for a short spell, I am a wild horse, leaping into the air, snatching imaginary objects from it, whirling like a dervish, submerging my snout in the snow, smearing my whole body with it, releasing the day's pent-up need to play for playing's sake. When I have exhausted myself, Harry leashes me again. But that feeling of weightlessness induced by play doesn't leave. It lingers, and I literally dance around the leash, around Harry's heaviness, all the way home.

March 20, 1977

I attended a lengthy rehearsal today at Marina's, in preparation for a performance of Handel's *Messiah* at Christ Church Cathedral. It will take place on Good Friday of the penitential week leading to Easter. Thanks to lessons with Brunhilde, Monique is now a "lyric" soprano, Marina a "mezzo", new identities conferred by Brunhilde based on the timbre, range and register of their voices.

According to their choir master, who is British-born and carried his British accent across the ocean with him, Handel's *Messiah*, in its massiveness and *grandeur* and aspiration, was meant to exemplify the British Empire itself in 1741, its finely wrought *arias* and *recitatives* emblematic of its royalty, its massive choruses symbolic of the British people, the very pillars on which Handel's architectonic structure was built.

But that was just the British talking, Marina said. George Frederic Handel loved opera. And the *Messiah* was really an opera on a sacred subject; the subject in Part II being redemption after death and resurrection. Sure, the choruses do all the heavy lifting—stepping, leaping, running, ascending and descending—depending on the affection brought into being by the music, which is always moving, always becoming something else. And yes, the choir master is right, the melismatic passages with their florid expansions on certain key words called for extreme vocal agility, just as the towering chords called for unwavering strength, which can only come from breath control and a good diaphragm. So Marina says. She has sung the *Messiah* before and, sure enough, redemption is what you feel from head to toe as you sing those last chords and bow to the applause and walk off the stage.

Today Monique and Marina worked on a chorus from Isaiah, concentrating on the diverging melodic lines and melisma demanding so much agility and lightness as the sheep go off in every direction:

All we like sheep
Have gone astray
We have turned everyone to his own way.

They also worked on bringing climactic force to the inconclusive chord at the end of

And the Lord hath laid on Him, hath laid on Him,

leading to the dramatic moment of silence before the solemn explosion of sound on

The iniquity of us all,

which, the choir master said, gathers the whole meaning of what was said earlier into one solid, sumptuous block of harmony.

Monique and Marina keep reminding one another of what Brunhilde keeps saying, that the aliveness in the music, mirroring the expression in the text, must come from the very core of their own awakened bodies. How else could it awaken and stir the listener?

During the *Messiah* practice sessions, Marina has taken to caging the cockatoos and carrying them upstairs. Not to the master bedroom, but further back, to Desmond's den, for they became so disruptive at the last session even from the bedroom upstairs, hysterical almost, during *Let us break their bonds asunder and cast away their yokes from us* – as if the passage applied to their banishment and imprisonment in the cage upstairs. Ah the cage, another human invention, diabolical as the leash. Good heavens! I mean the lengths to which humans will go to have us behave like them. To rule everything. Good heavens!

On Wednesday morning, with the sun prematurely warm for mid-April, Monique drove to the cabin beyond Lost River and took me with her. Like Matthew, I love the pickup truck. With no back seat, I sat in the passenger seat, and the mere novelty of sitting beside the driver and not behind, the momentary equality it signifies—tiny indulgences so easily passed over by humans—filled me with perfect, if momentary, joy.

Monique talked the whole way.

"Now Daisy, there's no fence to jump over at the cabin, but it doesn't mean you're free to run loose when we get there," she cautioned, sensing the excitation mounting like a primal force in my body at the prospect of adventure into the unknown wilds of Lost River and beyond. With the city flying past us, she talked on.

"So I brought a long rope with me and a stake, because we're not alone at the cabin, you might think you're alone, but you're not, I soon found *that* out. All six acres are full of creatures flying, creeping, roaming, living in trees and tree trunks, in the brook, in holes in the ground, and they're just getting used to *me*—like I'm the new creature on the block. So what will they think of you? I don't know. But you can't be a bull in a china shop. You can't act as if you own the place, because, let's face it, it's their territory. Even *I* didn't barge in and take over as if they weren't there. I'm just waiting. Hoping they'll get used to my presence, see me as just another neighbour. So we'll use the long rope, and the stake, so that *you'll* be a good neighbour as well."

Soon we were moving through mountains more immense at every turn in the road, their steep faces still patched with snow glistening in the morning sun.

Monique rattled on.

"I know everybody thinks I've gone crazy, going on one wild tangent after another, selling *Tête-Folle*, buying a truck, renting a cabin in the woods and, worst of all, leaving everyone behind like I was some Buddhist monk, like I've abandoned them, but it's not as if I hurled myself off a cliff, I'm still here, besides I *had* to do this, Aunt Irène *told* me to do it ages ago, before the mad rush to get married, and I didn't listen. No wonder I was so unprepared for everything. So not self-sufficient. So terrible in bed … "

In slightly over an hour, we're joggling along the winding dirt lane leading to the cabin, the truck swishing past the bushes and saplings on both sides. Once there, Monique immediately screws the metal stake into the ground and ties me to it with the long rope, for she knows me. Knows my ever-growing compulsion to chase things — a canine seven-year-itch, she calls it. The craving is such that I don't discriminate, I'll chase anything that moves, from a butterfly to a garbage truck.

"For the time being, you can just get used to the smell of things right here in the clearing," she says. And she is right, the communion of smells inhaled in one breath is intoxicating, a veritable feast for the olfactory sense.

The log cabin itself, small and weather beaten, stands at the crest of a gently-rising slope of forest detritus and dirt clustered with yellow-green wild grasses and early blooming wild flowers, some purple, some white. At one end, close to the door, is a lean-to stacked with firewood. The clearing around the cabin is also small and strewn with stones and fragments of leaves, bark, twigs, branches and pine cones. A large pile of fresh black earth lies at its far edge. Miraculously, the entire clearing at noonday in April captures the sun, which also filters through a stand of tall and leafless white and yellow birches beyond the pile of black earth. Except for the murmurings of birds, and the sound of a rushing brook in the distance, it is quiet. So quiet. Like a neighbourhood holding its breath, sizing up the new arrivals. But, as Monique says later, when you really listen, it's anything but quiet.

Inside the cabin, the logs are soot-gray and caulked in between with a once white putty-like substance. A black wood stove with pipes leading to a red brick chimney stands out from the back wall. The kitchen and living room are all rolled into one living space, and at the far end are two bedrooms, barely big enough to hold the beds — a built-in double-bed in one room, and two single cots in the other — all covered with gray wool army blankets. On the wall opposite the stove is a threadbare olive green couch. And beside it, a stern high-backed rocking chair. And on the floorboards below it, an almost round braided rug of many faded colours. The windows are also small and unadorned, their panes divided into four, and the sun is streaming through them and lying in squares on the floorboards.

I lie on one square and absorb the sun's radiance and early April warmth, while Monique brings in wood and starts a fire in the stove. She then carts supplies from the truck and makes lunch. After she's eaten, she ties the long rope to my collar, again going on about the prickly porcupines and raccoons and skunks and hedgehogs and rabbits and deer and here we were, marching unannounced into their territory, and even if the land didn't belong to *them*, they belonged to *it*. She goes on incessantly, as we thread our way through trees and saplings, stepping over fallen branches and boulders, until we reach the brook, an extravagance in itself, tumbling and swirling and falling over itself as if in a frenzy to get somewhere else. We follow it all the way to the beaver dam where the waters pool and eddy in foaming circles.

"As I told you, Daisy, this is not a quiet place, in the freshet you can hardly hear yourself talk," she shouts as we back track, and indeed, the air is full of clicks and cracks and swishes and squawks and chirps and clucks.

And just as we reach the clearing two hopping robins appear in a puddle of sun, one trailing a piece of worm. Had Monique not held me taut, I would have chased them high into the sky.

On our return, I lie and watch as Monique nails boards together to create a rectangular enclosure about two feet high, beyond the lean-to. She then shovels the black earth into a wheelbarrow and pours it into the enclosure.

"This will be a raised bed for growing vegetables," she says, "tomatoes and cucumbers and beets and zucchini and herbs — as soon as the risk of frost is over. I put the bed there because it's sheltered and has its own microclimate, the owner said."

The owner is an American draft dodger. He lived in the cabin when he first came to Canada, but he wasn't Henry David Thoreau, he told Monique, and before he died of loneliness or starvation, he landed a job selling cars in Lachute, and now he runs a service station and a car wash there.

After sundown, we sit on the couch in the living room. Aside from Monique stoking and feeding the fire, we do precious little. I lie and stare at her, and she stares at the fire through the grating in the front.

"I guess you're wondering what I'm doing here, aren't you Daisy, sitting and staring at the fire," she says, massaging my back and ears.

I do wonder. Is she conversing with spirits? Her mother? Aunt Irène disguised as flame? Is she calculating the future? Pasting together the past?

"For now, I'm just being," she adds, "something I'm not really good at."

With darkness creeping covertly into the cabin, Monique leashes me and takes me out into the clearing to relieve myself, but no further.

"We have to step lightly," she whispers, "the whole place comes alive at night—like the den at home when Aunt Irène was still in it—that was her time, and for some animals, it's their time too, this is when they get things done, build their dams, hunt for food, breed…"

We then retire for the night. I sleep on the bed at Monique's feet, because the floor will get way too cold when the fire dies down. As the poet said, April is the cruelest month. And full of contradictions.

In late morning of the next day, with Monique sitting on the stoop and me close beside, the two of us soaking up the sun, the phone rings, jarring as an alarm clock. It is Mark. He is waiting at the bus terminal in Lachute, and could she pick him up.

Monique hangs up and we hop into the truck. On the ride over, Monique is unnaturally quiet, gathering herself together, as it were, rearranging things in her head, things she's put off or pushed aside.

We pull into the bus station and there he is, in a baseball cap and jean jacket, the set of his shoulders listing to one side from the load of a packsack. But we hardly know him. One eye is swollen shut, the cheekbone beneath it, indeed, the whole side of his face a shiny blotch of red and purple and blue. Still, I greet him as one returned from a far country, leaping into his arms, lavishing him with kisses, consumed with delight at seeing him. He sets me down and turns to his mother.

"Don't be too shocked by the look of me," he says, pulling at the peak of his baseball cap, "I'm fine, nothing's broken."

But Monique *is* shocked and barrages him with questions.

"Where have you been, how did it happen, what did you do?"

When he doesn't answer, we walk to the truck and climb in.

On the drive back, with me on his lap, he comments on the scenery, the lack of traffic. This is what he needs, a break from the city, time to regroup, so he thought he'd come up here for a week or so, charge his batteries, commune with nature, listen to the birds singing.

But Monique is insistent.

"So what happened? Were you in a fight?"

"I guess you could call it that."

"A fight with who?"

"With a guy on St. Lawrence Boulevard, he was yelling at his girlfriend on the sidewalk outside the bar, his head an inch from hers, and she looked scared as hell, and when I told him to cool it, he hauled off and hit me hard, caught me off-guard."

"Did you punch him back?"

"Yeah, I landed a few punches, but Chuck was there and pulled me off him."

"When did this happen?"

"Last Saturday night."

"And did you go to work on Monday?"

"No, I called in sick, I couldn't go in looking like this, could I, so I told them I'd call when I was ready to come back, but that wasn't good enough for the manager, he didn't like me that much anyway because I made more sales than he did—I sold more in one week than *he* did in one month—camping equipment, tents, sleeping bags, lanterns, Coleman stoves—"

"Are you still drinking too much?"

"Oh, there you go again."

"Well, I'm worried about it."

"Well, don't be."

"Were you drinking when you got into the fight?"

"Look, the guy was threatening the girl, Mum—"

"Okay fine, you were being the Good Samaritan, fine you can stay here, get better, and while you're getting better, you can think about yourself and who you are and where you're going, 'cause you don't seem to know, and this is a good place to think about it—in fact, I'll go back today, leave you on your own for a while—you can even keep Daisy, she's good company and she loves you, although you won't have the truck, or any way to get around."

"That's okay, I'll manage. Leave me food and I'll be fine."

Monique stopped at the general store in Lost River, stocked up on food supplies, and we returned to the cabin.

Before leaving for the city, Monique took Mark on a tour of the property. And instructed him in the plain, practical lessons of everyday living at the cabin—how to build and tend a fire in the stove, how to dispose of garbage, above all, how to keep me safe in an unfamiliar environment. I could *not* run loose, she said, because nature has no mercy, does not care, is not sentimental—and I, Daisy, will chase everything in sight. She showed him the long rope and stake in the ground and, minutes later, she was gone.

With Monique gone, Mark stretches out on the sofa, hauls me up to lie beside him and wraps me in a suffocating bear hug. But his grip on me soon relaxes, for in no time he is fast asleep. I pry myself loose and wander aimlessly from place to place. Monique's sudden departure has left me feeling scattered, I admit. Still, I put a brave face on the unexpected turn of events, for when Mark awakens in late afternoon, he is not refreshed from sleep. In fact, he is exceedingly restless, pacing back and forth like a caged tiger, opening the refrigerator, closing it, opening the kitchen cupboards and drawers, closing them. By now, the sun has gone from the clearing. An almost melancholy gray has entered the cabin. And the floor is cold.

Mark at last stops pacing, goes outdoors and lugs in an armful of wood. After several unsuccessful attempts, the cabin choked with smoke, he manages to get a fire burning in the stove. He then takes me out on the long rope, but I can smell his dislocation, and we don't venture beyond the clearing. Back inside, he eats and settles in the rocking chair. But there is no rest in rocking, for immediately he is back on his feet, pacing again. And when I try to follow him, he orders me away, his rebuke so unprecedented as to confuse and dislocate me as well. With the fire now but a few red embers in the stove, he goes to the bedroom with the two cots, piles the wool blankets from one onto the other and crawls in underneath. I watch as he tosses and turns under the mountain of blankets, the floor icy and hard as iron underneath me. When sleep finally comes to him, I leave and hop up onto Monique's bed, lay my head on her pillow, close my eyes and wait for kindly sleep to ferry me away.

The next morning it is raining, the trees tossing and turning in the wind.

It is miserable and cold and lonely in the cabin too, for Mark remains buried under the blankets until late morning. When my whining at the door finally rouses him, he pulls on his clothes, tethers me to the rope and takes me out. But not for long. With the wind whipping through the clearing, the rain slapping hard against our faces, this is a merciless place, and we quickly take refuge inside. We are both soaked. Mark wipes his head and neck and, with the same towel, soaks up the wet from my coat, and immediately, he is at the stove, building a lattice of kindling and newspaper. Soon a fire is sputtering and crackling in the stove, and the dry, comforting smell of burning wood, its heat, transforms the place.

Marks feeds me, then eats himself. But soon he is pacing back and forth again, fidgeting with items in his pockets, opening and closing the fridge, peering at his face from every angle in the tiny mirror above the toilet. Finally, he pulls a pulp fiction paperback from his knapsack, lies on the sofa and begins to read. A few pages later, he is back up, closing the draft in the stove, wedging the front door open, muttering to himself, the fire is too hot, he says, has him in a sweat, now he is peeling off his clothes, rocking back and forth in the high-backed rocking chair, picking up his book, putting it down.

By mid-afternoon, it has stopped raining. Mark pulls his clothes back on and takes me out. We tramp through the sodden undergrowth all the way to the brook, now foaming and frothing and heaving its contents downstream at breakneck speed, the constant roar of it like a song with no end, shattering the stillness after the rain.

By the time we return to the cabin, the gray light is quickly growing into darkness, and the earlier warmth has vanished. Mark throws two more logs on the fire.

He then goes to his knapsack and pulls out a bottle of amber-coloured fluid.

"Time for a drink of rum before dinner," he announces, holding the bottle up in a triumphant gesture and looking down at me, his unlikely partaker in triumph. After a few drinks "on the rocks", he makes dinner and has me feast on the delicious scraps. By now, Mark is festive, the restlessness and agitation like yesterday. Night falls, and, with the fire burning brightly in the stove, he stretches out on the couch, the bottle of rum on the floor beside him, one hand holding a glass resting on his chest, the other replenishing the glass as it is emptied. As the evening wears on, I feel a sudden and premature need to relieve myself—probably due to the generous helping of delicious scraps that had constituted my supper—and there I am, whining at the door again, when Mark finally rolls off the couch and straggles over.

"Now you go out there and do your business, Daisy," he says, "and you come right back like a good dog—and no shenanigans, because I'll be right here waiting for you, d'ya hear me?" And with that he opens the door and turns me loose.

I run to a favourite gnarled and hardened tree just beyond the clearing and make a huge deposit. Indeed, I've barely finished when I spot something moving next to the lean-to. Like a racehorse exploding from the starting gate, I take off. A canine cannon ball. And in a matter of seconds, I have the creature in my clutches, my teeth embedded in its body, and I am shaking the life from its every living cell. But the coup de théâtre is short-lived. And quickly conceived as folly. For my head, snout and belly are seething with pain, excruciating pain, sharp as needles, leaving me yelping and helpless as a newborn. The animal hobbles into the woods, and Mark is there, standing over me, leading me by the collar, like a martyr to her martyrdom, my head crowned with thorns, so to speak, Mark chastising me as he goes.

What was I doing chasing porcupines at midnight? Why couldn't he trust me outdoors, even for one minute? And what a fine fix we were both in now. Inside, Mark falls to his knees, wedges me between them, stuffs a piece of kindling in my open jaw, holds it there with one hand, and attempts to remove the quills with the other. But he's lost his grip, his strength, and cannot hold me. For I am overcome with fear. Struggling to break free. Free to suffer my torments alone. I escape onto Monique's bed and lie there. Good heavens, I say to myself, so much for your heroic aspirations. When Mark attempts to approach me again, I bare my teeth. When he persists, I growl. He finally gives up and shuffles back to the couch. Soon he is snoring loudly. The hours pass and I lie there inconsolable, ready for death to take me to the land of catkins hanging from hazel trees and cauldrons spilling over with food and drink, and creatures of my species, white and wild and innocent as snow and, as Monique would have it, in charge of their own bodies.

May 1, 1977

It has been a harrowing fortnight. But finally, I have come home to heal. April was indeed the cruelest month for me. For in the woods beyond Lost River, April had resurrected in me that primal mix of memory and desire to hunt down a badger. And in a fateful case of mistaken identity, I had had a close to apocalyptic midnight encounter with a porcupine.

The morning after, Mark had called his mother. Less than two hours later, Monique burst into the cabin, ordered Mark to pack his bag, and with me lying on his lap, she drove to Lachute and turned him out. Not even at the bus station. He was full of apologies and explanations, but Monique wouldn't hear any of them. Once Mark was out, she settled me on the seat beside her, covered me with a blanket and drove straight to the animal hospital in Montréal. When we arrived, she lifted me into her arms and, with all the gentleness of a winged angel, bore me up the stairs and handed me over to the veterinarian.

The events that followed are tenuously linked in my memory. For I was anesthetized for a period, the only way to remove all of the embedded quills. I was then sedated, the only way to relieve my post-operative suffering.

Yet, all of my recent sufferings are the result of an aspiring heart, so easily prone to indiscriminate acts of hubris and unbecoming grief. But little by little, I am healing. Reverting to my former created identity of living sculpture in the round, free-standing when indoors only.

I should mention that on the first and second day of my convalescence at home, following my release from hospital, Monique and Marina gave their two performances of Handel's *Messiah* at Christ Church Cathedral downtown.

Harry stayed behind to take care of me. Kathleen stayed behind also. She was not interested in dead composers from a dead culture.

Following the second performance, Monique and Marina returned here, the two still basking in the afterglow of the music. And tagging along with them, a young, freckle-faced tenor named Edward — and Brunhilde. Indeed, Brunhilde is every bit the other-worldly warrior-goddess I had pictured her to be, as if she'd been born for an earlier time, a time of breastplates and horned helmets and winged horses. But she loved the *Messiah*. Knew it like the back of her hand, having sung it on stages in Europe. As for the soloists in tonight's performance, she thought the mezzo could have been more tragic, more pathetic, in *He was despised*. In fact, she rose majestically to her feet and, like the consummate teacher, demonstrated how a certain passage *should* be sung:

> *"He was despised*
> *Rejected*
> *Rejected of men*
> *A man of sorrows*
> *And acquainted with grief"*

Followed by the dire details:

> *"He gave his back to the smiters,*
> *and his cheeks to them that*
> *plucked off the hair,*
> *He hid not his face from shame*
> *and spitting"*

she sang, almost spitting herself, her voice full of scorn, enough to fill a cathedral. Everyone clapped like an audience. But the after-concert radiance had been swept away by Brunhilde's iteration. Or so it seemed. Indeed, it opened up my own wounds, for here I was, smote upon by a porcupine, my hair plucked off by the veterinarian and acquainted with grief as never before.

But the entire *Messiah* performance had been a discovery for Monique. She'd felt the glory and honour and blessing flow through her body all evening, she said afterward, especially through the flares and sparks of the final *Amen.*

As for Mark, he is nowhere to be seen, since Monique drove him from the cabin, her anger like a whip, biblical in its proportions. Yet given our intimate experiences together, Mark is gathered strangely inside of me, an abiding presence of sorts.

June 25, 1977

The beneficence of summer is upon us, and I, for one, am happy to be alive after the tortures visited upon me in May, when I was again spread out on the operating table and carved open like a Christmas turkey, all to retrieve barbed pieces of porcupine quills buried in my chest and causing infection. Needless to say, being shorn like a sheep had its own mortification. But why talk of beauty? Why vanity? "Full many a flower is born to blush unseen," as the poem says. Besides, there comes a time when joy must come from the bare bones of life itself. Particularly during the agonies of illness and extended convalescence, which has confined me to the house and back yard.

But curiously, my agonies and the common string of anguish they stir in everyone in this house has kept the temple from falling into ruins, so to speak. For there they were, kneeling by my bed, gazing down upon me like the peaceful disposition of stars in one night sky. Good heavens, I thought, am I dying? Without knowing it?

Monique did not go to the cabin for an entire month. Again, she slept on the hide-a-bed in the den. As for the solidarity that illness spawns, it was momentary. A mere flash in the pan. Once my recovery was certain, Monique and Harry became prickly as porcupines with one another. And distant. In fact, she never filled him in on Mark turning me loose from the cabin—on my own—at midnight.

"Why *should* I tell him," she said as she swabbed my operative wounds, "he'd only say 'I told you so,' he thinks he's so right about everything, so sure, especially about Mark, *so* sure, wanting him out of the house and everything and look what happened…"

But Harry never asks for details. In fact, he asks no questions about the cabin or Lost River.

As for the children, Matthew has gone to British Columbia for a summer of tree planting, and Kathleen is preparing for a two-week stay at girl guide camp in the Laurentians in July. And when Monique mentioned that I was not yet healthy enough to take to the wilds of Lost River, Harry spun around.

"Go, go," he said, waving a dismissive hand, "if that's where you want to be, just go, *I'll* take care of Daisy. I'm not going anywhere."

And again she was gone.

July 30, 1977

In mid-July, with Harry having to return to work, Monique came home and took me to the cabin in Lost River. She invited Kathleen to come as well. But Kathleen refused point blank. What would she do in the sticks of Lost River? Talk to the trees? Count the sheep in the clouds? Commune with the logs? No thank you, she said. She'd stay with Harry. Besides, she and her friend Julie had volunteered at the YWCA day camp for the rest of the summer.

So again, I was alone with Monique at the cabin. I hardly knew the place, everything growing wild and furious, the air filled with the swish of leaves, the raised vegetable garden a jungle of green in all of its manifestations, the window boxes heaped with petunia and viola and trailing lobelia, the language of birds filtering through the trees, the smell of evergreen everywhere.

Given my unfortunate encounter with one of her "neighbours," as Monique calls the wild creatures with whom she shares the premises, she staked me to the rope—now short-hauled—lest I come to further grief. For she knows. The self-glorifying appetite holds not one ounce of reason. Besides, I am still a pale shadow of my former self, she says, not yet fully recovered.

Monique worked in the vegetable garden all afternoon, tying up the tomatoes and cucumbers, weeding, thinning out the latest rows of lettuce.

Evening came, we were basking in the afterglow of the sun, when a car pulled into the clearing and a wiry young man stepped out of the car. His hair, the colour of chestnut, was tied in a ponytail, and he wore a tie-dyed shirt of many colours, and blue jeans. A peace symbol was tattooed on his right forearm. He opened the back door of his car, pulled out a canvas guitar case, army green and brown, and a footstool, and walked casually toward Monique, like someone she'd been expecting.

Monique introduced me.

"Daisy, this is Rick, my landlord," she said, "and Rick, this is Daisy."

"Daisy," he exclaimed, looking me over in disbelief, "back home, Daisy's a cow's name, and you look more like an aging Hollywood starlet, with your blond wavy hair not quite hiding your bald spots, but that's okay, I don't suit my name either—Rick—like a hiccup—when it's supposed to be Richard, not Richard, the Lion-hearted, mind you, but Richard Burton, my mother loved Richard Burton, she saw "The Robe" five times, and then she gave me up to the world."

Back home for Rick was Manchester, New Hampshire, I found out later, and Rick was an erstwhile draft dodger, the owner of the cabin, who now ran a service station and car wash in Lachute.

Rick's deprecation of my name—and his—touched that same raw nerve. But better a name unbefitting, than no name at all—the lot of most cows on this side of the world, where all that remains of the sacred cow is the metaphor—and of course the expression "holy cow"—like "good heavens" for me. I've heard people say it but they don't mean it, even if it sounds like a sworn statement.

But out of sheer sympathy, I would think of this gentleman as Richard, even if Monique continued to call him Rick. Surely they were more than landlord and tenant, for even as introductions were proceeding, he was entering the cabin, lifting his guitar from its case, placing his footstool in front of a kitchen chair, sitting down and tuning his instrument. And there was Monique, all business, fetching song books from atop the fridge and piling them in order on the kitchen table as a matter of ritual. Straightaway, they threw themselves into their songs, Richard playing the chords, Monique on her feet beside him, singing *Puff the Magic Dragon, Where Have All the Flowers Gone, The Cruel War is Raging,* and on and on, ending with *Johnny's Gone for a Soldier,* one they'd just begun practising,

> *"Here I sit on Buttermilk Hill*
> *Who can blame me cry my fill*
> *Every tear would turn a mill*
> *Johnny's gone for a soldier."*

I lie and listen as they sing through their repertoire. Richard, a tenor, singing the harmony. And just as Richard is about to put his guitar back in its case, Monique speaks up. She wants to buy a guitar. She wants to learn to play it. And could he teach her how to strum, play the chord progressions, for she'd love to be able to sing and accompany herself in town next winter.

"Sure thing," he says, "be glad to," and with one hand on the back of the kitchen chair, he bows and sweeps a hand over its seat, gallant as a knight from King Arthur's Round Table.

"Sit yourself right down on this here kitchen chair," he says with an almost theatrical artifice, "and we'll start at the beginning, with lesson one."

Once she is seated on the chair, Richard goes to great lengths. Positioning her shoulders and upper arms, running his hands lightly over them as he speaks, "the guitar is like a lover," he says, "you hold it in your arms, love it well, and it will love you back a hundredfold."

"You sound like Brunhilde," Monique says, laughing nervously.

"Who's Brunhilde?"

"She's my singing teacher." And she tells Richard all about Brunhilde and her "whole-body, awakened-body" philosophy of singing, even as Richard is on his knees at her feet, holding her right calf muscle in the palm of his hand and lifting her lower leg onto the footstool.

"Now you are ready, ready to receive the guitar, and this is where it will rest its weary head," he goes on, as one delivering a poem, all the while running the palm of his hand up and down the length of her right thigh, as if smoothing the way for the guitar, making the rough places plane. He then rises to his feet, places the head of the guitar on her thigh, cups her left hand in his and places it in position on the neck, "and the right hand strums over the sound hole," he continues, taking her fingers in his, playing in turn with each of their tips until the angle and curve is exactly as it should be, "to touch is to feel oneself being touched," he almost whispers into the sound hole. With everything in position, he steps back a pace, surveys the situation and smiles his approval.

"What next?" Monique asks, as if in a trance.

"What next?" he echoes, and in less than a wag of my tail, the guitar is resting flat on the table and Richard is the preceptor of the universe, kneeling at her feet, holding her calf muscles in the palm of his two hands, like two precious gems, laying his head on one thigh, on the other, lingering in the space in between, fondling her fingers, kissing each curve, taking their tips between his lips, and there *she* is, holding him like the guitar a minute before, touching him, loving him, and he returning it a hundredfold, lesson one on a long and rapturous continuum.

And that was August. Days of quiet aliveness and sun, evenings of singing and one lesson after another in guitar playing and rapturous loving with the preceptor of the universe and she returning it a thousand-fold.

By summer's end, Monique had also bought the log cabin and six acres of woods from Richard, with Richard thrown in to close the bargain. Every evening, she waited for him, watched for him, the first star to appear in the heavens, so to speak.

September 5, 1977

Monique brought me to town and to the veterinarian after the Labour Day weekend. I hadn't made a one hundred per cent recovery, she complained to the veterinarian, I was listless and feverish in the evening, twitching in my sleep, and could there be bits of porcupine quill still stuck inside of me, living there like a parasite or foreign body, or had I just grown old from too much punishment. Monique's suspicions were soon confirmed. Fragments of quill had burrowed their way into my upper leg and chest, with abscesses forming around them. This called for excision and drainage of the affected areas and of course more shaving of my coat, my chest now white and hairless as an egg. The usual antibiotic treatment was also instituted.

With Matthew and Kathleen back in school and Harry back at work, Monique had to stay in town and take care of me, clean my operative wound, administer the antibiotics and provide some supervised form of exercise.

Again, there was that coalescence of caring around me. Again, I became the preserve of everyone's love. And again, after ministering to me, each one went his and her own way, all stiff inside themselves. When Monique engaged Kathleen in conversation, she replied in grunts and monosyllables. Matthew, flush with spending money after a summer of tree planting, was happy she was home, for he could borrow the pickup. As for Harry, apart from everyday civilities, he said little. Even when Monique showered him with praise for how well he cooked and kept the house and the garden. Even when she noticed the two hydrangea bushes he had planted in the back garden.

"You seem more at home here than ever before," she said, looking around the clean, well-ordered kitchen.

"This *is* my home, I was *born* here," he said, as if he'd peered into its overlooked corners and spied some portion of himself sitting there.

"You make me feel like a visitor," she said.

"You *are*," he replied.

Again, Monique slept on the hide-a-bed in the den. She gingerly lifted me up to lie at her feet, as I had lain at Aunt Irène's. And again I felt the aloneness of those final nights of sleeping with Aunt Irène. Her aloneness seeping into me. As if night were a dark valley of aloneness and we were walking through it together. And here it is again, forcing its way up into me, along with the ache in my chest, leaving room for nothing else.

Monique and I spent this morning at Marina's. A first choir practice session on the fall repertoire. The cockatoos had been caged and taken upstairs when we arrived. Why? Because they hate Edward. Edward is the young rosy-cheeked, freckle-faced tenor with one earring Marina befriended at the choir weekend in the Laurentians. Now he was rehearsing with them. Marina had amply warned Edward beforehand about Minerva and Modesta, who had shown an inborn antipathy for almost every man who had darkened her door. But it couldn't possibly apply to him, he said. He loved birds of the parrot family. And they loved him. In fact, the last parrot he owned he'd taught to sing the opening lines of George Frideric Handel's *Art thou troubled,* which goes as follows:

> *Art thou troubled*
> *Music will calm thee*
> *Art thou weary*
> *Rest shall be thine*

And to prove it, he went to the cage and commanded Minerva to step up onto his hand. Minerva is a conniving one and she feigned obedience, but once there, she bit him viciously on the thumb, the bite so severe as to require stitches and cause the loss of his right thumbnail, and he a research librarian at the CBC music library, thumbing through files all day long.

Edward is now studying voice with Brunhilde as well, extending his range, learning to mix the different vocal registers. In fact, Edward's voice has been a source of deep-seated confusion and consternation since puberty, he told Marina. There he was, since the tender age of ten, singing soprano in the boys' and men's choir at Christ Church Cathedral, when overnight his voice broke, cracked, fell apart, changed, and he no longer knew what he was. Or who he was. Or where to turn. Or how to sing. Perhaps he was one of those misfits, born too late. In another century, he might have had his testicles removed and sung soprano all his life. But today, no matter what, you kept your testicles.

For a while he thought he was a counter-tenor, for he had this magnificent falsetto. But for some unknowable reason, he was ashamed of it. Plus, he'd grown tired of singing with men, fuss-pots they were, always bickering, picking at one another, everything from jealous to downright possessive, and he longed to sing with women, to *be* with women, he *loved* women, and joined the Elgar Choir.

"Why don't you take lessons with Brunhilde, she'll tell you what you are," Marina said.

And Brunhilde did. She awakened the male tenor voice lying dormant in the depths of his body all these years.

Today's practice session begins with the three singers stretched out side by side in the supine position on the living room floor, one open hand resting on the diaphragm, for according to Brunhilde, the diaphragm is the force that through the column of air drives the sound, a singer's version of the green fuse driving the flower.

"Breathe in and feel it rise," Marina calls out, from where she lies, "breathe out and feel it fall, and in that same out-breath, release all of the tensions piled up inside your body from one week of regimental, unnatural living."

Once back on their feet, they bend over, fold their bodies in two and hum into their heads until every suture between every lobe in their skull vibrates from the hum. Then one vertebra at a time, they unfold like ferns and resume the erect position.

They then imagine Brunhilde's long string running from the earth's core, through their spinal column, up through the ceiling and high into the heavens above.

"You and the string are one," Marina goes on, "and before you can sing, you must own the ground you stand on."

Next is the warm-up. Scales, arpeggios, octave leaps, on every vowel and resonant consonant. Because the contemporary piece on the program, a biblical drama for narrator, choir and organ, entitled *Saul*, is like no other. Its score is a minefield of sharp angles and razor turns and colossal vocal leaps. But Marina is particularly thrilled to be singing it, for the piece was written by Egil Hovland, the Norwegian composer, and her cousin Inge had sung in his church choir in Fredrikstad for years. But one look at the opening section, with singers entering independently at half second intervals and slowly building to breakneck speed and *fortissimo* volume, settles it. They cannot practise it alone here in the living room. Edward, however has brought a recording. So they sit on the sofa and listen to that.

First the large, booming voice of the narrator, citing from the Acts of the Apostles:

> *And on that day a great persecution arose against the church in Jerusalem.*

And who is leading the persecution? Saul, of course. Not only is he breathing threats and murder against the disciples of the Lord, he is entering house after house and dragging off men and women and committing them to prison or bringing them bound in chains back to Jerusalem. And this after the disciples of the Lord have worked themselves to the bone making unclean spirits come out of many who were possessed and healing many who are paralyzed and lame. And as the narrator graphically describes the lawless scene, in comes the equally lawless dissonant and cacophonous choir depicting the whole of Judea and Samaria in shambles, and to add insult to injury, the organ, racing frantically down from the hills, always down, the keyboard at full swell, as the entire region descends into pandemonium. With all hell breaking loose, everything then screeches to a stop, and the narrator is back

> *Now as he journeyed he approached Damascus, and suddenly a light from heaven flashed about him. And he fell to the ground and heard a voice saying to him:*

In this case, four voices—soprano, alto, tenor, base—whispering to him *pianissimo*, imploring him repeatedly,

> *Saul, Saul, Saul, Saul,*
> *Why, why, why, why,*
> *Why do you persecute me?*

But with the cockatoos shrieking like persecuted Christians upstairs, the heart-stopping effect of the *forte* whispers was completely lost.

"Maybe the dissonance, the chaos, takes them back to the wild," Edward suggested, "back to their fear of predators."

But Marina has fewer and fewer explanations for the cockatoos.

"Who outside of the wild really understands the language of birds?" she said, without waiting for an answer.

After the practice session, we take our leave. But Edward stays.

"I think the cockatoos are jealous of Edward," Monique says on the way home, and she *thinks* she knows *why*.

October 15, 1977

It has been a fortnight full of circumstance. To begin with, Mark finally came around ... I had not seen him since the day Monique drove him from the cabin with whips, the morning after my assault on the porcupine, in future known as the defendant.

I was alone in the house when Mark arrived. The swelling, discoloration and abrasions on his face when I last saw him had vanished. So had his stubble of beard. And in its place, as if by design, that clean-shaven, wholesome look of a man grown from heavenly seeds. Overjoyed as I was to see him, I could not leap into his arms in the usual manner of greeting. But he sensed the frailty in my hindquarters, and the rush of solicitude it invoked brought him to his knees. He held my head in his two mighty hands and looked me straight in the eye.

"You know I didn't mean to hurt you, Daisy, you know that, I was half asleep and just forgot where we were for a minute," he said, "it's that simple." And there was Harry, coming through the back door after watering the shrubs and flowers, cutting Mark's words of reparation short.

"Well, well, look who's here, haven't seen much of *you* lately," said Harry, turning on the kitchen tap, washing his hands and pouring a glass of water.

"Yeah, yeah, well I've been working for a landscaping firm and this is a busy time," Mark replied, jumping to his feet.

"I thought you were working at Eaton's."

"I was, but this pays better, and I work full-time—and outdoors, I like working outdoors."

He then changed the subject and began asking about everyone, piecing the family back together, as it were ...

" Where's Mum?"

"Up at that place she has in the Laurentians, I guess. You've been there."

"Yeah, yeah, where's Matthew?"

"He's at this science fair at the college, he has an exhibit there on astronomy."

"And where's Kathleen?"

"She's babysitting for one of the neighbours, they just moved in this summer, that brownstone house with the yellow door just around the corner."

"And how's Daisy? Mum said she had more surgery."

"Yeah, more bits of porcupine quill buried in her leg and chest, forming abscesses."

"Is she gonna be okay?"

"We hope so, but the vet's not sure, quills dig their way in, sometimes enter a vital organ; for now we're just keeping her comfortable."

"When's Mum coming back?"

"I don't know."

"This week? Next week?"

"I never know. She comes and she goes."

"And you're not flying anymore, I hear."

"No."

"Not ever?"

"Not now."

"You're working downtown, Mum says?"

"Yep, somebody has to be here, Kathleen can't stay alone."

"Yeah, 'cause I was thinking about taking some flying lessons, learning how to fly, maybe even joining the air force."

Silence.

"So you don't think it's a good idea."

"No I didn't say that, but there's no war on, no crying need for pilots."

Silence. Then Harry again.

"But look, if you're serious, real serious, I mean, I know a guy at the recruiting centre, and if you really want to learn, get a real education, I'll introduce you to him."

"What about private flying lessons, could you teach me?"

"No, I couldn't. And I wouldn't. Best to learn from a complete stranger, I say. But, as my father told *me* way back, flying lessons are just flying lessons, what you need is an education for down here on earth. And flying lessons are expensive, like everything else these days, you won't be able to afford them on what *you're* making."

"I'd like to meet the guy at the recruiting centre."

"Fine, I'll go with you, introduce you to him."

"Okay fine."

Mark left soon afterward.

A week later, on a Monday afternoon, the appointed day for meeting the recruitment officer, Mark arrived at the house in a shirt and tie and sport coat. Harry came down from upstairs, ready to go, but when he opened the front door for Mark to pass through, Harry stopped abruptly.

"We're not going anywhere," he said, walking into the living room and sitting down.

Mark stepped inside and closed the door, keeping his hand on the door knob.

"So what's the problem now?"

"You smell like a tavern."

"Oh come on, I had two beers and that was two hours ago."

"You're not serious, and I took the afternoon off work just for this?"

"I'm not *your* kind of serious, *that's* what you mean."

"You're not any kind of serious. Nobody goes to an interview smelling like a still, and if drinking's your problem, you need to get serious about that, because that *is* serious."

"Aw screw it, I'll make my own arrangements," Mark said, turned the knob he was still holding onto, pulled the door open and walked out.

Harry then phoned the recruiting officer and cancelled the meeting. Something had come up unexpectedly at the office, he said.

Good heavens, I thought to myself, how fragile the face of aspiration, white and high and bloated as a cloud, yet so quick to darken, lose its form, or disappear completely.

December 5, 1977

Today, Sunday, Harry and I drove to Mount Royal. At the last minute, Kathleen decided to hop in as well. She had nothing better to do, she said, her best friend Julie, who's been taking lessons in Irish dancing since she was six, was performing at an Irish *fesch* in Two Mountains.

"Is that what you're wearing?" Harry said, looking at Kathleen as we prepared to leave.

"Yes."

"To the mountain?"

"Yes."

Kathleen, soon to turn fourteen, is already making fashion statements. Her ensemble for Sunday's outing was flamenco-pink tights, black patent leather knee-high boots and, pulled over a jacket, a green and yellow diamond-knit cast-off woolen sweater of Harry's, last year's Christmas gift from his father Ned, and on her head a yellow over-sized Rastafarian cap, her mass of curls spilling out underneath it like the contents of a weekend bag too hastily packed, and hanging from her earlobes, Aunt Irène's gold-leaf hoops, large as bracelets. Kathleen now loves Bob Marley and The Wailers. Loves reggae. Thinks the Rastafarian religion is better than Christianity because it's more than a religion, it's a way of life and not something people do on Sunday. In fact lately, she's been making Harry stop and listen to *Get Up, Stand Up*, and *I Shot the Sheriff*, and who is the sheriff, she says to Harry, then answers her own question—the sheriff can be any of the Babylonian kings of the Bible or others like them—still alive and well and living in Jamaica and in America and in every dark little unsuspecting corner of the world.

And sometimes of late, Kathleen's reggae music is the only sound we hear, its responsories and versicles echoing through the house as through a silent cloister, as if to say, take it and eat it, let it lift you up above the vapour and dust of earthly existence and all of its abandonments.

Beaver Lake itself, a tarmac for the arrival and departure of water fowl, was deserted when we arrived, the deciduous trees stripped of their foliage. Except for the odd squirrel padding through the light blanket of snow, the animals and birds seemed to be holding their breath, hiding behind barricades, sensing the nearness of winter aligning its forces. We walked, but not long distances. For much as I love the open spaces on Mount Royal, the pungent smell of resurrection from the cemetery nearby, I am still a convalescent, my reserves of energy swiftly depleted. On the trek back down to Beaver Lake, however, the sun broke through the sheer curtain of white cloud, inviting us to stay a while, as it were. We sat on one of the benches around the lake, set like chairs around a table, and took what remained of its warmth into ourselves.

We sat quietly, Harry and Kathleen on the bench, me in the space between, and Kathleen began with her stockpile of questions.

"When you were a kid and living alone with your dad, how did *you* feel?"

"That's a funny question to be asking me all of a sudden... I don't know, I'd have to think about it," Harry said. "Why do you ask?"

"Because I'm alone and living with you, that's why, Mark's gone. Matthew's always out somewhere..."

"And how does *that* feel?"

"It feels miserable. I'm very mad, very mad at Mum, like I don't want to even talk to her when she shows up."

Silence.

"Were you mad at your mother when she died?"

Silence. Then Harry again.

"I thought about her lately... when I planted those hydrangea bushes out back."

"Why's that?"

"Because that's what she was doing when I found her, she was planting two hydrangea bushes she'd just bought at the Atwater Market."

"She loved hydrangeas?"

"Yeah, she loved hydrangeas."

"And you found her?"

"Yeah, I found her."

"So what did you do? How old were you?"

Long pause, then,

"I was six ... I came home from school and there she was, in the garden, fallen over flat on her face, lying in a pile of black earth."

"So what did you do?"

"You don't want to know."

"Why? Yes I do."

"First I shook her, told her to wake up...and when she didn't move I went back into the kitchen...and I made myself a peanut butter sandwich and ate it and sat there at the kitchen table, waiting for my father to come home from work."

Silence.

"And what did *he* do?"

Long pause, then,

"Some other time, Kathleen, Daisy's getting cold, it's time to go," Harry said. "Let's go."

Back home at dinner, Kathleen picked up the subject where she'd left off earlier.

"Did Grandpa Ned blame you for just sitting there?"

"Yeah, he did. In fact, he was furious. What was I doing sitting there? he said, and why didn't I pick up the phone and call him. But I'd never called him at work, didn't know the number, still I could have done something more than sit there like a helpless dolt and eat a peanut butter sandwich...but seeing her lying in a pile of dirt, I just couldn't even think...I was paralyzed in a way...and I pretended everything was the same as when I left that morning."

"What was your mother like?"

Harry is quiet for a moment, as if thumbing through his mind, looking for an image other than the one of her lying face down in the pile of dirt.

"My father took all the pictures down, all the snapshots, and put them away, hoping I'd forget, hoping he'd forget too, I guess, and we never talked about her… still you'd think I'd remember what she *looked* like at least…what I *do* remember is her smell, and the touch of her skin, soft and smooth, her hands, her fingers, I know she was quite plump, and she loved her flowers — and her books — she worked as a volunteer at the Atwater Library, in fact, and she was planning to go back to school, she wanted to become a librarian, I remember her saying that, but of course she didn't get to do it."

"Is that why you planted the two hydrangeas, because she didn't get to do it?"

But Harry has answered too many questions already.

"I guess so… that's enough for now," he says, "and if *you* want to get to do things, you better get your homework done, tomorrow's another school day."

Kathleen goes upstairs, and Harry does the dishes and sweeps the kitchen floor, reaching his broom into the spaces on the sides of the stove and under the fridge, all the difficult to reach crevices and corners where crumbs collect and specks of dust and dirt collect and hide.

December 8, 1977

On Sunday, Harry was stringing outdoor Christmas lights around the front bay window, the evening oh so peaceable, with bloated snowflakes falling, floating weightlessly on wisps of air and twinkling like stars in the light of the street lamp, when the phone rang jarringly through the quiet.

Kathleen, who was doing her homework at the kitchen table, answered, then opened the front door a slit and poked her head through.

"It's Chuck, the weight lifter," she called out to Harry halfway up the ladder.

Harry came in, wiped his feet, brushed the snow from his shoulders and arms, removed one glove and picked up the receiver.

Immediately it was all Chuck the messenger, the bringer of news about Mark — bad news, I surmised, for the more Harry listened, the more uneasy he became, his feet fidgeting, his gloved hand fiddling, first with the telephone cord, then with the peak of his cap, pulling it down onto his forehead, lifting it off. He finally broke through the monologue.

"I'll be over… yeah, yeah, I know where you live." said Harry, and hung up. But for what seemed like a millennium, he sat there, forearms resting on his thighs, his gloved hand covering the bare one, taking the news into himself, that uncertain, wounded look, so visible after his heart attack in Vancouver, now returning to his face, as if one wound had reopened an earlier one. Then suddenly he was on his feet and, like a monastic, arranging things in orderly rows, putting his ladder and tools away, and calling Monique at the cabin in Lost River.

Mark had been in a fight in a bar two nights ago, he told her. The bar owner called the police. Mark was taken to the police station and let go in the morning. But last night, Chuck caught him stringing a skipping rope over the transom in their flat, the one he uses to chin himself. When Chuck asked what he was doing, he said 'nothing', but Chuck doesn't buy it, Mark's been bummed out lately, he said, too bummed up to go to work, his face and fists are battered and bruised, his ankle swollen — sprained when he lost his balance during the fight — so he can't do much….

Harry then listened to Monique, but he soon grew restless and impatient.

"Look, I'm going there right now…no, don't bother your head," he replied, "no, you're having a great time where you are…hold on for now at least…I'll call you…"

Harry hollered up to Matthew in the attic, explained where he was headed and why, leaving out the worrisome details, and ordered him to hold the fort until his return. But Matthew is *insouciant,* as Aunt Irène would say. Disconnected. Unplugged from life on the ground floor. At midnight, with Kathleen asleep and Harry still not home, he climbed into the attic and went to bed.

Truth is, Matthew never really came home after his summer of planting trees in British Columbia. He eats here, goes back and forth from Dawson College and sleeps in the attic. In a sleeping bag. He also keeps a telescope up there. A purchase he made with some of his tree-planting earnings. He wants to be an astronomer, he announced to Harry, upon his return. All from lying flat on his back exhausted after twelve hours of planting and looking up and seeing the evening sky for the first time, he said, the meteoroids, meteor showers, noctilucent clouds, even the heliacal rising at sunrise, all things he never noticed in Montréal, the night sky was like this immense happening place, without the chaos, and without the racket, everything predictable and in its place, yet infinitely more interesting than this boring speck of dust, this aimless particle we're living on down here, he said.

And Harry had seemingly understood.

"Yeah, I thought that too at your age, everything far away, far up, is better."

So with Matthew sequestered in the attic, I was left to hold the fort from the Oriental rug at the front entrance, my head resting on my outstretched forepaws, every nerve and sinew poised to strike despite my weakened condition.

A profound quietness had penetrated the house when Harry's van pulled into the driveway. In seconds, there he was, unlocking the door, nudging it open with his foot, holding onto Mark with one arm, carrying his rucksack with the other, leading him limping into the den, easing him down onto the stuffed chair in the corner, returning to close the front door.

And there I was, foolish as a nine-tailed fox, my entire body wagging, straining to capture Mark's attention, given my failing hindquarters.

"Don't, don't, don't try and jump," Mark cautioned me through his bruised and swollen lips. I slavishly licked his two hands and swollen knuckles, thinking oh good heavens, what a sight you are, sitting here in the dim light of the lamp, your two legs apart, one eye just a slit, your face puffed and shining with bruises and lacerations like a professional boxer, battered in one round and fearfully contemplating another.

Harry moved quickly. He opened the hide-a-bed, made it, eased Mark down onto it, and removed his shoes and socks, jacket, and shirt, Mark wincing as Harry removed his pants and sock from the swollen ankle. Once he'd settled Mark in, he switched off the lamp.

'Good heavens, I thought, oh helpless soul of me,' no longer able to scramble up and assume my post at Mark' s feet, as I had done so dutifully with Aunt Irène, with Monique. But before frustration spilled over into whining and whimpering, there was Harry, stretching out on the other half of the hide-a-bed, flat on his back in his clothes, taking my animal place, as it were, my abiding presence beyond words, and there they lay, like two weary soldiers, till sleep closed fast around us.

December 1, 1977

The day after bringing Mark home, Harry dragged Matthew's mattress down and laid it out in the den, and this is where he's been sleeping ever since. Before settling in himself, he lifts me up to sleep at Mark's feet on the hide-a-bed.

Monique came home the next evening, close to midnight, crept into the den and beheld us lying there — three wolves sleeping in a den. Of necessity, she slept in the connubial bed in the master bedroom. Indeed, except for Kathleen, everyone is lying in another person's bed, as travelers do, sleeping and waking in new surroundings, seeing the world around them from a new place.

Every evening, Harry pours warm water into a white enamel basin, adds three tablespoons of Epsom Salts and has Mark soak his ankle in it. He compresses his cheek and eye, dresses the abrasions on his knuckles, all things he learned to do in the RCAF, he tells Mark. Other than comment on the matter at hand, the two say little. But I can almost see the slow procession of thoughts winding through their heads.

Finally, toward the end of the week, Mark breaks through.

"Remember how you said I wasn't serious about anything ... well I wasn't really serious about hanging myself either."

"How are we supposed to know that?"

"'Cause I don't have the guts to do that either."

Long pause…then Harry.

"I'd forgotten all about it, until the other night, but I tied ropes together every night when I was a boy, so you must get that from me…"

"I didn't think I got anything from you."

"That's how I put myself to sleep, tying ropes together in my mind, hanging them out the window and letting myself down into the garden…But I never had the guts to really do it either…I was only six and seven, that's how I put myself to sleep…tying ropes together…like people tie sheets…"

"Did you want to run away?"

"No, no, but for a long time after my mother died, I pretended she came to the garden at night…that's where I saw her last…so you must be desperate about something too if you're tying ropes together…and how desperate do you have to be before you do something…about the drinking to start with…"

Long pause…then Mark.

'I can't stay here much longer…I gotta get back to work ... "

"Did you know, my mother soaked her feet in this basin right here…?" Harry said, "and so did I when I stepped on a nail."

Mark looked down at his foot immersed in the healing solution.

"Did you use Epsom Salts too?"

Yeah, we did," Harry said.

"Different problems, same solution."

'Same basin.

And that is how the conversation ended. Everyone's feet in the same basin.

January 3, 1978

Christmas Day arrived, and Harry and Kathleen roasted the turkey in a slow oven in a brown paper bag. Indeed, the entire day was about as jolly as a brown paper bag. Harry's father Ned came and fiddled forlornly with his new corncob pipe, a gift from Harry. Matthew appeared for dinner then disappeared into the attic. Mark came, the wounds from his latest battle almost completely healed, And with him a French-speaking woman named Chloé, who looked somewhat older than Mark. Monique came on Christmas Eve, slept in the den and left after Christmas dinner. The dinner was a listless affair. A cold coming together of individuals. There was no singing of Christmas carols. No after-dinner visit from Marina and Desmond and Kirsten. Yet through it all, one moment shines. After dinner, Chloé, Mark's French-speaking friend, came and knelt beside me. Mark had told her all about me, she said, and she'd been longing to meet me. Good heavens! I thought, and there she was, with her dense crop of short black hair and black inquiring eyes, full of gravity and grace, bending down, touching me, her regard so attentive, as if to say "What are you going through, Daisy?"

"I'm suffering from an acute case of ecstasy," I wanted to say and instantly rolled over onto my back, my four legs swaying in the air like the branches of a barren fig tree, my private parts exposed to her in an act of total self-surrender. And unlike others I know, she didn't flinch.

January 27, 1978

Again last night I had a dream. A foretaste of what is to come — later rather than sooner, I hope. In the dream, I am liberated from this failing canine body of mine, freed from the obscurities and mysteries of daily life in this house and escorted into paradise under a canopy of heavy gold brocade held aloft by four winged caryatids soaring up, up, up, until we arrive at a celestial entrance in the uppermost reaches of the cosmos, the entrance exhaling a fragrance, an intoxicating amalgam of Dr. Ballard's fresh from the can and the cow dung I'd smelt in the Saguenay, and as if by some beatific form of serendipity, there is Aunt Irène standing among a conference of birds, like Sweeney among the nightingales, singing in her faraway bird-voice *Quelle est cette odeur agréable,* so very apt given the aromas, and lying at her feet below the conference of birds, Ebony, the object of my green envy on earth, black and sleek and self-indulgent as always, now decorated with gems, bells and banners, as are the legions of resurrected animal martyrs gathering around me, slain before their time—sacrificial offerings, for the sake of their skin, their heart, the feathers on their tail, their big or small horns, their teeth, their tusks, their nails, their bones, or even their bile and now finally elevated to heavenly states of blissfulness and blessedness, the whole scene a paradise unto itself, until a gargantuan porcupine, in another *coup de théâtre* of sorts, burst in on me, its needles long and sharp, shooting like rays of sun from his spinal column. Needless to say, my compulsion to chase it, coming from that same frightful inner necessity, brought me to, and there I was, back down on Earth again, relieved to see the bright face of morning, sufficient to soothe my melancholy as the days of winter darken round my ever-growing frailness.

February 14, 1978

Today, St. Valentine's Day, Mark came to visit in the evening, accompanied by Chloé, who again showed that rare ability to pay attention, to me at least. And again I would have gladly been St. Valentine, allowed myself to be beaten with clubs and stoned and beheaded, for just one moment of her rapt attention.

Mark quickly caught Harry's attention when he announced that he'd been to the Canadian Armed Forces' recruiting office, passed all the aptitude tests, the medical examination, the physical fitness tests and was waiting for his first assignment.

If Mark's news came as a thunderbolt to Harry, he did not let on.

"Good,' he said, continuing to sweep the kitchen floor, "you know you might have to leave town, go someplace else for training camp."

"Don't worry, I need a change of scenery anyway," Mark said.

Then Harry turned to Chloé. Did she want a cup of tea or coffee, a piece of cake, something to put Mark's news into perspective in his own mind, or so it seemed, because he hadn't swum across the English Channel or climbed Mount Everest or snowshoed to the North Pole.

Yet I could feel, floating in the air around us, a quiet jubilation, a fragile hope even, hovering over our heads like a single-winged angel or ruby-throated hummingbird.

March 15, 1978

Today Marina and Monique practised choruses from *Dona Nobis Pacem* by British composer Ralph Vaughn Williams, the *pièce de résistance* on their spring program.

They concentrated on the second movement, which, according to the conductor, called for a bloody-minded, sabre-rattling, martial tone.

> *Beat! Beat! Drums! — Blow! Bugles! Blow!*
> *Through the windows — through the doors — burst like a ruthless force,*
> *Into the solemn church, and scatter the congregation;*
> *Into the school where the scholar is studying,*
> *Leave not the bridegroom quiet — no happiness must he have now with his bride;*
> *Nor the peaceful farmer any peace, ploughing his field or gathering his grain;*
> *So fierce you whirr and pound, you drums — so shrill you bugles blow.*

After an hour of practice, we all repaired to the kitchen, where the two ate pickled herring and bread, sipped tea and talked and talked into the late afternoon, Monique unburdening herself to Marina, confessing that she'd fallen hopelessly in love with a thirty-year-old American named Rick she'd met in Lost River, even describing his long wavy locks of chestnut hair tied into a pony tail, his star-spangled headband, his earring, the peace symbol tattooed on his forearm, and how serendipitous that she should be singing *Dona Nobis Pacem* on the heels of meeting a pacifist, and how easily, how spontaneously, he abandoned himself to his passions, and how contagious it was, miraculously passing over into her, everything happening in a flash like some dazzling illuminating awakening of her body, once dead as a dried-up tree, dull as a rock, now risen from the depths of somewhere, all five senses alive again.

Had she told Harry about him, Marina wanted to know.

No she hadn't, but she planned to at some point, she was screwing up the courage, waiting for the right moment.

There is no *right* moment, Marina interrupted, the right moment is *now*, she couldn't hold with the hare and run with the hounds, as they say here, besides, one secret, one lie, is not so bad, but it leads to another and another and another. She never lies to Desmond. She tells him absolutely everything he wants to know, but of course, Desmond doesn't mind, humans are not monogamous, never have been, he says, all the combined wisdom of China and India and Africa, all the teachings of Paul, Augustine and Thomas Aquinas, could not make humans monogamous, some just pretend they are, in fact, Desmond even loved hearing all the spicy details about Marina's passionate liaisons—with Edward, for instance, they gave him an appetite when he lost it, like the apples in the Garden of Eden.

But Harry was another person altogether, Monique said, Harry did everything solo. If she told Harry about Rick, he might say "go, go," he'd said it before, and maybe "don't come back," already she was treading on dangerous ground, she was more like a visitor now anyway, and Harry—even Kathleen and Matthew—seemed to need her less and less, Harry did all the cooking, all the cleaning, all the parenting too. He's like a shepherd in his own pasture, tending his flock, because he owns the house, he was born in it, as he always reminds her, he's never lived anywhere else, yes, she knows, she'll have to tell him all about Rick, but she won't tell him the details, that he's a draft dodger, that he hates war, she won't tell him how head over heels she is, how alive she feels with Rick, how he'd brought her to life, like Pygmalion in her Greek mythology course at Concordia, no, she won't humiliate him, because she knows how humiliated *she* felt after the incident in Vancouver.

What incident in Vancouver? Marina asks.

And Monique confesses all the lurid details surrounding Harry's heart attack in Vancouver.

Marina runs short of words for a moment, as if adjusting her image of Harry to fit the moment.

"Maybe Desmond is right after all," Marina says finally, "I should stop blaming everything he says on the war."

Mar 23, 1978

In late April, Harry was promoted to the position of Director of Flight Operations for Air Canada. Following his appointment, he travelled to various cities in Canada, a good will tour of sorts, to meet the people with whom he would be working. As a result, I was shipped out to Lost River, where I spent another month.

How splendid the scene upon my arrival there—the log cabin swimming in sunlight, the clearing a sea of wild flowers, soft winds blowing the fragrant resins of fir trees into my nostrils, birds calling from the cloister of trees beyond the clearing, the rushing water from the brook.

We spend the days outdoors, Monique bent over her vegetable garden, hoeing, digging, raking, and planting seedlings, then filling the window boxes and pots with geranium, petunia, viola and trailing lobelia, as I lie watching the welter of life around me, my body skewered to the spot, hot and helpless as a pig at a pig roast.

In the evenings, once the last beams of sun have fallen, Monique builds a fire in the stove, uncases the new acoustic guitar she purchased this winter and sits at the table piled high with her songbooks. She's barely tuned the instrument, begun to play and sing, when a car pulls into the yard, the front door opens and in walks Rick—again in that familiar, easy fashion I remember when he was still the landlord.

And in that same annoyingly easy fashion, just last evening, he again raised the painful issue of my name.

"Hi there Daisy," he said, "the dog named after a cow, when you could have *been something,* you could have been a contender, learned a few tricks and been Rin Tin Tin or Lassie or Pal, you're still that good-lookin'."

And again last evening, after the singing, he did what he always does—put his guitar away in its case and, like a seasoned performer striding onto a stage, walked over to Monique, removed the guitar from where it sat on her lap, lay it on the kitchen table, and immediately fell to his knees at her feet, reverent almost, as if in a place of worship, and immediately it was she, removing his headband, loosening his locks, combing through the head of wavy chestnut hair, pulling his face to her body, unbuttoning her blouse, cupping her bare breasts in her two hands and presenting them like jewels for him to kiss and fondle and in no time he was carrying her in his arms, laying her on the couch, removing all of her clothes, removing all of his and entering her, diving to the bottom, filling her with himself, and she, moved to helpless tears.

Once their passions were spent, they pulled their clothes back on, sat on the couch and stared into the fire flickering in the stove, her head resting on his shoulder.

"Have you noticed anything?" Monique asked suddenly, still staring at the fire.

"Noticed anything?"

"Yes, noticed anything...my breasts bigger, my nipples darker...anything like that, because I've missed one period already and I'm late for the second."

"You can buy these do-it-yourself kits at the drugstore now, they'll tell you if you're pregnant even before the doctor does."

"No, I prefer to see a doctor."

"Then why not see the doctor you saw for your other kids?"

"No, I don't want to do that."

"Why not?"

"Because it's not my husband's baby, that's why."

"You're sure, are you?"

"Yes, I'm sure."

"Or someone else's?"

"There *is* nobody else... Is there a doctor in Lachute?"

"You're *that* sure it's mine are you?"

"Yes, I'm sure."

"I thought you said we didn't need to worry about that..."

"I thought I didn't, but—"

"Well make your appointment, there are doctors in Lachute, Saint-Sauveur, Sainte-Agathe, everywhere. I'll go with you if you want, 'cause we need to know where we're going," Rick said.

And with that, he stood up, bunched his chestnut curls together and corralled them into a ponytail with an elastic band pulled from his pocket, stared for more than a minute at the flames slowly petering out in the stove, as if seeing them with new eyes, kissed Monique goodnight on the head, picked up his guitar and walked out.

Monique lifted me up to lie in the warmth left over from Richard's body. And there we sat. Watching the last wriggles and twitches of flame struggling to stay alive in the stove, watching the last of the logs fall apart as night closed in. By the time we went to bed, the cabin had grown cold. Again Monique hoisted me up onto the bed and swaddled me in a gray army blanket from one of the cots.

A few days later, Monique rose early and drove to her appointment with a doctor in Saint-Sauveur. By mid-afternoon, she'd returned. Stepping through the cabin door, she looked as she did after a singing lesson, flushed, red blotches on her face and neck, in a daze, standing there at the open door, almost like a prospective buyer, studying the logs, the floor, the furniture, the stove. Then she snapped to attention, went to the bedroom, changed into her 'cabin clothes' and brushed the tattered remains of my flaxen-haired coat. And she talked.

"Well that's it, Daisy, I'm pregnant," she blurted out, "and I haven't even told Harry about Rick, how stupid is that, and now I'm going to have his baby. I wish Marina were here, she'd know what to do, but she isn't, I'm *really* in charge of my own body now, isn't that the truth. I'm like the raccoons and foxes and trees out there, they're in charge of their own bodies too, and most of me is delighted about it, and so is Rick, I *think* he is, he said so, I *hope* so, even if he doesn't quite believe it's his, again this morning he said, are you sure it's mine, are you sure you want to keep it, of course it's yours, I told him, of course I want to keep it, it belongs to me, it's growing in my body. But Rick will be over tonight. After work, he said. And we'll talk everything over and make plans."

She rambled on, studying the four walls of the cabin again, the floor, the sleeping accommodations, the stove, "but how in the world will I ever tell Harry — and Kathleen, and Matthew, and Mark — they'll hate me for it, maybe they'll even hate the baby, how do other people do it, and why didn't I think of all this beforehand, why am I always so unprepared?"

We ate supper, and Monique threw fresh logs on the fire. But the guitar remained in its case, the songbooks atop the refrigerator. She simply sat at the kitchen table, arms resting on it, hands clasped together, and waited for Rick to come. It grew dark, and Rick did not come. Was he working late, she thought aloud, and called the service station. Was he at home, watching the New York Yankees? No, he was not. Perhaps he'd gone mountain biking in Saint-Jovite with his American buddy, Woodrow, who worked as a landscaper at the Gray Rocks resort and golf course. He'd been doing that lately. No, of course not. Not when he promised to come. Not now, when she was carrying his child. It grew late, the quiet and cool of outdoors seeping into the cabin. Still she sat there. No sound but the spitting and sputtering from the stove. Then in the dark and quiet, a dawning realization. Again, she lay her head down on her arms and wept. Not those helpless tears of old. No, overwhelming sobs, seismic in their proportions, a mix of rage and grief, rising from a newborn, more sensuous self, shattering the natural quiet of the cabin. And alternating with the sobs, uncontained outpourings of words addressed to me, seated on the frigid floorboards under the table.

"I knew it, I knew it, deep down I knew he wouldn't come...just from the way he was this morning...the blank look on his face... the pretend smile...still wondering if the baby was really his, he doesn't really want the baby, I could tell... but I just didn't face it, and now he's like a baby himself, sulking... hoping I'll have an abortion perhaps, who knows, and if I don't, what... I may not see him again...not ever..."

On that inconclusive, unresolved chord, the lamentations slowly subsided, and the unearthly quiet of earlier returned. Good, I thought, and moved from the frigid floorboards under the table to the oval rug. Nothing left to do now but watch the bloated tears drop silently onto the table, one by one, as if counting out the share of ecstasies given to her in equal abundance.

The waiting days that followed filled Monique with a vague sense of something like shame, she said. The shame then gave way to something more solid. And from that day forward, it was as if a new, unseen presence now occupied the cabin, an *éminence grise,* wielding power over the event of things. Monique walked with a different gait. Sat on the stoop in lengthy sessions of silent thought. Stared at the green retreat of trees. And in the evening, she played her guitar.

Rick finally did come, a little over a week later. The sun had just left the clearing, leaving an immoderately warm evening behind. He stepped out of the car and, innocent as a lamb, bent down to greet me in that cursory way of one who never left. He then opened the back door of the car and retrieved an immense bouquet of flowers in manifold shapes and colours, and strode smiling toward Monique standing at the cabin door. He reached out to hand her the flowers, but her hands were on her hips as she stood there stone-faced, blocking the entrance.

"Little pig, little pig, let me come in," he recited, feigning the meek and supplicant voice of the wolf in sheep's clothing. When Monique did not budge, he answered for her.

"Not by the hair of my chinny chin chin ..." he chanted in an almost English choirboy voice.

"Then I'll huff and I'll puff and I'll blow your house in," he continued, affecting a kind of mock threat.

I then beheld the hellish fury of a woman scorned unleashed before me.

"Go," she said, her two hands still planted on her two hips, "and take your flowers with you."

He paused, as if rummaging through the cast of characters in his mind, looking for someone more suitable, watching his sandals toy with the gravel beneath his feet. Then easy as you please, he flashed the peace sign.

"Peace," he said, reaching down and placing the bouquet at her feet, reverently, as on someone's grave. He then turned, sauntered back to his car and drove away.

"And don't come back," Monique hollered, stomping on the bouquet and trampling it to pieces.

Back in the cabin, she sat at the table again. And again she wept. Quiet weeping, barely audible, like that steady summer rainfall you get after the dust and heat. It all came to an end without my barely noticing it, and there she was, reaching for her songbooks atop the fridge, holding her guitar in her arms, tuning it, singing through her repertoire, ending with the most recent addition,

> *Hush little baby don't say a word*
> *Mama's gonna buy you a mockingbird*
> *And if that mockingbird don't sing*
> *Mama's gonna buy you a diamond ring*
> *And if that diamond ring is brass*
> *Mama's gonna buy you a looking glass*
> *And if that looking glass gets broke*
> *Mama's gonna buy you a billy goat*
> *And if that billy goat don't pull*
> *Mama's gonna buy you a cart and a bull*
> *And if that cart and bull turn over*
> *Mama's gonna buy you a doggie named Rover*
> *And if that dog named Rover don't bark*
> *Mama's gonna buy you a horse and cart*
> *And if that horse and cart fall down*
> *Well you'll still be the sweetest little baby in town*

She put the guitar away in its case and closed the lid on it and— on the long list of "*and if's*" already impossibly long—stoked the coals in the stove and added more wood. Again, we snuggled together on the sofa as the silence grew deeper, watching the flames, listening to them flap and swoosh against the updraft of air as they danced, swerved and leapt in seemingly wild abandon. Once they'd petered out and fallen exhausted into the embers, we crept into bed and slept.

I dreamt I had been swept up into the heavens in a fiery chariot and carried on wings of flame into a paradise populated by choirs of bulls, riderless horses, elephants and camels and lions, all of their primal energy and grace, beauty and strength, now fully returned to them after the long fall from brotherhood with humans, and sharing its green pastures with them, flocks of sheep and lambs, mystical white and fleecy, herd upon herd of cows, and in their midst, some of my own species, their coats glimmering gold, they too restored to their former naked beauty. How blissful was it to be among the blessed, I thought in dog-dreaming, when came the blood-curdling claps of thunder, tearing me away from the dream, a dream that spoke to me in that stentorian voice we attribute to prophets when preparing the way for what is to come, I daresay. For I know now, in dog-knowing, that I have entered the inner circle of death, even as Monique is being pressed more deeply into life by the throbbing fetus growing inside her.

July 1, 1978

For the time being, I am a full-time, if not permanent resident of Lost River. When Monique decided to make this her permanent home, at least until the baby comes, she decided to keep me here as well.

No more choir, she announced to me one day, at least not for now. No more courses at the university. And no more going home, for she hasn't told anyone she is pregnant yet. Again, she is waiting for the right occasion, and the right occasion has not presented itself. Richard may have flown the coop, vanished into thin air, she may have ordered him to "go and not come back," but a thousand-fold of him was left behind, is still gathered strangely inside of her, judging by her evenings of loud, uncontained grief, imploring him—the phantom man who made her flesh so willing—to please walk through the cabin door again. On other evenings, she sits in the straight-backed rocking chair, fondling her

growing belly and whispering intimacies and endearments to the baby —
and to him — as if *he* were a throbbing presence within as well. And she
flits like the leather-winged bat from one to the other.

As for the days, we spend them outdoors. Monique working in the
sprawling garden, planting fruit trees, me recumbent and untethered,
watching the never-ending *tableau vivant* of birds, bees, butterflies,
squirrels chipmunks, the armies of creepers and crawlers parading
before me. Chasing them is now beyond my power and feeble means.
Add to the frustration, the latest wrinkle — the inability to lick and smell
my own genitals. Mostly, I lie at the foot of an immense dying balsam fir,
its trunk riddled with holes bored by pileated woodpeckers. It too is
ready to topple over into the earth, were it not for the leafy arms of
neighboring evergreens holding it up, stoic as camels carrying their
burden.

Yet, life urges and pushes forward. As the poet said, "So much
depends upon the red wheel barrow," on the indulgence of trees and soil
and small wild flowers, on a ripening green tomato, all of them poised to
move us into a new and simpler intimacy. So much so that Monique put
the question to me one day, standing in the hot noonday sun, hands
planted firmly on her hips.

"What kind of a man would walk away from seeds he planted
himself, his very own flesh and blood?"

She then spun around, marched into the cabin and slammed the
door, leaving me stranded and untethered on the outside. That did it.
From that moment forward, the hours, the days, the evenings, the
agonies, seemed to magically transform into tiny little nuggets of
magnificent sense. And lately, the quiet little wisdom of waiting.

October 20, 1978

In autumn, Monique reaped what she had sown. The squash and
pumpkins, the cucumbers and tomatoes, the scarlet runner beans and

zucchini had grown in such profusion that she carted them off in the back of her pickup and sold them to a market in Saint-Sauveur.

Her belly had also grown to such a size that she began asking questions. Why was she being kicked in the ribs on both sides? All at once? Was she having twins? Like Yvonne and Irène? Shouldn't she ask her doctor? And what if it *were* twins, she needed to know. A full two weeks before her scheduled appointment, she drove to see her doctor in Saint-Sauveur. And indeed, an ultrasound the next day confirmed it. She was carrying twins, she announced to me when she came home in early afternoon.

We sat together on the stoop and, after an interim of stunned silence, she talked until the last streak of sun had stolen behind the stand of trees.

"Why is everything so different from what I expected, how did I get into this fix anyway, forty-two years old, having twins with no father when all I wanted to do was learn to stand on my own two feet, stand up to Harry, the know-all, the one with the pat answer for everything.

"So what did I do instead? Allow another know-it-all to take over, teach me how to play the guitar when I could have bought a book and learned to play chords on my own. But, there I was, a door hanging and swinging on hinges and he barged right in, Captain America from the Marvel Universe, and me falling for it hook, line and sinker, and what did he find? That exciting stranger inside of me Brunhilde talked about. He'd unbolted the door and entered places nobody else had ever been, and by some miracle I wasn't afraid.

"I loved his erection, and like you chasing the porcupine, Daisy, I didn't think of the consequences. You never know what's enough until you've had too much. The same with Rick, pouring himself into me evening after evening, all swallowed up in it, then riding into the sunset, the same Rick who wouldn't go to war because of the consequences, he would say.

"What is more unreasonable than building great glowing cities and creating beautiful people of all kinds to live in them, then blowing them all to hell, that's what Rick would say. And didn't I do the same? Desert my own flesh and blood? Kathleen and Matthew and Mark?

"That's what we do, create things, then walk away. My grandmother did it, my mother and Aunt Irène, they walked away from the farm. Aunt Irène walked away from Yvonne in Chicago, then from Curt in Chicago. So no. Enough walking away. I'm staying right here with these two babies.

"You didn't ask to be born, did you?" she said finally, looking down directly at them now moving around, holding her belly in her two hands like a globe of the world whose contours were constantly changing. And with that, we got up from the stoop, went into the cabin and ate supper.

The very next day, a truck came and hauled away the two cots in the second bedroom. The day following, Monique drove to Saint-Sauveur and returned with a sewing machine and bolts of material to make blankets and towels and diapers, she said. The following week, two cribs were delivered and all the paraphernalia to go with them— mattresses, rug, dresser and changing table. Would it all fit into that tiny bedroom? No. So she set the dresser and changing table on either side of the wood stove.

And she went to work, the sewing machine whirring on the kitchen table like one consumed by a mighty purpose, bolts of cloth and styrofoam and zippers and spools of thread piled on the table and floor around it, the whole cabin "looking like my mother's shop off the kitchen with all its hats and wigs and hair and felt."

First she made a plush cushion for the straight-backed rocking chair, then a throw for the sofa, and curtains and blankets and towels.

And the week before Thanksgiving, a steady procession of workers; two carpenters who built a small extension off the bathroom, a plumber who installed the piping to accommodate a washer and dryer, and a technician who installed the appliances.

Then Marina. Fresh from her Thanksgiving weekend with the choir at Lake McDonald and a three-day smorgasbord of singing. She stayed a week and slept on the sofa in the living room.

"You should have come to the choir weekend at least," she said to Monique, "we practised Antonin Dvořák's *Mass in D* for two choirs, one choir for each baby, they would have lapped it up like milk, after food and shelter, that's what babies *in utero* need - music - the best preparation for life, the best antidote to agitation and *in utero* claustrophobia."

"Was Edward there?" Monique asked, abruptly changing the subject.

"Oh Edward. Brunhilde helped him find his voice lost somewhere inside him, and he fell crazy in love—not with her, but with his own voice—now he thinks he's too good for the choir, he wants to be a baroque tenor, a soloist, ever since Brunhilde had him practise, *"Where e'er you walk, cool gales shall fan the glade"*. You know, that famous one, well, he thinks he was born to play Jupiter and sing that aria in Handel's opera."

"So you don't see him anymore?"

"No, he could never forgive Minerva for biting his thumb, I should train her better, he said. Even in the beginning, the cockatoos terrified him. In the end, I terrified him too, I might bite off the finger hanging between his two legs," she said, falling into fits of laughter. Then she too abruptly changed the subject.

"So what happened to Rick? You were so much in love a month ago," she asked, sober again, and aching to know.

"He disappeared," Monique said, after a pause, her grief surfacing anew, her eyes glassy with tears. She wiped them away with the back of her hand, then continued, anger now rising to meet the grief.

"He didn't—he wouldn't—completely believe he was the father. Are you sure, are you sure, he kept saying. He even offered to take me to an abortionist he knew in Saint-Sauveur. How come you know so much about abortionists, I said to him."

"Did you look for him after he disappeared, where he lived, at work?"

"When I was feeling so abandoned, yes. Desperate, yes. But then one day I sat on the stoop and something snapped. Snapped shut. Suddenly. Like it snapped open in the beginning."

"Why haven't you told Harry at least?"

"Oh I don't know, I felt so ashamed."

"But he's there waiting... how long can you keep him waiting..."

"The babies can't be Harry's, that's for sure. And I never told him about Rick, he may suspect something, I think he did, because he stopped calling me all of a sudden. Kathleen never calls anymore either. And neither does Matthew, there's no phone in the attic, he says."

"But shouldn't Harry know something, something about your plans, you've left them all hanging there by a string, Kathleen, Mathew, and Mark too..."

"No, I've been speaking to Mark out in Portage la Prairie, at the Air Force Base. He's passed all the tests and now he's learning how to fly. But I didn't tell him anything. Why distract him from what he's doing, why upset him?"

"So how will you manage up here alone, aren't you taking everything a bit too lightly?"

"I'm not alone, I have Daisy, and a whole alive neighborhood out there."

"But how will you manage when the babies come?"

"I'll manage. For once, I'll manage. And who knows what will happen next? *Something* will happen, who knows what that will be … nobody ever knows …"

"That's it, you're going overboard, giving birth is not something to do alone. I'll come, when you're ready to go. I'll come, I'll stay a few weeks, I'll sleep on the sofa, because don't you remember what it's like, the bull-strength it takes, the push, to get a baby through that cramped little passageway, and now two, you forget, and worse still, you'll be looking all around for the father, your heart will break over and over again when you see Rick staring at you through the babies' eyes. No, no, I'll come."

Marina helped Monique assemble the cribs, hang the curtains and arrange the new equipment in the new bathroom. Then she too left.

And here we stay in the gray of November, that old and satiated season. Even as the days grow shorter, my own days ever shorter, the babies grow longer.

November 10, 1978

My body seamed with scars is now wracked with the greatest grief. How suddenly do things change. There I was, my far-reaching desires put away, my love for my family burning like a sacred fire. There I was, preparing to leave this world and be instated into the beatitude of the next, a transition I had made so frequently in my dreams, when the bone-cracking news was delivered, grief then gathering around us like a tempest around a mountain.

As Monique so often says, who knows what will happen next? Just how light and superficial should one be when making plans? For there she was, making room for the growing bodies within her, touching them through the wall of her taut belly, listening through a stethoscope to the distant drumming of their hearts, talking to them as she talks to me, apologizing for their absent father, singing to them in the evening, the guitar askew on her belly, when the phone rang.

The uneasy tone told me it was Harry. And like clockwork, as she listened to Harry, a car pulled into the driveway, and Marina walked through the cabin door.

Monique threw down the receiver and sat bolt upright on the edge of the straight-backed rocking chair, splotches of red on her neck spreading to her face and arms, hands holding her large belly like a fragile parcel.

"So what happened?" she said, in a whisper almost, not even daring to look at Marina.

"Harry will tell you everything when you come," Marina said and wrapped a strapping arm around Monique's shoulder. "But he's still alive. It was not a flying accident, it was a car accident. Mark was on leave in Winnipeg when it happened."

"Was he driving?"

"No, his buddy was driving."

"Were they drunk?"

"I don't know. Harry will tell you the details. He's flying to Winnipeg as soon as possible to see him, to see the doctors, the people at the air force base."

When Monique continued to sit there in disbelief, at a loss as to what to do next, Marina took over. She gathered her necessities together and packed them into a weekend bag. And with the evening shrouded in dusk, and the wind whistling at the windows, we drove to Montréal in Marina's car.

We drove in silence, Monique staring at the road ahead, her body stiff, afraid to speak, afraid to look right or left, as if any move would make things worse, she said to Marina.

"You can sleep at my house if you want to," Marina said, as we pulled into our driveway. She then helped us out of the car and drove away.

Harry was sitting in the dim light of the small table lamp in the living room when we arrived. Kathleen and Mathew stiff on the sofa across from him. They all rose to greet us. Harry, chivalrous as ever, helped Monique out of her coat and hung it in the hall closet. And then the strangled look from all of them, staring in startled silence at Monique's bloated belly, enough to fill her with shame, she told me later. Shame for how she looked. Shame for not having told them sooner. Not knowing where to look or what to say, she stood where Harry had taken her coat, nailed to the floorboards, as tears of shame rolled down her cheeks, landing one by one on her protruding belly.

As for Kathleen and Mathew, they reached down and, each in turn, ran their fingers through the remains of my coat then promptly went upstairs, like theatre goers walking out on a performance, preferring not to know how it ends.

Once Monique had composed herself, entered the living room and sat down on the sofa, Harry sat down again himself.

"Don't be too shocked," she said finally, looking up at the recently repaired ceiling, then down at her protruding belly, "I'll explain all this later of course, just tell me everything about Mark."

Mark was in Saint-Boniface, Harry said. He was with a buddy, also training to fly; they were on a three-day leave, the buddy driving his father's car. They'd both been drinking and drove into a tree on a lonely two-lane road at two in the morning outside Saint Boniface. Who knows where they were going, Harry said. The buddy was killed on impact, and had another car not driven by and called the police, Mark would be dead too.

As it was, he had serious injuries to his head and lay unconscious in the intensive care unit at St. Boniface Hospital. And he was flying out there at midnight tonight. She could come too, if she wanted, he could arrange it, but given her condition, she might be best to stay put, he would bring Mark home anyway as soon as he was fit to fly.

Monique decided she would stay. Hold the fort. Not that Kathleen and Mathew needed her — or even wanted her around — and how could she blame them, she said. But I, Daisy, needed her. No one else could have me swallow the analgesics I was taking every four hours.

We slept in the den of course, now a refuge for dissenters, like the high hills for wild goats. Slept in a manner of speaking only, for Monique could not find a position that would appease all parties. She lay on her back and whispered to the babies. She lay on her side and beseeched the gods. She wept into the pillow. Sleep did come at last, and when we woke next morning, the house had been deserted, Harry flown to Winnipeg, Kathleen and Matthew gone to their classes.

Monique pulled on her housecoat and walked barefoot into the kitchen.

"Well look at this," she said, stopping dead in her tracks, astonished at the new burgundy vinyl counter tops, the new shelving unit in the pantry, "and look at this," she exclaimed aloud upon seeing the bowl of exotic fruit on the kitchen table, "pomegranates and kiwis and mangoes, and "look at this, will you," she went on, opening the cupboard doors, all the vinegars and oils, dried figs, dried cranberries, risotto rice.

"Perhaps I shouldn't feel so ashamed, perhaps there's another woman here, making meals at least, and look at this," she said, opening the refrigerator, peering into the shelves, "Kalamata olives, Manzanilla olives, anchovies, capers, hummus, mango chutney, We never ate those, I never bought those," and before she had a bite to eat, before she even thought to feed me, she searched through the upstairs, scoured the clothes cupboards, inspected the bathrooms, looking for further evidence of "another woman."

She was still searching when Marina arrived with a plate of muffins fresh out of the oven and wrapped in aluminum foil.

"No news yet?" Marina asked.

"No news yet," Monique echoed, taking two mugs from the cupboard and pouring coffee into them.

"Mmm, delicious coffee," Marina said, after a first sip.

"The coffee maker was all prepared for me this morning, I simply had to turn it on," Monique said, "and whoever makes the coffee grinds the beans."

"That's Harry," Marina was quick to add, "on the weekends the two of them, Harry and Kathleen, they shop and they cook and they make meals for the whole week. In the beginning, he would phone and say, "How do you make this, how do you make that?" But now, he's a *cordon bleu*, and Kathleen, she's the *sous-chef.*

"So there's no other woman — in the kitchen, I mean?"

"Just the woman side of Harry. Why do you care so much about no other woman anyway…?"

"I don't know, but I do," Monique was saying when the phone rang.

"Let me get it," said Marina, running to catch it on the first ring. She identified herself. "Yes, it's me, Harry — Marina — I'm here with Monique," and she handed the receiver to Monique now standing next to her.

"Are you at the hospital already?" she asked, so tentative, easing herself down onto the edge of the straight chair by the phone, one hand holding the receiver, the other holding her belly. Within seconds, she'd dropped the receiver and was gripping the seat with both hands.

"He died," she said, her voice numb and faint, "before Harry got there." And for a minute she sat there, staring wide-eyed into space, as at some phenomenon beyond the here and now, out of reach, the receiver swinging helplessly from its cord inches above the floor and slapping against the wall.

"Come,' Marina said, lifting her onto her feet, folding her arms around her and leading her into the living room, "come, sit down on the sofa."

And there they sat. On the sofa. Clinging to one another through the hours of morning and into the early afternoon, their mighty grief seeping into me. And mighty it was, coming at the expense of an intimacy dear to all of us, for I too had felt his body close to mine, smelled his sweat, soothed his desperation. I too could feel the pain, and it swept through every chamber of my heart, as the two mourned and keened like abandoned animals.

November 30, 1978

Harry flew home from Winnipeg on November 13 with Mark in the cargo. And again grief and anguish ran rampant through the house. For

Mark's dying was not the serene transformation I, for one, aspire to, was not the culmination of a proud and accomplished life, leaving behind a hundredfold of oneself as incitement to others. No. it was a crude and fiendish death, often fingering the young and foolish embarking on their first steps. And it left everyone paralyzed. And speechless.

"Did you see him?" Monique managed to ask Harry, the whole family converging on him in the living room upon his return.

"Yes, I saw him," he replied, head down, voice faltering. And before he could say more, he went to the kitchen, poured a shot of rye on the rocks, and returned, sinking into one end of the sofa.

"They said he died about an hour before I got there..." he continued, now threading his fingers through Kathleen's tangle of hair, for she had curled into the crook of his arm on the sofa, head back, eyes closed shut.

And for a long time they sat there saying nothing, as if satiated, if not frightened, by Harry's words and unwilling to hear more.

I, of course, was immediately drawn to the large black suitcase Harry had stationed just inside the front door, for the smell of Mark, indelible as a tattoo in my memory, came wafting through it.

"What's in that big black suitcase?" Kathleen asked finally, opening her eyes and noticing me, conspicuous by my presence beside it.

A moment's hesitation, and Harry spoke up again.

"They're Mark's things...clothes and personal effects...things he brought out west, and there's more to come..."

The suitcase and its contents seemed to come disturbingly alive, even threatening to Kathleen and Matthew, for the two promptly rose to their feet and crept past it up the stairs.

Monique, on the other hand, was instantly curious, wanted to look inside, see what was left of him, she said, and asked Harry to open it. Without a word, he carried it into the living room, laid it on its back beside the coffee table, unzipped it, lifted its top and eased it down onto the floor, oh so gingerly, almost reverently, as if it were something disturbingly alive. And there they lay. Mark's jeans, T-shirts, shoes, socks, sweaters, neatly folded and laid out in rows, his electric razor, Swiss army knife, wristwatch, the scent of his pheromones escaping from the suitcase like a genie from a bottle.

At the sheer sight of them, Monique lay her head back on the chair and covered her face with both hands, tears rolling like glass beads down the sides of her face and collecting in tiny puddles in her ears. Once she'd regained a measure of composure, Harry reached into the suitcase and pulled out a large brown envelope.

"These are letters," he said, pulling them out and examining them. "They're all from Chloé."

Who in the world is Chloé?" Monique asked, annoyed almost at not knowing.

"A girlfriend…I met her once or twice…she came to the house here…with Mark… in the few weeks or so before he left for the training camp."

Good heavens, I said to myself, Chloé…how could I forget, the one who'd looked beyond my blemishes, peered into my soul and seen the breadth and depth of me when I exposed myself to her in that shameless way of animals. Had she peered into Mark's soul too, I wondered, had he exposed himself shamelessly to her…

Had anyone thought to inform her about Mark, Monique asked. And had *he* written letters to *her*, and would these letters tell her something, at least, ease her longing to know more about him, lying alone, dying alone, in a hospital bed miles away from home.

"We'd better get in touch with her…tell her what happened… return the letters at least…" Harry said. He would do that soon. "Perhaps she *does* know things we don't know," he added, closing the lid on Mark's belongings.

"I thought he'd stopped drinking," Monique continued, that old familiar, forlorn hope creeping back into her voice.

"Yeah, he *did* stop drinking for a while…I spoke to the officer at the air force base, and he'd been impressed with Mark, he'd performed well in everything - physical fitness, teamwork, pilot training…"

"So what happened? He sounded so upbeat on the phone two weeks ago."

"Who knows? We may never know…"

And there they sat, the anguish of unknowing sinking ever deeper into their own private thoughts.

Again in the days that followed, I was barred from attending the funereal rites. And again, I was relegated to Marina's care among the cockatoos, now grown hateful, Minerva more hateful than Modesta, exhibiting symptoms of histrionic personality disorder, says Marina, exploding into fits of melodrama and rowdiness when she is not the centre of attention, a disorder prevalent among captive birds prized for their beauty apparently, which of course would never happen in her native jungle where beauty counts for nothing except perhaps for attracting a mate and is certainly not an end in itself the way it is here, Marina says.

Beauty is not an end in itself for me either, by the way. Give me rather, a feeling of inclusion—and at the risk of sounding presumptuous—inclusion as an equal, albeit different, member of the family. Mind you, in the two weeks since Mark's burial, I *have* felt included, indeed I have felt like the holy rivers of Babylon running through the holy ground of grieving, for each in turn, Harry, Monique, Mathew, Kathleen, came and sat by me, seeking my canine form of mute solace. And heavy as the burden of sorrow is, each has turned to his and her own way of making sense of it, all of their feelings gathered inside of them, like the tightly bound twigs the cockatoos pick at.

But again, life surges forward, does not slip backward. Harry returned to work. Kathleen and Mathew went back to school. And I was left to confer a modicum of serenity on Monique—and the babies now restless and kicking at her ribs. All week she sat there, like a partridge sitting on eggs. Good heavens, I thought, we're back to where we started.

On the Sunday before he returned to work, Harry drove to Chloé's apartment on Christoph-Colomb Avenue to return the letters. And to my immense delight, he took me with him. Immense delight until I saw the iron spiral staircase, rooting me to the spot. Harry picked me up in his arms, and we climbed in circles to the second floor.

Chloé greeted us cordially and invited us in. With her hair now longer and swept up into a loose mound on top of her head, and the scoop-necked topaz-coloured dress, she looked like the figurehead on the bow of Nordic clipper ships I'd seen on a book cover at Marina's—beautiful, aged and toughened by weather and rough seas.

Harry handed her the envelope containing the letters, reassuring her that he had not read them, she then thanking him for his *courtoisie* and *discrétion* and ushering us into the living room, which doubled as a work room for making jewellery. Making jewellery was a hobby of hers, not a living. To earn a living, she worked for a large travel agency downtown. She then offered her condolences and apologized for not attending the funeral rites.

But Harry clearly wanted to know more, for he settled himself on the sofa like someone keeping an appointment in a waiting room. Would he like a glass of wine, she asked finally, seeing him firmly installed with no intention to leave. Yes, he would. When she returned with two glasses on a small tray, Harry took a first sip and spoke up.

Did Mark write letters to her as well, he asked.

"No, he did not," Chloé said, "he phoned instead. Once a week. Sometimes twice." He said the telephone suited him better. The truth was, he said to her over breakfast one day, way back before he left for training camp, that he wouldn't write to her because he couldn't spell, never learned how to *spell* properly—because he never learned how to *read properly*.

"Well he never really worked at it, he never *liked* school." Harry interrupted.

"Was he really that bad at school? Chloé inquired.

"Bad enough, that's why I sent him to boarding school."

"He said he was a misfit at school … always …"

"At boarding school he did very well at public speaking, entered contests, won prizes and everything …"

"Yes, he told me about it, he showed me the medals he won."

"He didn't get that from *me*, I'm not much of a talker."

"Oh he was a talker, as we say in French, *il avait la langue bien pendue*," Chloé said, adding that on first meeting him, he made an instant impression. In fact, on being introduced to her by a friend, a chance meeting at lunch hour in *Carré Saint-Louis*, she thought he was a student of theology or philosophy because he sat beside her on a park bench – in the glaring heat of the noonday sun—and launched into the five proofs for the existence of God—no other man had ever talked to her about the existence of God. And certainly not in a first encounter in *Carré Saint-Louis*, which was not Hyde Park after all, she said.

"That was just bluster. A cover-up. He never liked books or studying, he quit college almost before he got started," Harry said.

"I know, I know, he told me all that," she continued, "he felt like a misfit at the college too, and he was desperately looking for a place where he *could* fit, if not on earth, maybe in the sky."

Some people are born too soon, he told her one day, some are born too late, and some are born at just the right time. He was born too late. He should have been born centuries before, in the centuries before books, when people learned from other people, before words became squiggles and lines and curlicues on a page, almost impossible to decipher—or spell—his mind always so disconnected from his body, he said.

"Is that why you pay so much attention to your body?" she'd asked him, "you know, working out, building your muscles, getting always stronger…"

"In his body, he felt like someone," Chloé added finally.

Did she know about his drinking, Harry wanted to know.

Yes she did. That is what scared her away in the end. When he drank, he was even *more* physical, a brawler, *un bagarreur*. And of course, always defending the weaker one, the persecuted one.

"You should stop drinking," she said to him one day.

"I can stop when I want," he said.

"You sound just like my father," she said, and she told him about her father who died alone in a cheap hotel room on Berri Street, just two years ago last August; he was fifty-two and already old from too much punishment.

But when Mark joined the Armed Forces, he *did* stop drinking, she said. Before he left for basic training camp, he had come and stayed with her for two weeks, and for those two weeks she had allowed herself the luxury of loving him as he was then, a man alive in his body, a man who loved to touch and taste and smell, pleasing her in all the little details other men passed over. (Because he'd been to basic training camp for would-be lovers, I longed to interject, had I had the words…)

"Why don't we meet in Ottawa?" Chloe had suggested. After basic training in Petawawa. She would fly to meet him when he was on leave.

"Great," he said, "we'll celebrate." But at the last minute, he told her not to come. And he gave no reason. But then he called her drunk from a bar where he was celebrating with his buddies. He called again from Portage la Prairie weeks later, so contrite, so full of apologies and excuses and promises. So like her father, the greatest promiser of all—he would take her and her brother to Belmont Park, to the *Carnaval de Québec* in Québec City, they would see the ice sculptures, they would go racing down the toboggan slide on the *Terrace Dufferin*, he would show them where he was born in Beauport, they would see *la Chute-Montmorency*, they would spend a week at the ocean in *Old Orchard Beach*, waves splashing over them — but he never kept any of his promises. Not even one.

Mark again begged her to come to Winnipeg on his first leave from Portage la Prairie, but again he cancelled a week or so before. He had to go visit his best buddy in Winnipeg who hadn't qualified, who'd been let go, and was bummed out about it. She didn't believe him this time. Her father had loved his buddies too. Oh sure, he loved his family, but he loved his buddies more and his liquor best of all. So the very next day, before she was truly swallowed up in the relationship, she wrote Mark her last letter, the Dear John one, and sent it special delivery.

"I don't know if he received that letter… but that was the end for me…in Mark, I was resurrecting my father, in a way, bringing him back to life in another man's body," Chloé said, "but now he is dead and I must let him be dead, and I must let Mark be dead too."

Then came the speechlessness that follows revelation, Chloe putting the words she had just spoken carefully away, as a bird tucks its songs inside its bill, leaving Harry to stare at the parquet beneath his feet and twirl the stem of the wine glass in his fingers, as if pondering Chloé's way of letting someone be dead He then lay the glass down on the tray, slapped his two hands down onto his thighs, his own form of wordless punctuation, and said, "okay, we're on our way up to Mount Royal now, Daisy and I, to the cemetery, to visit the grave… would you like to come?"

She seemed caught off-guard by the invitation. But then she said "yes", disappearing and reappearing in corduroy slacks, walking shoes, light-brown suede jacket and an excessively festive red and yellow scarf. And we were off to Côte-des-Neiges Cemetery.

When we reached the grave, the late afternoon sun also seemed excessively festive as it beamed down on the limp flowers lying on the freshly-turned black earth. We stood there, Chloé mute, her shoulder steeled against the gusts of wind, Harry mute and still as a statue, as if hoping to hear what he had not heard, see what he had overlooked, understand what he had misunderstood. When the sun fell away completely, I grew restless from the cold ground seeping into my vitals, a sign to Harry that we should go.

"It helped to see the grave, to see where he is, to make an end," she said to Harry when we dropped her off at her apartment. Before leaving us, she slid the van door open and spoke directly to me.

"You know, we had a dog named Cécile, tiny, all bones and skin, not beautiful like you, Daisy," she said, "but so loyal, so compassionate, and when my father came home drunk, nobody would talk to him, nobody would listen to him, my mother wouldn't sleep with him, he slept on a couch behind the kitchen stove, and Cécile, *she* would sleep with him, *she* would listen to him talk and talk and talk himself to sleep."

And with that, she said goodbye, slid the door closed and climbed the spiral staircase to her apartment.

When we reached home, Monique plied Harry with questions.

How well did Chloé know Mark?

Had she slept with him?

Did she know about his drinking?

Was she in love with him?

Did he write to her too?

Did she cry?

Harry answered her questions as best he could, even passing on the revelations about Chloé's father, his drunkenness and how he died.

"Sounds like she's older and wiser than her years," Monique said, finally.

"Also sounds like she trusts dogs more than humans, wouldn't you say, Daisy?" Harry said, looking down at me, then back at Monique.

"By the way, did you know that Mark had a problem with spelling — and reading?" he asked.

"Who said?"

"Chloé said. Mark told her all about it."

"Well he didn't tell *me* ... maybe I wasn't paying attention...or maybe he was ashamed of it and hiding it ... maybe he didn't *want* me to know, maybe I didn't *want* to know ..."

"Didn't *want* to know ...?"

"Didn't *want* to know, because I'd be ashamed of it too in a way ... think it was *my* fault ..."

"*Your* fault …?"

"Maybe that's why you sent him to boarding school … so you wouldn't have to be ashamed of it either … because you wouldn't see it, *I* wouldn't see it, it would remain a secret, even on weekends, he never brought his books home, or his homework … only his speeches, and they distracted us from everything else …"

In the silence that follows, Monique goes to the clothes cupboard, puts on her coat, wraps a scarf around her neck, leashes me, opens the door and takes me out into the semi-dark of early evening. And as we walk, she talks to me, the one and only receptacle for her secrets, I daresay.

"Adults, children, we all have our secrets stuffed away inside us … and once in a blue moon we open a door, sometimes just a crack … but it's touch and go—if the other's not standing right there on the threshold when the door opens, ready to receive it, we don't come in, and we certainly don't invite ourselves in, especially if we're ashamed to begin with, and, bingo, the secret goes back into hiding.

"You and Aunt Irène, you stood on the threshold for me … but me, no … I never stood there, I never stood still long enough, not for Mark, not for Mathew or Kathleen either," she rambled on to me as we walked up one street and down another, as in a game of snakes and ladders.

A few days later, Marina drove Monique back to the cabin, and I went along with them.

"Why leave so soon?" said Marina on the way, "is it the babies, the blind fury of creation happening inside you?"

"No, no," Monique said, she simply felt *persona non grata,* especially with Kathleen—and even with Matthew, who was still holed up in the attic.

"Hermits love their cells, the safety of them," Marina said, "I know from Desmond."

In any case, they'd gone back to school, Monique added, and they certainly did not need her in the kitchen with her boring meat and potatoes and brown gravy, when Harry was serving up artichoke ravioli and mango chicken and trout salad with fresh dill dressing.

"And what did they say about your big belly?" Marina went on.

"Oh, they paid no attention," Monique said. In fact, when she announced to Kathleen that she was having twins, she fired back with, "I thought you said babies were too much responsibility, isn't that what you said when you didn't let Daisy have pups, remember that?" and walked away. And when she told Matthew the twins would be born in January, he launched into a long lecture on the disposition of stars in the night sky in January, on constellations with binaries growing into red giants and others becoming red dwarfs, so scientific she could not keep up with him. Matthew liked facts. Scientific facts. To him the earth was hurtling through space at eight hundred miles an hour, the sun was standing still, the stars were made of hydrogen and helium, and the sky was a vast open ever-expanding space, when to her it's just the opposite, the earth is standing still, the sun journeys across the world every day, rising and setting every morning and evening, the stars are tiny lighthouses shining in the night sky keeping her from total darkness.

As she expected, they never asked about the father. Children don't want to know anything about their parents' sex life. Kathleen didn't even want to hear her mother sing, Monique said. They expect their parents to be rocks, not rolling stones. Big rocks. Too big to be moved.

But she did tell Harry about Rick, and again, she left out the humiliating details, like his disappearing-into-thin-air act. Harry never liked draft dodgers anyway, she said, he thought they should stay where they were and fight for what they believed in, instead of running away. What else could she tell Harry? ... that she was like a tree growing in the woods around the cabin, a tree growing at both ends, with sap now running through it, and branches growing this way and that way and the other way, a tree standing there no matter what, letting itself be ... he'd think her beyond foolish if she said all that ... no, what she did instead was apologize to him for leaving him hanging there not knowing. But some day soon, she promised him, she would sit down with him and talk about the future.

"Some day soon?" Marina repeated.

"Yes, some day soon."

"Will the day just fall like a flaming comet from the skies and knock you flat on your back?"

"Some day soon, these two babies will fall from my belly," said Monique, and no, they would not knock her flat on her back. For once, she'd be prepared, stand on her own two feet.

Two babies entering the world in the blinding cold of mid-winter were more than enough to contend with. Such was the prevailing wisdom. Until the blessed event transpires, I have been consigned to Harry's care, considering my own ailing condition, more suited to ignoble ease than strenuous activity. Still, the exigencies of living with Harry have been taxing enough, for he has taken to visiting Mark's grave every day, fair weather or foul. He comes home from work shortly after 2 p.m., loads me into the van, and we drive to the cemetery, walk to where the grave is and stand there, alone among the stone-faced memorials, in a form of mute ritual, Harry looking down at the frozen earth now carpeted in snow, studying it, as it were.

While the comparison pales, I sometimes feel like that Skye terrier in the 1800s who sat on his master's grave for fourteen solid years. Waiting, I suppose, as dogs do. Is Harry waiting too, I wonder, as my legs shake and tremble with cold among the tombstones. And for what? Some apocalyptic display in the sky? A resurrection? Or is he waiting for Mark to tell him something? To discharge his secrets from the grave, new untold revelations? Or is it Harry keening in that wordless way of his …

On Christmas Eve morning, against all rules of common sense, we drove through blistering wind and driving snow to the mountain and trudged up the hill to Mark's grave. Good heavens, I thought, was I an elephant in Hannibal's Carthaginian army climbing the Alps? Sensing my fatigue and flagging resolution half way up the hill, Harry led me back to wait in the van, swaddled in a blanket, while he put in his time at the grave.

On Christmas Day we went again. And again I waited in the van. But when he returned, we did not head home but wandered aimlessly through the maze of snow-swept streets behind St. Joseph's Oratory, up one deserted slope and down another, like Bedouins ploughing through a sandstorm. And like Bedouins, we did not celebrate Christmas in the usual Christian fashion. There was no tree. No outdoor lights. No gift-giving. Harry simply served a meal of green pea mint soup, beef rib roast with sweet potato and steamed broccoli. Kathleen, Mathew — and Ned, Harry's father — whom we picked up after our wanderings — joined Harry for dinner. Sadly for me, a slave to my appetites, there were no scraps, one of the downsides of living with a *gastronome*.

Food aside, it was a glum affair. Once they'd licked their platters clean, Kathleen and Mathew excused themselves and left to be "with friends". Leaving me, of course, alone with Harry. And Ned, who is grimness incarnate, smoking his pipe.

Once the table was cleared and the dishes stacked, we repaired to the living room, where the two spoke in platitudes, mostly about the weather and the perilous condition of the highways and byways. Then unexpectedly, like a stiff gust of wind from the north, Harry barged into the lull with a question. Sudden it was. And calculated, I suspect. And for Ned, like a wolf raid on a flock of sheep.

"Where did you put all the pictures of Mum, Mum and me, and all three of us, after she died, and that large album of snapshots, what happened to that?"

Ned's whole body, even the pinstripes in his suit, stiffened, and for one long and equally stiff moment, it seemed as if the question would harden like plaster to the ceiling. Ned finally removed his pipe from between his lips.

"That was fifty odd years ago … I put them in a box, in the attic … "

"Here in the attic …

"Yes, up there in the attic …"

"Why in the attic?"

"It was all over … so I put it all away."

"Put it away …"

"Yes, put it away."

And that is how the conversation ended. With three bereft words, straining and cracking and breaking under the burden, as a poet once put it.

The very next day, Boxing Day, Harry climbed the ladder into the attic, searched high and low until he found the box of photographs and the album, and carried them down and into the living room and, as gingerly as he had opened Mark's suitcase, opened the cardboard flaps on the box. And there they were. A silver-framed, black-and-white portrait of Ned and Ella on their wedding day, she in long white satin, he in a three-piece suit, standing at the open church door. And, lying underneath it, a framed colour photo of Ned and Ella standing in a field, the grass high and wild and green around them, Ned in an opened-necked, cream-coloured shirt with sleeves rolled up and a wide-rimmed straw hat pushed back from a seamless brow, and Ella, in a summer dress, her plump body pressed into his side, two arms holding him possessively, like something precious that might escape her hold, the two smiling as if helpless to do otherwise.

And in the album's black pages, black and white and colour snapshots capturing signal moments in all seasons—Harry in his white christening robes, Harry under the Christmas tree, Harry a toddler cupping a dahlia bloom in his small hand in the garden, Harry sitting on his mother's lap on the wrap-around verandah, Harry on a park bench at Beaver Lake sitting between his parents, Harry at five on the way to the library with his mother, Harry at six leaving for his first day of school, his mother holding his hand. Then nothing but blank black pages. Harry fanned through them, slowly, as if contemplating the void, then closed the album and laid it on the coffee table. From the array of framed photos and snapshots spread out on the living room floor, Harry selected four, setting two on the buffet in the dining room and hanging two on the blank wall in the kitchen.

Then true to ritual, we hopped into the car, drove to the cemetery and stood at Mark's grave. Perhaps if we stand there long enough—and every day—something will jump up, rear its head. For even in dog-grieving, nothing that is part of one, like my own mother, for instance, is ever truly lost, could ever truly cease to exist or disappear like pictures into an attic.

January 15, 1979

Last night's dream bears recording on these pages. For while it was picturesque, it was interrupted before reaching its natural end, an unfinished symphony, as it were.

Bernadette Griffin

In the dream, Mark and I are flying low in an airplane built for two, skimming the surfaces of buildings and mountains and oceans, Mark, the pilot, me, the co-pilot, irrational and, I daresay, presumptuous for a dog, but dreams being dreams, we fly and fly, round and round the earth, over all of its civilizations, advanced and less advanced, old and not-so-old, and still, Mark cannot find a suitable place on which to land, and why? Who knows, who knows the impenetrable mysteries in the realm of the human psyche, I say to myself, even as we are running out of fuel and, in desperation, are forced to make an emergency landing on a long narrow strip of cirrus cloud that looks deceptively like a runway with a washboard surface, but we are duped, clouds being deceptive, not what they look like, for the landing strip cannot hold us, and no sooner have we landed than we are plummeting to earth like a potted plant from the top of a spiral staircase, when through some miracle of fate or benevolent act of divine providence belonging only to dreams, we light on terra firma, oh so gingerly, like a sparrow lighting on a branch.

"Where are we?" Mark asks, looking around him, visibly stunned, as if waking from a dream within a dream, for we seem to have landed in a verdant virgin forest, forest that bears a striking resemblance to the woods around the cabin at Lost River, with birds singing, frogs gurgling, crickets chirping, Canada geese honking overhead, while in the background, the constant roar of a waterfall, a sound I know so well, inducing us to step further into the woods and standing there, almost disguised as trees, none other than Marina and Monique, the two singing, songs without words, but with an energy that could only come from the awakened body Brunhilde had insisted upon, and before them, sitting on a tree stump, the turntable from Marina's living room, so that even before we get our bearings, the entire forest is a cacophony of sound—a Babel of languages really—all sensuous, expressive and unique to each inhabitant.

"This is my eureka moment," I say to Mark in dog language, "who says you can't go home again," my entire body wagging like a national flag, immersed in the world from which I'd come, from which Mark had come too, I dared to think, when a larger-than-life-size officer of the law, uniformed in red with gold brocade trim, appearing out of a copse of bushes, handcuffs Mark, leashes me, and marches us to the edge of the forest, down a flight of concrete steps and into a Disneyland, or could it be Coney Island or Las Vegas, with flashing neon signs illuminating an immense plaza laid with mosaics, where loud, piped-in music is playing as brown and black bears skate on roller blades amidst a chorus line of elephants in pink tutus dancing on the tips of their toes.

"Keep moving," the officer orders when we stop and stare. He prods us past the rippling fringes of a fairground with a shooting gallery and rattling tin plates and, further on, an enormous round turquoise swimming pool filled with marine animals—dolphins and whales and porpoises—all performing their tricks and all wearing sunglasses with neon-lit frames, and just as we come to a corral wild with cowboys on bucking broncos and throngs of spectators egging them on, I am violently heaved back into the real world by the machinations of a backhoe down the street. I look around and Mark was nowhere to be seen, no officer of the law either, thanks be to the canine god, for there I was, all alone, listening to the infernal backhoe, the final dream scene arrested and lying unfinished in the brain cells where memories are stored. Ah, those machines, hell bent on destruction of any kind, dreams included.

February 16, 1979

Monique delivered the babies on January 18. And hours later, Marina delivered the news to all of us here in Montréal. The babies—a boy and a girl—had come into the bleak mid-winter of January kicking and screaming, Marina said, furious at being evicted from the womb and thrown into the snow and cold with no good explanation. As for Monique, she had pushed and pushed till her face turned purple, then wept and wept for joy—a joy mixed with loneliness, Marina said to Harry, of course she was present, but she was not the father, and what could be lonelier than giving birth without the father at least close by—an eye-opener to Harry, a shocker, for Monique had purposely spared him all the devilish details about Rick's ungraceful exit from the scene. As for the babies, they looked like cherubs dropped straight down from heaven with chubby red faces and dimples in their chins. The girl she named Darcy. (A variation on Daisy, I like to think.) And the boy she named Mark, because he looked like Mark when *he* was born, and what better way to remember Mark than to have another carry his name through a longer life.

Harry receives all of these revelations, even those about Rick, in his usual wordless manner, as if collecting them and storing them away in his mind, like a bee stores pollen in a hive, and he waits, perhaps for the bitter to somehow become sweet. And every winter afternoon, we drive to the cemetery, climb the hill, and stand at the grave.

february 28, 1979

After Monique brought the babies home to Lost River, Marina stayed for another two whole weeks, then shuttled back and forth every weekend, taking me with her, and leaving the shrieking cockatoos at home. And caged. She even locks the cages and confiscates the key, because Desmond, who is now retired, says they are bonkers, insane, and he is threatening to turn them loose on the world, winter or no winter, if she doesn't do something—donate them to the zoo or ship them back to where they came from and where they rightly belong.

Desmond's patience is a delicate veil, Marina says, and it is wearing thin. But, first things first. Now she is busy at the cabin—cooking the meals and doing the laundry, feeding and stoking the fire, taking me out for walks in the woods—a perfect excuse to wear her snowshoes made in Norway—while Monique breastfeeds the babies, changes their diapers, bathes them and rocks them to sleep in the straight-backed rocking chair. Once asleep, she lays them in Moses baskets, as Marina calls them, even if we are thousands of miles from the warmth of Egypt, from the reeds and bulrushes along the Nile.

Last Saturday, cold or no cold, Marina loaded the babies into their Moses baskets, carted them outdoors, and lay them on a makeshift wooden platform she'd cobbled together, "to breathe the brisk cold air of February into their cells and stretch their lungs." This was after Marina had loaded Monique into her pickup truck and sent her packing to Lachute and a few hours alone with her raging hormones, for come Friday, she was fighting off acute attacks of cabin fever. Unexpected yes. And puzzling. Just when she thought she had everything sorted out and in its place.

On weekend evenings, Marina and Monique sit and sing to the babies, everything from Brahms' *Lullaby*, which Marina sings in German, to Monique's *Hush Little Baby*, don't say a word, a lullaby with "a long list of promises, one as lame as the other," Marina said when she heard it, but the babies don't know, don't care, especially don't care about words. Once they are asleep, the two friends, almost like sisters now, sit on the sofa buried under a mound of blankets and talk, the fire burning brightly in the stove.

And what do they talk about? Everything. Like what is she doing up here, alone in the woods with two babies, Marina wants to know, what is she hoping? Is she hoping that Rick will suddenly appear, swoop in like Superman in his scarlet cape, see the babies, his own creations, beautiful as himself, and fall in love with them? Not on her life, Monique fires back, even if he glows in the dark, she will not let him cross the threshold, "not on the hair of my chinny-chin-chin," she adds mockingly, recalling the last time he'd come and begged like the wolf in the Three Little Pigs, always so ready to slip into another character when it suits. No, she's learned her lesson.

As for living here at the cabin, the babies were conceived in this cabin, their hearts began to beat here, Monique says, and the winds, the smell of earth and woods and wood-fire, the sound of rain and trees and creatures living close by, have passed through her into their bodies. And she wants that body way of knowing to pass into their bodies too, and like the birds and foxes and porcupines, have their own mind and be sure of who they are. And what else does she want?

To learn about herself. Just as Aunt Irène begged her to do—before the mad rush to get married. And learning about herself means going back to the beginning. Back to her mother's beginning, to Aunt Irène's beginning, in the wilds of Saint-Honoré, to her grandmother's beginning in Roberval, because she carries their personal history with her, their ancestry lying in a helpless heap inside her body.

Most of all, she wants to stand on her own two feet and say to all of them gathered inside her, "See, I've done it." I've stood there, like the trees, through wind, rain, snow, sleet, heat, cold, and not only do they stand there, but they keep growing at both ends—and producing foliage in the middle, like all those creeping, crawling, crouching creatures fending for themselves, and of course the birds, she said, forget what the bible says, because they too fend for themselves, she'd seen it with her own eyes, they *do* toil and spin and reap and sow, they *do* take care of themselves, and so could she. Because she'd never done it.

And what if she runs out of money? Marina asks.

If she runs out of money, she'll rent an apartment in Lachute and get a job. At least Darcy and Mark will have a mother. And they won't have to listen to a cock-and-bull story about their father dying and watching over them from heaven, like her mother and Aunt Irène were told. She'll tell them the whole truth about him and she won't sweeten it. And about herself, if they ask. And why not?

Just listening to Monique touches a raw nerve in me, arouses that vague longing to go back to the beginning, to where I came from, so picturesque in my dreams. Here in the wilds around the cabin, I too have watched my fellow creatures toil and spin and reap and sow, and what more respectable pathway to salvation is there, I think. Small wonder I stooped to folly and chased a porcupine. For what is required of me now as a family pet? Not productiveness. Not procreation. Not acts of heroism. Nothing but to stand on my four legs, look beautiful and discharge my bodily wastes out of doors. Face it, I say to myself. This is a modern world, with machines to toil and spin and reap and sow.

Then again, without sounding vainglorious and high-flown, traits I despised in Ebony the cat, there have been moments in my dog's life when my physical presence, with all the beauty and mystery and nakedness it contains, seemed to keep members of my human family from dying, mostly of deprivation or unquenchable longing. Longing for what, you might ask. For the trees and streams and wilderness from which *they* came, origins sometimes seen as too lowly for self-regarding humans, who fancy themselves God's masterpiece, a ready-made work of art drop-lifted down from heaven onto the place beneath. Good heavens!

March 20, 1979

I have been handed over to Marina's care for a week while Harry travels to Portage la Prairie in Manitoba. His daily visits to Mark's grave are not enough. He wants to speak to Mark's superiors at the training camp, go to Winnipeg, drop in on Frank and Myrna Cunningham, the parents of Mark's buddy, killed outright in the accident.

Marina's house, once a bedlam, is now more like the sea of tranquility on the moon, for Kirsten has moved to Barcelona to learn Spanish and continue her studies in flamenco guitar playing, and the obnoxious cockatoos, Modesta and Minerva, have gone to the Granby Zoo, a donation, Marina called it, and while she pines for their presence, I dote on their very absence, for I had lost my ability to tolerate them, much less calm them.

It all came to pass when Desmond retired from his job as travelling salesman for Caterpillar Tractor, an unnerving event, not for Desmond, but for Modesta and Minerva, who became more unmanageable than ever. Demented is more like it. It was as if Desmond had come home and brought a Caterpillar Tractor with him. And they could not tolerate Desmond being downstairs when he should be upstairs in his den, tying flies or preparing to go fishing.

"Decide," Desmond finally said to Marina, on the brink of dementia himself. He wasn't going from the zoo "out there", he said, wagging his arm at the front door, to the zoo "in here," so make up your mind, "either they go," he announced, "or I become an unmanageable wild animal and you donate *me* to the Granby Zoo."

Marina, who since coming to Canada, sees things from two different places, understood Desmond. Retirement can shorten one's life. Madness can shorten one's life. But the two together could kill Desmond in one fell swoop, she said. So the deed was done. The cockatoos, cages and assorted accoutrements were stoically assembled and driven to the Granby Zoo.

For me as witness, the whole operation was a cruel reminder of Jean-Marc, my first owner, forced to choose Clarke and get rid of me. But the Granby Zoo was just a stone's throw away, Marina said, and once Modesta and Minerva had adjusted to life in a real zoo, she would go and visit them, because they were not merchandise, not things you return to the store or give to charity when they don't fit or don't suit.

March 29, 1979

When Harry returned from Winnipeg late last evening, he immediately came to take me home. Kathleen had just returned herself, fresh from March break at a *plein air* resort in the Eastern Townships with her classmates and again, teeming with questions. Questions about Harry's trip to Portage la Prairie and Winnipeg. Had he spoken to the officers in command at the training camp? What did they say? Did he go to the road where the accident happened? Did he go to Winnipeg? Talk to the parents of Mark's buddy?

Harry poured himself a rye on the rocks, sank wearily into the sofa, and talked and talked. The officer in command at the training camp had little to say. Mark had done exceptionally well in basic training. He'd also performed well in occupational training in Portage la Prairie. His buddy who was killed in the accident had done exceptionally well in basic training. But he'd been let go from the occupational training in Portage la Prairie. When Harry asked why, the officer was not at liberty to say. But everyone said, everyone knew, he was Mark's best buddy. They hung out together. A week after his buddy was discharged, Mark was granted a three-day leave for high performance. That's when the accident occurred. During that leave. He took the bus to Winnipeg, but he never made it back to Portage la Prairie.

Harry then drove to Winnipeg, where he'd arranged to meet with Frank and Myrna Cunningham, Mark's buddy's parents. They lived in a small bungalow in Saint Boniface, friendly people, but still broken up over "Alex", their only son. They'd had a daughter as well, a second child, but she too had died young, of meningitis when she was five. In their living room, Harry said, Myrna had set up a sort of shrine to Alex, a square table and over it a white lace tablecloth, and on the tablecloth a large framed coloured graduation photo of Alex from Red River College.

"What did he look like?" Kathleen asked.

"Well, he had white crooked teeth, a smile as wide as the Red River, which ran close by their house, freckles, short light brown hair in tight curls, like yours, and blue, blue eyes. Not what you'd call good looking," Harry said, "but an open face, a fearless look in it."

And on either side of the photo, Harry went on, vigil lights burning, and fresh flowers from the flower shop every week, his mother said. And in the foreground, two plastic models of fighter planes mounted on stands, models Alex had built as a young boy.

"He should never have joined the armed forces," his father said, "never even tried, but he loved airplanes and was bound and determined to fly one." Oh, he knew how the army felt about homosexuals, but they didn't have to know about it, it was none of their business, Alex said, people lied about all kinds of things to join the army, to go to war. So he joined. And he hid the fact. He loved being in the Forces. Loved being physically fit, loved the drills and the discipline and the orderliness, most of all the camaraderie, because he never had a brother. Then out of nowhere, one of the young men sharing living quarters with him asked him if he was homosexual, then two others refused to shower or sleep in the same room with him. And when Alex was called up on the carpet, he no longer denied it, he no longer wanted to deny it. He'd done so well in training that it wouldn't matter to those in command, they would look the other way. But a few days later, he was let go.

Alex had just been home a week when Mark showed up at his front door. On a three-day leave he'd hopped on a bus to Winnipeg, hoping to see Alex. Mark wasn't gay, Alex said. No, they were simply buddies who'd become the best of friends. Alex borrowed his father's car that evening, and the two drove downtown. "To let off steam," Alex said. But from what the bar owner told Frank Cunningham later, Mark got drinking at the bar and decked a guy a few stools away who was complaining to the bartender about the place being "full of faggots." Alex managed to muscle Mark out before the bar owner called the police, loaded him into the car, and the two sped off in the slapping wind and pelting rain, out beyond the outskirts, along a flat and deserted country road and into a tree. They weren't going anywhere in particular Frank Cunningham thought, Alex often took the car and went for long drives to nowhere special, especially when he was in a stew about something.

"I guess Alex didn't know about Mark and his drinking," Kathleen said.

"I guess not, if he took him to a bar," Harry replied. "But Mark never admitted he had a drinking problem, perhaps not even to himself ..."

"Maybe he was too ashamed ..."

"Maybe."

"But look at his buddy, he wasn't ashamed ... to be gay, I mean ..."

"Yeah ..."

"Maybe that's what Mark liked about him ... he wasn't ashamed."

"Yeah,"

"So his parents knew he was gay?"

"Yeah, they knew ..."

"And they were all right with it ... that's cool ..."

"Yeah, they seemed fine with it ..."

"... And Mark took the bus all the way to Winnipeg ..."

But Harry's glass was empty, his supply of words exhausted, and Kathleen knew it. She wrapped her arms ringed with bracelets around him (she's confiscated all of Aunt Irène's jewellery), pressed her head into his shoulder, and there they sat, breathing in the quiet after the avalanche of information. Even after Kathleen went to bed, Harry sat there, hunched forward now, elbows and forearms on his thighs, fingering his empty glass, turning it round and round.

The next day, Kathleen drove with us to the cemetery. As the three of us climbed the slope to Mark's grave, me composing the rearguard, we passed a sad procession of brand new mourners, the early April sunlight streaming down upon them like a consolation as they tramped through the snow. Again at Mark's grave, Kathleen wound her arms around her father's body as he stood there mute as always, head bowed, staring at the mound of snow caught between melting and freezing.

"Shouldn't we put a tombstone there to mark the place where he's buried?" Kathleen said to Harry as we drove back home in the van.

"Yes we should... when the ground thaws ..."

"Why do you go there every single day?"

"Because he seems more reachable there somehow ..."

"Reachable?"

"Yeah, reachable. I don't want him to just disappear."

"Disappear?"

"Yeah, disappear into the ground or into heaven or into the attic, the way my mother did ... first lying in a pile of earth, then nowhere ... gone ..."

"But they died."

"Yeah, they died, but they didn't have to evaporate into thin air."

"Do you talk to him?"

"Sometimes."

"What do you say?"

"I say things ..."

"What things?"

"Things I could've said before and didn't."

"And does he talk to you?"

"No, not so far ..."

"But he was such a talker ..."

When we reached home, Kathleen raced upstairs and, with the abandon of a light brigade charging headlong through a field of artillery, sent the Beatles blasting through the house:

"It's been a hard day's night
And I've been working like a dog ..."

... working like a dog, good heavens, not *this* dog. Such a lame comparison when I haven't done an honest day's work in my entire life—to earn my daily bread, that is, but the Beatles come from the British Isles and probably meant the border collies that herd sheep for a living in the highlands of Scotland. And while we're on the subject of dogs who work for a living, allow me to make a correction to scripture, it's not the shepherd who layeth down his life for his sheep, it's the sheepdog.

April 25, 1979

Again, I've spent three days confined to the infirmary at the animal hospital. More abscesses in my chest, requiring more perforations and incisions and drainage, more sheering of my coat, more agony and suffering. And much as the veterinarian means well, that piped-in music with no beginning and no end, just an interminable middle, more suited to a massage parlour, strikes the wrong note. It certainly did nothing for the hyperbolic dog one cage over, who retched and heaved and moaned interminably as well, all of which brought me back to my incarceration at the SPCA and the miseries attending it. Yet I felt the most fortunate of patients. Why? Because I had visitors. Get well cards are fine and dandy, but visits are far better. After visiting Mark's grave, Harry came to visit me, a further inducement to recovery, for I am not yet prepared to be wrested from this world and hurled into the next like a stone from a catapult, before my own house is set in order. And Harry knows it. I can tell. Upon my release on Friday last, he toted me through torrents of rain and wind, my body again swaddled in his rain coat, laid me on the back seat of the van and, moving gingerly through all the stops and starts and jolts of rush-hour, delivered me home. And a deliverance it was, for there was Kathleen, the earthbound angel welcoming me with hot water bottles, one for my hindquarters, one for my forequarters, waiting for me on a plush new bed—just when I thought I had forsaken the vanities of this world. But I saw no pigeons, you know, like the ones in my dream, who sing and pray and carry the soul away, thanks be to the canine god, if there is one. No, I am still breathing regularly. I can hear my heart steadily pounding like a great convulsive drum, as that hyperbolic poet said. For how can I die when the world still weeps for another? Another as divine as myself. No, I cannot go for good and forever. Not right yet at least.

Again, Harry hovers over me like the pigeons in my dreams, administering the antibiotics, swabbing my operative wound with disinfectant, serving me beef consommé in lieu of tap water and chopped liver instead of Dr. Ballard's in cans, all remedies to beef up my hemoglobin count after losing so much precious blood. And of course he lifts me up and down the back steps into the yard, even watching me as I relieve myself, examining the look and scent of my exudations.

But for all of the solicitude, the consommé, the hot water bottles, the plush bed, that vague longing for Monique sits like a hard lump in the pit of my stomach, gnaws at my marrowbones. Pining for her presence, I watch and wait for her to turn the handle and step through the open door as she once did. Ah me … if life's little wisdom is to wait, should it not mention how long…

June 19, 1979

To my veterinarian's disbelief, I have made an astonishing, if not lasting, recovery. Death did not stop for me, at least not as predicted. Beware of false prophets, they say. I am now up and hobbling around the downstairs as Aunt Irène once did. An unholy sight, I daresay, with my hairless chest, purple and knobby as a cluster of Concord grapes, all from the gentian violet bactericidal applications, not to mention the diabolical Elizabethan collar I wear — uneasy lies the head that wears the crown, you might say — well try the Elizabethan collar.

During this latest convalescence, Harry took a week of his vacation time to minister to me. To fill in the gaps between ministrations, he purchased wood and assorted other posts and knobs and tools and built a stairway to the attic, all to replace the metal ladder flush against the wall. A stairway to the stars and Shangri La, Kathleen calls it. In his off-school hours Matthew pitched in and, once it was built, he bought a brand new futon to sleep on, hauled it up the new staircase, then spent three days furnishing his "pad." And predictably, when he'd finished, he invited Harry up to view the attic now transformed — and to see the night sky sometime in mid-June, Matthew insisted, before he leaves to go tree planting for the whole of July and August in the forests of British Columbia. And on a cloudless night, mild-mannered and moonlit, shortly before Matthew left, Harry carried me up the new flight of stairs to Matthew's attic. And there, through his "catadioptric telescope with a 3.5 inch aperture," a "find" in a garage sale, almost a giveaway, Harry viewed the night sky in June. Not as he'd seen it countless times from a pilot's cockpit. But as never before.

For two whole hours it was Matthew, the budding scientist, the voice of reason, holding his father's attention. Instructing him. Lecturing him. Leading him through the heavens, like a tour guide with an encyclopedic knowledge of the destination.

"There on the western horizon is the evening star Venus," he began, "covered in clouds of sulfuric acid reflecting seventy per cent of the sunlight hitting the horizon. And to the upper left of Venus, Mars, bright as many stars, and to the southeast, the Leo the Lion constellation, part of the Virgo Galaxy Cluster, the richest gathering of galaxies in the local supercluster containing some 3,000 galaxies, centered on the giant M87 galaxy, which has a total mass of nearly eight hundred billion suns, making it one of the most massive known to man," Matthew said. "And located about five degrees north of the planet Mars, the asteroid Vesta, a chunk of rock three hundred and twenty miles in diameter, whose lighter surface soil reflects light some six times better than the moon's much darker surface — a whopping thirty-eight per cent of the sunlight striking it."

And on and on he went, urging Harry to look for this and watch for that and, last but not least, to scan the vast open field of quasars and twinkling pulsars in search of meteor showers, "tiny specks of space dust," he said, "that burn up during their fatal encounter with the Earth's upper atmosphere," his running commentary crammed with numbers and scientific data and astronomical facts, all directed at the audience of one peering through the aperture of the telescope.

As an encore, Matthew expounded on the "mystery of miraculous coincidences," where each new creation becomes a creator in its own right and sows the seeds of the next creation all the way up the ladder of complexity, a theory encouraging to me or anyone else on her last legs and never permitted the pleasures of procreation. Good heavens! Imagine. Sowing the seeds of the next creation without even knowing it. Cold comfort, but comfort nonetheless.

On this note of comfort, the lesson in astronomy came to an end, and Harry carried me down the staircase. What a disappointment, I thought to myself as we descended, listening to Matthew. How disconcerting to be told that all those multitudes of stars and galaxies and superclusters, so cool and distant and serene, so numinous and mysterious, are nothing but raging fiery furnaces. How heartbreaking to be told that Vesta with her big radiant heart is nothing but a chunk of rock. That the moon, a lustrous abiding presence in the sky since time immemorial, is not even green cheese, but more rock and more soil where nothing grows and nothing shines, nothing a cow would ever want to jump over, much less walk on. Ah, those telescopes. Another human invention. Don't believe what you see with the naked eye, they seem to say.

June 28, 1979

Today, with Harry having flown to Toronto for a business meeting, and Matthew gone to plant trees in British Columbia and Kathleen working the long shift as a counsellor at the YMCA day camp, I was shipped off to Marina's. In fact, I spent the better part of the day with Desmond, as Marina had gone to the Granby Zoo and a first visit with Modesta and Minerva. Desmond refused to go with her. For the same reason he didn't visit prisoners in Bordeaux jail, or cattle in the stockyards down by the port, or dog shows at the convention centre, he said. Besides he is busy. Busier than ever since his retirement from Caterpillar Tractor, for he's polishing the first draft of his book, applying the "second coat," he says.

"What book?" Marina had said, flabbergasted when he first mentioned it, "a book about tractors, fly fishing, tying flies?"

No, no, a book about horses, he told Marina. Horses in the wars. Horses in World War I, World War II, the Boer War, the American Civil War. It's a book he's been writing for years. In the den. When everyone thought he was tying flies for his fishing trips, he was writing his book about war horses. Yes, for sure, he did tie flies to go fishing, he told Marina, tying flies, fishing, standing knee-deep in water, waiting for the fish to bite, also gave him time and space to think about the horses.

And today, with the new typewriter he just bought sitting on the kitchen table, Desmond was creating a typewritten draft from his handwritten manuscript. During pauses, he talked to me, as if I were Marina or knew all about war.

"Dogs too, they know all about war," he insisted. They got roped into them too. Like the horses. Well-bred horses. Millions of them. In cavalries on the front lines, pulling ammunition trains, soup kitchens, bread ovens, soldiers' supplies, medical supplies, hauling them through two feet of mud and slime and slush and snow and ice. All the way from Germany to Russia even. He saw them after the war with his own eyes. Teams of two and three, long dead in fields of mud, shot and left alone to die.

"You couldn't forget them," he said.

He'd never really forgotten Beauty either, the horse on the farm in South Durham in the Eastern Townships, the horse his father taught him to ride. Oh how he loved that horse, how he loved riding her, through the fields and trails through the woods. But then she broke her leg. And he blamed himself, for getting her to jump fences, on his own, without knowing how it should be done, too much of a smart alec, too stupid to know better, and with her front leg broken, his father took her up into the woods and shot her.

"Don't come," his father commanded him, leading her into the woods. But Desmond *did* come, crept into the woods at the other end of the field, and from a hiding place flat on his belly behind a thick row of evergreens, watched. He was fourteen. And something snapped in him that day, he said. The flimsy string that held everything together inside of him snapped open, and everything fell out—the father, the boy, the world he thought he knew. Even the sun never shone quite as bright after that.

Sometimes he thinks that's why he ties flies, he's putting everything back together, tying them into something beautiful—at least to the fish.

I listened, paws outstretched in his direction. Good heavens, I thought to myself when he'd finished, how could everything depend on a flimsy bit of string.

Desmond had just returned to his typewriter, I had just begun brooding over the indignities of dying, when Marina walked in. She was back from the Granby Zoo and sorry she went, another big mistake, for Modesta and Minerva knew her immediately, she said, and made a scene, so embarrassing she pretended not to know them, but the other visitors, they loved it, of course they loved it, because they love foaming at the mouth and freak shows and mad bulls and red blood and will walk a hundred miles to see it. So no, she will not go back. Minerva and Modesta do not need visitors. None of the animals needs visitors.

July 4, 1979

If my state of health allowed, I was to spend the summer months in Lost River with Monique and the babies. That was the plan. And on Friday of Canada Day weekend, Marina took me there, me so overjoyed to see Monique that I lost control of my bladder, another new compounding problem, not to put too fine a point on it, and emptied its contents on the front stoop, right between the two pots of flaming red geraniums. The way the stream of urine came slapping down, splattering onto both pots, it could have come from an elephant. Good heavens, I thought to myself, what a shameful way to begin an extended visit to someone's home. But Monique didn't fuss. She mopped the urine up and mercifully disposed of the subject in short order, deflecting attention to the babies, Mark and Darcy, now six months old.

Once we'd settled in, Marina and Monique brought the babies out into the sun and sat them on a blanket in the "garden of earthly delights" as Marina calls the clearing and surroundings. And while Monique weeded and hoed the vegetable garden, trained the vines of tomato and scarlet runner bean on their trellises, corded the newly-delivered pile of wood into the lean-to, Marina entertained the babies.

One small mercy. I was not tied to the stake like the early Christian martyrs. For there's no need. I have lost my ability to run, much less give chase. Free rein is now an invitation, of sorts, to savour what cautious pleasures my disabled body allows, like the scent of green leaves and damp tree bark and excreta of animals. My inner promptings, however, are not disabled. In this patch of wild, my beastly side and the vigour attending it look for any excuse to spring to the surface and win back all that dignity staring me in the face from the woods around. For life is a medley of extemporanea, as someone said, even in this patch of wild, one never knows what will greet the day. Indeed, no sooner had Marina left to go back to the city than we had a visitor, unexpected and unannounced. He came in the early quiet and gray of dusk. In fact, he walked through the cabin door as if he'd been here yesterday. Richard, that is. The preceptor of the universe, with that same easy smile, same faded jeans and T-shirt, same gold locks corralled into a ponytail, same star-spangled head-band and symbol of peace tattooed on his arm.

Monique stopped drying the dishes and stood stock still, as if frozen to the spot at the sight of him smiling so benignly.

"Don't be so shocked," he said, his two arms raised in the hands-up position, "I said I'd be back. Didn't I say that? Well here I am and dying to see you, even if it took a while …"

And there he was, straddling a kitchen chair, resting his arms on its back, Don Quixote back from his travels, recounting his adventures with his sidekick—first back home to the US, and when that was worse than his worst nightmare—back up to Canada, to Montréal, Ottawa, Toronto, he and his buddy Woodrow, the one who worked at the Gray Rocks resort golf course, the two trying to go from immigrant to Canadian citizen … and all the endless rigmarole and red tape involved …

"And it's still not a done deal, in fact, it's going to take longer, a whole lot longer," he said. But he wanted to get back here and patch things up, see her at least — and the baby of course.

"Where *is* the baby?" he said, his eyes scouting all around the cabin, then lighting on the Moses baskets sitting empty by the stove.

"It's the *babies*," Monique said, in a matter-of-fact monotone.

"Oh … more than one?"

"Yes, two."

"One, two, three, four, who cares, I'm here to see them."

"They're in bed for the night."

"Where?"

"In the nursery back there."

"Can I grab a quick look?"

A long pause, then,

"Yes, I suppose you can." Monique said, and led him to the bedroom where Mark and Darcy lay sleeping.

He looked down at them, first one, then the other, but for one who is glibness incarnate, words always falling off the tip of his tongue, he seemed tongue-tied and said nothing.

Back in the living room, he still said nothing, in fact, he looked decidedly uneasy, shifting his weight from one foot to the other, eyes flitting here and flitting there, from the pile of diapers, to the Moses baskets, to the assorted toys strewn around the living space, as if trying to absorb the change of scenery now redesigned and reimagined for babies.

"I guess I should have come earlier… before bedtime … maybe tomorrow?" he asked, not bothering to sit down.

"They're asleep by eight,"

"At seven then."

"Fine, seven."

And dependable as the trains, there he was at the stroke of seven the next evening, on the floor with Mark and Darcy, sitting in the yoga position in front of them, talking to them, reciting *Itsy Bitsy Spider*, his fingers marching up and down their fat little bellies, playing Pat-a-Cake with their fat little hands, This Little Piggy Went to Market with their ticklish little toes. And so it was, one evening following another, all week long, Richard wooing the babies, breaking into their angel hearts and winning them over.

"I guess an hour-a-day father is better than no father at all," Monique mused, after he'd come and gone all week.

On Saturday, to Monique's astonishment, Richard came early, had dinner with her, fetched his guitar from the car and sang to Mark and Darcy before they were carted off to bed: *Jimmy Crack Corn, Foggy, Foggy Dew,* and *That's my Heartstrings:*

> *"Who comes running through the house*
> *With muddy, muddy shoes*
> *Who can say I need a dime*
> *And know you can't refuse*
> *Who can tear the house apart*
> *Just going up the stairs*
> *Who looks like an angel*
> *When he kneels to say his prayers*
> *That's my heartstrings*
> *That's my boy*
> *That's my heartstrings,*
> *That's my girl."*

Once the babies had been settled for the night, Monique was moved to fetch her own guitar from its case, as if to show off what she'd accomplished, the various chord progressions in various keys, the many strums and rhythmic variations she'd almost mastered, and in no time the two were singing and playing as if the end were the beginning—songs they'd once worked on together, Monique even performing the latest additions to her repertoire: *Four Strong Winds,* and the most recent of all,

> *"Come all ye fair and tender ladies*
> *Take warning how you court your men*
> *They're like the stars on a summer's*
> *morning*
> *First they appear and then they're*
> *gone"*

But if Richard had come to repeat history, play the errant knight returned from his adventures, or better still, the Superman who swoops down between the songs and cavalierly removes the guitar cradled in her arms, only to fall to his knees between her out-stretched legs, he had grossly miscalculated, for when he *did* try to lift it from her hands, she grew fierce as ten furies rolled into one.

"Don't touch my guitar," she fired, jumping up from her chair, putting the guitar back in its case and slamming the lid shut.

Ten furies were not enough, for there was Richard, disbelieving, forcibly pulling her body into his, pressing his lips to hers, pushing her toward the sofa, muttering as he went, how can you say *no* to me, when I taught you everything you know about the guitar, everything you know about sex, and just as they reached the sofa, there I was, the black dog of Satan, beastly and vicious, leaping into the fray, clamping my teeth down on the calf of Richard's leg. And to further weaken his purpose, there was Monique, standing over him, impudent and arrogant as a valkyrie from the great hall of Valhalla, brandishing his guitar like a club over her head and threatening to dash it to pieces on his.

After a raucous struggle to pry himself loose and a long litany of obscenities, obscenities you would not expect to hear from a conscientious objector, Monique called me off. Once I had released him, she thrust the guitar into his hands, and he was on his way, a wounded soldier limping from the battlefield.

Victory or defeat, heroic exploits do exact their toll. In the heat of battle, I'd been swung through the air like a medieval flail, slapped to the floor, kicked with Richard's free foot, anything to pry himself loose from the almighty grip I had on his leg. Indeed, every kick, slap, swing had shortened my life a little, and any more of these gyrations would surely have spelt the death of me. All well and good considering my infirmities. In any case, heroism in two's or three's or more inevitably gets to be a bore. But what if the foe were to return? What then?

Once the battle was over, once Richard had gone, Monique would sit and stare into my soul, as it were, extol my wonders. She also sponged me down with a solution of warm water and Epsom salts, Harry's remedy for everything. But I had no urge to gloat. Immediately, I felt ten years older. The beast within not dead, but spent.

Overspent—and not "myself", as Monique put it, the morning after. And to rule out further injury from the revolutions and convolutions imposed upon me in the heat of battle, I would have to see a veterinarian.

Again, Monique was on the phone to Marina. And before the noonday sun had reached the clearing, Marina was back in the cabin, sitting at the kitchen table, listening to a blow-by-blow description of the previous evening's hostilities, followed by a retrospective look at every evening of last week, beginning with Richard's appearances and how he had captivated the babies, won their hearts, tried to win hers all over again, then forcing himself on her when she resisted, her account culminating in a detailed recital of my achievements—"titanic," she said, given "my weakened condition and failing every day."

Her description had barely struck home, than Marina was on her feet, hands gripping her tangle of hair on both sides, and she was shouting.

"Never mind titanic this, titanic that, wade too far in and you can't get out, what if Richard returns? What kind of pickle will you be in then? What titanic thing will Daisy do half-dead? And Mark and Darcy, what about them?" she railed on, Richard was the father after all, and fathers have rights too, would he kidnap the babies in the middle of the night, and who would come to her rescue then? The porcupines? The raccoons? The butterflies? The trees? Would they protect her? Would they protect the helpless babies? Monique interrupted too.

"I'm sure he doesn't want the babies," she said, "and he certainly doesn't want another run-in with Daisy."

But Marina wasn't sure of anything. That was that. *She* would stay. The police were not crouched in the woods waiting for Richard to show up, they were miles away, she said, and who knows what Richard might do next, when he obviously thinks he can do anything, Americans are born thinking they can do anything, it's in their blood.

Early next morning, with Marina to look after the babies, Monique lifted me into the pickup truck and drove to a veterinarian in Saint-Sauveur—a young Japanese woman whose walls were lined with framed colour prints of all twelve animals in the zodiac constellation, my species numbered among them, I'm proud to say, and all twelve heavenly generals of the healing Buddha.

Monique proceeded with a lengthy history of my fateful encounter with a porcupine and its lasting effect on me, fragments of quill still migrating into my vitals, causing recurrent infections, etc. She then briefly described yesterday's encounter with a "stranger" trespassing on our property, wanting to fish in her brook, Monique said, not heeding the "BEWARE OF DOG" sign, and the scuffle that ensued, a trumped-up story to be sure, making little of my heroics. But such is human guile, presenting the whole, but imaginatively rearranging its pieces.

"Her vital signs are good," the veterinarian said, but given the traumas already sustained, the surgeries, the recurring abscess formation, she could not spin straw into gold, I could not be expected to live that much longer, much less be a guard dog.

"In an isolated place like that, what you need is a German Shepherd or a Rottweiler," she said.

Monique paid and we left. Imagine, a German Shepherd or a Rottweiler. Good heavens, I thought to myself on the way back, a changing of the guard is imminent, I'm reaching the tail end. The truth had finally struck home. Nothing would save me now, not even the twelve heavenly generals of the healing Buddha. As they say, my goose was cooked.

Marina and I stayed for the rest of the week, and Richard did not return. In an effort to placate Marina before we left for the city, Monique posted two large signs at the entrance to the road leading to the cabin, one reading PRIVATE PROPERTY, NO TRESPASSING, the other BEWARE OF DOG—when there was no dog there to beware of, another glaring example of that human haze over the hills of honesty.

July 15, 1979

Harry was entertaining a young woman when we arrived home, the two at the dining room table eating dinner. Good heavens, I thought to myself, surely not another imbroglio with no good end, apparently common as sin among humans. But no. The young woman was none other than Chloé, Mark's ex-girlfriend, whose letters we had returned after Mark's passing.

I arrived just as they were finishing the main course, which was ginger-marinated pork tenderloin with sweet potato and asparagus tips. Before embarking on the next course, Harry took the time to settle me in, as it were, as Marina explained that I was "under observation," after being involved in another "scuffle," she called it, good heavens, hardly an apt description of the events, but understandable given the social circumstances. "Under observation," really, I thought to myself, an endangered species would be more like it.

They were eating the dessert, Peach Ambrosia, when Harry broached the subject of Mark again. He'd been to the training base in Portage la Prairie, and according to the officer in charge, Mark had been a great recruit in basic training and in occupational training. Harry went on. He'd also gone to Winnipeg and visited the parents of Mark's buddy killed in the accident, and it might be comforting to know that Mark didn't lie to her, Chloé. He *did* take the bus all the way to Winnipeg. He *did* visit his buddy, who'd been discharged a week before for being a homosexual. And according to the parents, his buddy was really broken up about it. So he hadn't really gone drinking with his buddies. That wasn't the plan.

They finished the Peach Ambrosia, and Harry poured two cups of coffee.

"I didn't plan to tell you anything else," Chloé began, but you seem to want to know everything ..."

"What else is there ..."

"It's the letters ... when I looked through the letters, I found the special delivery one, the dear John one ..."

"Was it open, the envelope?"

"Yes, it was open, he must have opened it before he went to Winnipeg."

They sipped from their cups in silence. Then Harry again.

"Did Mark ever talk to you about me?" he asked.

Chloé seemed caught off guard by the question.

"You know, before he went away to basic training, or after ..." Harry added.

"Why do you ask?"

"Because I'd like to know."

"Well, he *did* say he admired you."

"Admired?"

"Yes, admired. Everything about you."

"Is that all?"

"No, he said he wished he could be more like you …"

"More like me?"

"Yes more like you, then you might have liked him better, he said."

"Is that why he joined the air force?"

"I don't know, maybe …" Chloe said. "You know, I told you how he felt like a misfit … he said he only knew what he was *not*, that's why he liked the feeling when he drank, because when he drank he was *somebody*, a brawler maybe, but somebody at least." And maybe if he got off the ground, he told her, somewhere high above the earth and everyone on it, maybe the sky would tell him who he was.

" … Anything else?"

"I don't know … did you ever ask *him* any of these questions?"

"No, I guess I didn't …"

They drank the last of the coffee and as Harry moved to clear the table, Chloé came and knelt beside me. And again, it was as if she was encountering me for the first time. I could feel my sutured wounds prickle. If only I could roll over onto my back, my four limbs uplifted, and in a paroxysm of willingness, expose every fiber of my being. The "whither-thou-goest-I-will-go" position, Monique calls it. Ah me. Set a high value on physical spontaneity and it goes, like dew on the grass. Still there she was, massaging my ears and laughing at my tail slapping helplessly on the hardwood floor.

She said goodbye and left. With Harry gone to drive her home, I dozed in the dark, pining for an end to my afflictions.

Last night I had the strangest dream, a disturbing dream, to put it mildly, the disturbance clinging to me, even as I crossed the threshold into consciousness. Don't fret, I chastised myself, dreams are dreams, fabrications to make the night pass more quickly. Yet it left me shaken. Frightened even. For in it, the floodgates of heaven open without warning, and torrents of rain fall with an intensity not seen since the great deluge in biblical times, and like the great deluge, threatening to consume all that lives and moves upon the earth, while there I am, a spectator on a hill high as Mount Ararat, watching the natural phenomenon unfold on this vast terrain stretching out below me as far as the naked eye can see, the scene of an "us-and-them" scenario, on one side the animals — elephants, lions, tigers, caribou — as well as horses, cows, sheep, goats and every other species living on Earth, and on the other, the most immense gleaming-white ocean liner — a twentieth century Noah's Ark, if you like — into which humans are streaming via a gargantuan gangplank, a most disconcerting sight, for once they are all on board, the gangplank is raised and the ship floats off, leaving the legions of animals standing there in the pouring rain, the rising waters lapping against their undercarriages, all in a state of confusion and dismay, at a loss as to what to do next.

Surely this was just a bad dream, I thought, when I'd come to my full senses. Everyone and his country cousin knows that Noah marched two of everything into the ark with him, everything that moved, everything that breathed — wild animals according to their kind, all species of cattle, creeping things, fowls of the air and birds that fly. Even a humble farmer like Noah, with no book learning, whose job it was to simply walk with God and increase and multiply and fill the earth, never had to think twice about it, for he instinctively knew that we were all worth saving, foresight alone telling him that he would die of hunger and, I daresay, loneliness, without us. Isn't that why Monique found a reason to take in another dog before I die?

September 10, 1979

I finally met my successor. At the cabin on Labour Day weekend. Not my "replacement," Monique said, for I could never be replaced, blandishments made to humour me, level my path, for I entered the cabin and there he was, sitting in a princely position on his hind quarters by the stove, observing me from a distance, not a hackle raised. He is a male, black and tan Doberman Pinscher named Henry, well past his prime I daresay, judging by the white hairs here and there on his snout. His previous owner? A man in his late seventies, a lifelong ski bum, who lived alone on the edge of Saint-Sauveur. He'd tumbled off a ladder while washing his storm windows, fractured his collar bone and refractured the leg he'd broken the previous winter on a ski slope he could normally ski blindfolded. He was carried off on a stretcher and to the hospital in Saint-Jérome, leaving Henry to fend for himself. When a neighbour delivered him up to Monique's veterinarian, she called Monique. Would she like a homeless, well brought up, home-schooled guard dog, a Doberman Pinscher, for protection? If not, she would call the animal rescue shelter. Monique did not hesitate. She would give it a try.

For the first week or two, Henry was grief-stricken, Monique said, morose even, eating little and restlessly moving from place to place in the cabin. But little by little, he had come round and was making the best of a bad bargain. When the babies were asleep, Monique took him out into the woods, where the familiar sights and smells and sounds seeped into him, helping him get his bearings and remember who he was, she said. By degrees, she had also won his confidence.

Adjusting to the creeping, yelping babies was another hurdle. She acclimatized him to Mark and Darcy in small careful doses. It helped that Henry was seven years old, knew his limits and escaped into his crate when he needed peace and quiet.

No excitement sprang from Henry's soul upon meeting me either. If anything, he was complacent. Indeed, he showed all the conceits of a dog of independent means, if such a creature still exists, for he barely looked at me. Still I tolerated him. Which in dog language says, "for all of your ascendancy, you too are part of the flesh of this world, you too will eat and get eaten in due time."

Monique now also has a babysitter coming in three times a week. A plump woman named Blanche Lamontagne from Lost River, past middle age, who comes in running shoes, jump suit and *bandeau* in her hair, prepared for strenuous activity. She never bore children of her own because her husband didn't want any, she told Monique, he said the house was too small, when really, he was sterile as a mule. And just as cantankerous.

"A babysitter's all fine and dandy, "Marina said, when she heard, "but what about Richard?" Had Monique heard from him? Had he phoned?

"No, he hasn't come, hasn't phoned," Monique said, but she thought she'd seen him in her rearview mirror once or twice, following her in his car on the road from Lachute after shopping trips.

"Richard gives me the creeps," Marina said, even if she'd never met him, and why was Monique stuck on living in the back woods all by herself with two babies and nothing but an old, worn-out dog for protection.

"Henry will attack if I tell him to," Monique protested, "the vet told me so, he was trained by the previous owner to attack men, not women, and he knows the difference, he smells the different hormones and pheromones."

"And something else, the choir is short of sopranos, even the conductor is wondering why you dropped out," Marina insisted.

Monique had to admit, she did miss the choir, especially when she heard the frogs and perching birds and the chorus of leaves as the winds sift through the trees.

But other things were pressing, weighing her down. She had a dream in which she was standing in a large open square, all alone, with throngs of angry people behind a barricade hurling stones at her, Kathleen and Matthew in the front line, shouting and throwing stones too, and how could she blame them when she'd walked out with no good explanation, no wonder Kathleen found the cabin boring, no wonder Matthew was holed up in the attic.

"Have they seen the babies?"

"No."

"Six months, and they still haven't seen the babies …?"

"No, and now Matthew's gone out west for the whole summer."

"That's it," Marina said, "a family's not a set of building blocks you take apart and put together again just like that, it's not that easy."

"And not everything is explainable either; there isn't an answer for everything."

"Still, everything matters."

With the babies restless and waiting to be fed, the conversation ended and the two sat down to supper, Mark and Darcy in their highchairs, holding each morsel of food set before them in their fat little fists, examining each as if seeing it for the first time, then stuffing it into their little mouths as if nothing else mattered but the never-ending present.

After supper, with darkness raining down, Marina put on her fleece, found the flashlight and went out for a long walk in the woods.

"The moon is almost full," she announced when she returned, euphoric almost, "so bright, so shining, I never had to use the flashlight."

And later, with the cabin deep in sleep, the almost-full moon shone down on me through the small square window, its light licking my wounds, lulling me to sleep, and again I heard him, that faraway owl, hooting.

September 30, 1979

As the poet said, how good life is, how incorruptible, how impossible to deceive, not even by strength or willpower or courage. I say this for I suspect that I am coming to the tail end of it, pardon the canine metaphor. Life is slowly and painfully forcing its way through my body one last time, leaving room for nothing else but the two of us tied together as if climbing a steep mountain, and on the way up, passing in review the wellsprings of my joy and all the dark evergreen of my sorrows and griefs and woes. Oh how jubilant they have been, how harrowing, served up to me in mouthfuls. And I fully present in all of them. Catching them on the fly, as it were, like a Frisbee floating easily through the air, knowing it cannot float forever.

For in my lifelong affair with fate, I have been like dice, first rolled out from a cup onto the terrain of the canine world, then onto the table of humans. Like others, I was not able to cast myself out. Yet no matter how I tumbled, I was always somehow ready to begin again and again. And when put back into the sometimes bitter cup of fate, my instinct was to pull back into the centre of myself. And to wait. For again, as the poet said, "life's little wisdom is to wait." And what was bestowed upon me in return? The great grace to survive. Survive you say? Yes, survive, for the new will contain something of the old. Or will it? For I am also overcome with fear. Please someone, let me know, comfort me in passing, tell me that the hundredfold of dog left behind will pass over into those I've left behind, pressing them more deeply into life, even as I pass over into death.

Good heavens! How every bone and sinew of my body aches. Hang on, I tell myself, as you hung on to Richard's leg, as you waited to be called off. The end will come and take you … soon ….

October 2, 1979

Mid-afternoon on Saturday, Marina called.

"I'm coming over," she said to Harry. And with Kathleen going out to a movie with her friends, and Matthew working weekends at the planetarium, Harry insisted she come for dinner. He loves to cook and make a show of it. A show not lost on Marina, of course, who thinks that appetite comes when you eat, no matter what appetite.

On the menu: Honey-glazed salmon steaks grilled on the barbecue and, with it, a pot-pourri of eggplant and red and yellow peppers *en papillotte,* served with perfumed basmati rice on the side.

Harry served the main course, they began to eat, and between mouthfuls, Marina filled Harry in on the latest news. First about the cockatoos, Minerva and Modesta, she no longer paid any visits to the Granby Zoo, but she'd telephoned, the cockatoos had been transferred to a rehabilitation centre, thousands of miles away, in the Oakland Zoo aviary for parrots and exotic birds. The news came as a blow at first and then a relief, a consolation, a blessing even, because their behaviour had gone from bad to worse in a few short weeks at the Granby Zoo. It had been one uproar after another, not only did Minerva and Modesta pluck one another's feathers, they plucked the feathers of all the other birds as well, but what broke the camel's back was the affair with an African gray parrot, a male, who'd fallen madly in love with Modesta, and when he dive-bombed her in a kind of foreplay that was more like a frenzy, she bit him, viciously, the zoo keeper said, not a love bite. But Marina was not surprised, what does Modesta know about love, about sex, nothing, she said, again answering her own question. The sad truth is, Modesta and Minerva should never have left their natural habitat in Australia. Desmond was right on that one. Instead, she'd driven them crazy by having them live like shut-ins, in a space too cramped, too constricted, and none of the give-and-take of living with others of their kind, virtues in the natural habitat all turned into faults in a house built for humans.

As Harry cleared the table in preparation for serving the dessert, Marina turned the conversation to Monique and the babies. The babies, Mark and Darcy, were almost ten months old, crawling everywhere, eating like horses and growing like weeds.

"Do they look like the father?" Harry asked, slicing and serving the upside-down apple cake.

"How do I know, I never saw the father."

"Why, where is he?"

"You don't know about him? Monique never said about Richard?"

"I never asked."

"Well you *should* know."

And flouting all the rules of discretion, written or unwritten, about what was right or wrong or about who should know what, Marina barged right in and told Harry everything. Everything she knew about Richard—as a person on the outside looking in, that is, because no one can know everything about everyone. A worm living in the earth knows more about soil. An eagle soaring in the sky knows more about the winds. Besides, she and Richard had never crossed paths. Still she knew this much. He was an American, a landlord, peace-lover, war resister, draft dodger, minstrel, guitarist, teacher, all rolled into one. And last but not least a lover—a phantom lover, appearing and disappearing as he pleased, and just when Monique thought he'd disappeared for good and forever, just when she'd slammed the door shut for good and forever, in he swoops like Superman in his cape and tries to win her back, more like a wolf parading as a lamb, forcing himself on her when she said no, but luckily Daisy was there, leaping in between, sinking her teeth into his calf muscle and holding on and on and on while he kicked and swung and pitched her this way and that way in the air, and Daisy _in extremis_ even before the battle had begun.

Who knows what might have happened if Daisy hadn't been there, Marina said, and that malevolent streak comes racing headlong through every vein and artery in my body. Yes, who knows …

The account of my exploits was followed by a full description of Henry, the Doberman Pinscher who is my successor. With a dog born and raised in the Laurentians now on guard, Richard would think twice about coming back, although Monique thought she'd seen him following her in her pickup truck, on the road back from Lachute.

A lull in the monologue followed, as Marina ate her apple upside-down cake. After a long gap, Harry returned to the subject of the babies. Were they healthy, sleeping through the night, did they look alike?

Sitting in the clearing on Labour Day Weekend, Marina said, they looked like two fat rosy little elves crept in from the woods, breathing the wild smells into their lungs, crawling around in the clearing, discovering the earth and everything in it for the first time. If she could, she would take them home herself, to replace the cockatoos, and that would send Desmond back up to the den.

October 3, 1979

Perhaps the analgesics Harry has been giving me rocked me to sleep, for Marina slipped out without my knowing it last night. In fact, when I did come to, it was morning, and Harry was bustling around in the kitchen like a man on a mission, brewing fresh coffee and making waffles in his new waffle iron, for him and for Kathleen, who had just shuffled down from upstairs in her slippers and dressing gown, yawning and stretching, still caught in that foggy space between sleep and waking. The two sat across from one another at the table and ate the waffles doused in maple syrup. But my vision had blurred over night, and I could scarcely distinguish one from the other until they spoke.

"Why did you get me up so early?" I hear Kathleen say, "where are you going in such a mad rush on a Sunday morning?"

"I'm going to Lost River. To the cabin," Harry answers.

"Why up there? You never go up there, is something wrong?"

"I don't know, I'm just going … I got you up to look after Daisy, she seems to be fading fast, that scuffle she was in up north was too much for her, so keep her comfortable, her pills are right there by the coffee maker."

In another foggy, fast-moving blur, Harry is up and out the door and on his way to Lost River.

And I am left with Kathleen, who is leafing through the newspaper. I could be left with Moses enveloped in mist on the summit of Mount Sinai, or in the haze of a Chinese water colour, it wouldn't matter. It wouldn't change my fate. Forms fade before my eyes, even as I too drift away. The kitchen floor tiles are stone cold. Indeed, I am cold. And heavy as a giant boulder.

After several futile attempts, I finally manage to lift myself onto my spindly legs and make my way to the hall closet, my place to be in thunderstorms and other fearsome occurrences, its darkest corner ever and always offering the same warmth and solace. My promised land now.

And here is Kathleen, swift on my heels. Spreading the wool blanket over my body still trembling from the exertion. It is dark here. A safe place to be. And to wait. So much of my life has been waiting. Waiting for the thunder to pass. Waiting for Monique to come home from choir practice, from Vancouver. from the cabin in Lost River. Waiting with Harry at the cemetery. Waiting for Mark and Marina to finish their lessons in love-making. Waiting, waiting, waiting. And now waiting for Harry … how I wish he had taken me with him to the cabin … where I could sink into the soft earth beneath the aspens … once and forever … what a time to be excluded from human affairs … for who knows what will transpire in the woods on the edge of Lost River … everything so complicated with humans … so unpredictable … so individual … they don't like mystery … things they can't explain … or master … or measure … when he drives in, will she think it's Richard and call the police …

Caught in the thick of the moment, will she set Henry the new Doberman guard dog on him … or will she be like the trees and expect the unexpected … let him in … ah, the black bat swoops down on me, and I am full of fear … and this when I've been dying slowly … serenely … knowing that I won't be made into glue or soap or sent to a taxidermist … knowing her, she'll load the babies into the wagon and take him for a walk in the woods, through the soft trail strewn with needles and pine cones, to where the ravens' nest is … perhaps he'll see the way the ravens swerve, turn somersaults in the sky … like stunt pilots … at the sound of human footfalls and babbling babies …

Will she take him to the waterfall that never stops falling … walk him through the neighbourhood, as she calls it … already I lie in a dazzle of light … kindly light, white as bone … will they step over the crackling twigs around the aspens already gold on Labour Day … where she plans to bury me, because their gold is so close to the colour of my coat … in the glory of my days, she surely meant … surely, she'll point to where I met the porcupine … attacked the innocent porcupine, is more like it, minding his own business, a turning point in my canine history heaped up in my body, all of its joys and sorrows pinned to my heart …

Here is Kathleen … a shadow coming to me, bending to me, the analgesic to swallow … my tongue dry as parchment … no strength to drink … no desire … and will she, who has learned the wonder and wildness and language of trees and wind and birds and bees, will she now be more able to decipher his language … manner of speaking … like me, so hopeless with words … see his ancestry assembled inside him … and the wind of wildness blowing through her … will he let it blow through him … will it invite further exploration … will he allow questions with no answers, admit other solutions, other remedies than his Epsom salts for all ailments …

And that electric current of desire that ran through Richard … into her … can it create new miraculous connections … ah come sweet death and take my breath away … if I were with them … if I had words … I would say don't look for me "under your boot-soles," as the poet said … don't look for me buried in the earth … or in dog-heaven in the sky … if I am really part of you , as you say, if we are all hitched to one star, let part of the hundredfold of me, the steadfastness, forgiveness, the devotion—and that little wisdom to wait, ancestral graces inherent in my species—pass over from my still centre into yours … and look for me there … almost too close to notice … oh good heavens … everything good … even dying … takes the longest patience …

About the Author

Bernadette Griffin is the author of *Scenes of Childhood*, a fictionalized memoir inspired by her childhood in Québec City, Canada, published in 2007. Prior to writing, she worked as a professional musician, reaching local and national prominence as founder and conductor of two prize-winning choral ensembles, *The Donovan Chorale* and *Les Chanteurs d'Orphée de Montréal*. She lives with her husband in Montréal in winter and on the Kingston Peninsula in New Brunswick during the extended summer months. She is the mother of five children and has five grandchildren.

Scenes of Childhood

With her Irish story-telling lilt, Bernadette Griffin spins tales of literary fiction based upon her early years in Quebec City in the 1940s and '50s. We meet Johnny and Marie-Ange, their marriage reflecting the French-English component of the city. We meet Johnny's sister, the flamboyant Francie, who makes salads at the Chateau Frontenac for Premier Duplessis. We meet the string of neighbours who move in and out of the first-floor apartment on Rue St. Joachim. We know there will be trouble with the tavern next to the church and with sharp-tongued neighbours who keep their eyes on everyone's private lives.

The inspiration for the title comes from Robert Schumann's suite of short piano pieces, "Scenes from Childhood."

CPSIA information can be obtained at www.ICGtesting.com
Printed in the USA
LVOW131942110613

338071LV00003B/467/P